CHAINED
GUILT

For Jackie, Terry and Jacey

ACKNOWLEDGEMENTS

I would like to thank my editor Susan Hughes who took my words and performed magic! Thank you for all of the advice, contacts and encouragement with this project. I would also like to thank Lois Benoit who pushed me to finish and share my work with the world. Last but not least I would like to thank my family and friends who have always encouraged me to follow my dreams.

PROLOGUE

It had taken me longer than I'd planned, but I'd finally tracked the bastard down; it now appeared the odds were stacked in his favor.

"Detective David Porter!"

The voice calling out had a strong Russian accent. I knew the voice. No mistaking it. Prodinov. I looked around and tried to figure out which direction it had come from. I obviously had company in the dark, box-filled warehouse. It was late, and the temperature had continued to drop. The inside of the building was as cold as the outside. My teeth chattered and my fingers tingled in the subzero temperatures. This was one element that definitely favored the Russians; they were used to the cold. Houston was cold about one month out of the year, but it was nothing like this. I tried to block out the bone-chilling temperature and focus on zeroing in on Prodinov.

"So you come all the way to Russia to die? For me to kill you like I did your brother? Didn't you learn from his mistakes? He never saw me coming, but he should have. You are a much better detective than he was; I'll give you that. But you will die tonight. Shoot him down!"

Gunfire rang out across the warehouse. I dropped to the cold cement floor and rolled behind a wall. I frowned, still unable to pinpoint his location as he taunted me. I was hit in the shoulder, losing blood fast as three Russian hit men closed in on me. I had to figure out what my next move was going to be. I should have known Alexander Prodinov would have some hired goons try to take me out. No way would a coward like him let this be a one-on-one battle. But if he thought I had traveled all the way to Russia to die, he was sadly mistaken. I had also promised him when he took his last breath, I'd be standing over his cold, lifeless body. My "vacation," as I'd told my superiors, was anything but.

"Revenge has a way of making people better at what they do. I'm a killer, Mister Porter, and a very good one. Unlike you, I do what I do for fun, not for a paycheck. They've written books about me, about my skills. When will you figure these things out? No matter how good you are, you lack the talent and the brains to win against me. I am simply better than you are."

"I didn't come here to die!" I shouted back at him. "Death will come to one of us, I promise you."

The words had barely left my mouth when another barrage of gunfire whizzed past my head. Bullets ricocheted off several crates around me. I ducked behind one, wincing as a splinter left a trail of heat across my cheekbone. I saw the exit and, crouching now, focused my gaze on it. I sprinted for the door, hoping I wouldn't be gunned down before I reached it. Ignoring my wounds, ignoring the cold, I charged forward. I heard the echo of footsteps behind me but knew I couldn't stop.

"Run, Porter!" Prodinov bellowed, laughing.

With the trail of blood I left behind, I knew I would be easy to track down come daylight or flashlight. The only hope I had was the cover of night and the thick Russian forest that surrounded the warehouse and stretched on forever. It was a bone-chilling fifteen degrees, and my body wasn't used to this type of weather, but losing myself in the woods was my only hope.

As I ran, I heard animal sounds I didn't recognize. Every so often I made out a set of eyes watching me. They could probably smell the blood and waited for me to keel over so they could pounce on me. I stumbled, nearly tripping over a fallen tree branch in the eerie blackness. Whether I died running or got shot down by Prodinov's goons, they'd never find me.

I heard voices, too close for comfort, so I dove for cover behind a fallen tree stump and burrowed deeper into the thick overhang of an immense oak. Glancing over my shoulder, I was relieved when no flashlight beams cut through the darkness. They, too, navigated the woods with the help of a quarter moon. They didn't see my tracks.

"Track him down and put a bullet in his head. Then bring his body to me," Prodinov had ordered his men.

I held my breath as they passed by me. My heart pounded, keeping time with the throbbing in my left arm. It was a relatively clean wound, in and out, no broken bones, but I had no idea how badly I was bleeding. No time to create a makeshift bandage, even if I had the supplies. This couldn't be the end for me. Bleeding out alone in the middle of Russia?

Suddenly I heard the low, fierce growl of a dog. Its eyes, two yellow moons, seemed to pierce my flesh as it looked at me. I could barely make out its silhouette in the dark. Maybe it wasn't a dog but a wolf. I couldn't be sure. Whatever it was, it sniffed and snorted like it had just found its next meal. My only advantage was my gun, which I'd already drawn. If I didn't deal with this soon—and quietly—

the animal would expose my hiding place, and we'd both end up dead anyway. I slipped the silencer onto my weapon, controlled my breathing, and pulled the trigger. And like that, the beast was gone.

I left my dubious shelter and ran as quickly as I could. The snow, two feet deep in places, certainly didn't offer the best conditions for making a clean getaway. Breathing heavily, quickly growing weak and tired, I forced myself on. Quitting wasn't an option. All they had to do was hit my tracks with the flashlights, and I would be exposed. Finally, after what seemed an hour but was probably only minutes, I saw a glow of light up ahead. As I crawled closer, I realized it was a small, dimly lit log cabin. I had no idea who the owner was, but this was probably my only chance of making it out of this mess alive. I rose to my feet and staggered through the woods, weaving my way through the trees until I came to the back door. I banged weakly on it.

"Help! Is anyone home? Someone please help me! I'm an American police officer!"

I was hesitant about stating I was a police officer—even worse, an American one. Attitudes in Russia could go either way with that announcement. It would either save my life or ultimately seal my fate.

"Who's there?"

The voice was female, soft and motherly.

"My name is David Porter! I'm an American police officer," I explained, catching my breath. "Men are chasing me. Please help!"

Seconds later, the door opened.

"Come. Come in quickly," the woman said, stepping back to let me in.

The cabin was sparsely furnished and quiet. A fire burned in the fireplace, producing the only light in the room.

The woman, probably in her late fifties, grabbed the straw broom leaning against the wall beside her and went out to sweep my snow tracks off her back porch. I watched intently from the window, leaning against the roughly-hewn wood wall for support.

She returned and glanced warily at me, especially at the gun in my hand.

"You're hurt," she said.

Despite my gratitude, I had to know. "Why are you helping me?"

"How about a thank you, American?"

"I mean, yeah, thanks, but why are you risking your life to help me?"

Before she could respond, the sound of voices approaching caused me to straighten in alarm. A fist pounded on the door several times. Prodinov's men. I glanced from the door to the woman, who had placed a finger over her lips, gesturing for me to remain silent.

"Shhh. I will take care of this."

I was more than a little nervous about what was about to happen. She could easily turn me over to the Russians. I made sure my gun was ready to fire and waited. They may get me, but I would take at least one of them with me. I wasn't afraid of dying, but I was fearful that my wife and daughters would have to live without me around to protect them.

The woman stepped toward the door and opened it a crack. As a part of my military training, I had learned several languages, one of them being Russian.

"Excuse me, ma'am," came a gruff voice from the other side. "We are looking for an escaped convict, an American. Have you seen anyone or heard anything tonight?"

She didn't respond. I was in trouble. Perhaps she

was pointing or whispering something to them. I couldn't tell from where I stood. Maybe she was afraid because the bastard had told her I was an escaped convict. I couldn't be sure of anything.

"Ma'am, have you seen anyone out here tonight?"

The voice grew noticeably aggravated.

"No," she replied. "It's been quiet all night. I haven't heard a thing or seen anyone. What does this American look like? Do you have a description? What is he wanted for?" She paused. "Should I be worried?"

"No need for you to worry yourself over the details," the man replied. "Do you mind if we look around? It will only take a second."

"Yes, I do mind, actually," she said. "I have a sick father upstairs in the loft. I take care of him, and I'd rather he not be disturbed. We are letting the cold air into my house. As I said, I have seen no one! You understand that, don't you?"

A long silence ensued. The men were probably trying to figure out if they could believe her or not. The moment of truth—my moment of truth.

I thought about waiting until the men left, but then I remembered Prodinov. I should use this chance to show him what he had gotten himself into. I quietly slipped out the back door and made my way around the side of the cabin, staying close to the structure and wary of casting a telltale shadow in the wan moonlight. I hoped the sound of snow crunching beneath my feet would not give me away as I hid behind a car parked in the front. I ducked down behind the left front fender and waited. Why did this car have to be so damn small? Trying to hide my six-foot-three-inch frame behind a car I could probably flip over by hand would be a test in itself. I continued to listen as the woman talked to Prodinov's men. My wounds ached, but I had no time to cry about it.

"If you don't have any more questions, I'd like to get back to my father," she was saying. She started to close the door. "I do hope you find the man you're looking for. We don't need criminals running around out here."

"Yes, ma'am. Have a good night."

She closed the door and the three men, bundled in long, heavy coats to ward off the bitter chill, stepped down off the porch and headed back the way they'd come.

I emerged from behind the car and, without hesitation, fired. One. Two. Three. Three shots, three dead Russians. As I anticipated, they had let their guard down after talking with the woman and I made them pay. Did I feel bad about ambushing them? Not one bit. They would have done the same to me.

The door of the cabin flew open. "Oh my God!" the woman screamed.

She stared down at the bodies in her driveway, their blood creating dark pools on the pristine ice, and then looked at me, her eyes wide with fear.

"Who are you? Are you some kind of killer? Are you even an American cop?"

Wincing as I bumped my shoulder on the car as I rose, I stepped from my hiding place. "Yes ma'am, I am," I assured her. I reached into my jacket pocket and took out my badge, showing it to her. "Relax. I'm a good guy. Have you ever heard of Alexander Prodinov?"

"Yes, who hasn't?" she stammered, returning her gaze to the men on the ground. "That evil man gave Russians a bad name. He's a vicious serial killer."

I slowly walked toward her, not wanting to frighten her more than she already was. "Well, those men were working for him," I explained. "They were trying to kill me. I am here in Russia trying to do the same to him. A few years ago I was tracking a serial killer in the United States, and it turned out to be Prodinov. He killed my brother in my home while he slept." I paused, swallowed hard. It was always difficult to remember. "For no reason, other than to prove to me how good he was. One day I will kill him."

"I'm truly sorry about your brother," she said. "But you know killing him won't bring your brother back."

I was grateful she had saved my life, but I wasn't exactly in the mood for a sermon. "Of course I know it won't bring him back. My brother being murdered is just one more reason for me to do away with this monster. You know what he is. He's killed many people, including children. He kills for pleasure. The world would be a better place without him."

"I understand what he has done, but judgment is not yours," she said. "You are bleeding badly." She gestured for me to come inside. "I used to be a nurse. I can patch you up until you can get to a doctor."

"I need to get rid of those bodies," I remarked.

"Let's get you cleaned up first. If you die those bodies won't matter so much will they?" she said as she turned to go inside.

I followed and shut the door behind me. I settled in a chair near the fireplace while she gathered some first aid supplies from under the kitchen sink. The cabin was small, but comfortably warm. I found myself relaxing.

"You never answered me earlier. We aren't the most liked here, so why did you help me?"

"Take off your jacket and shirt," she ordered.

I did as she bade and watched as she removed packaged squares of gauze from the kit, some antiseptic, and a mesh-like bandage roll, and focused on cleaning and bandaging my arm. It didn't appear she was going to answer my question. I didn't really care why the woman had helped me. I was just glad I was still alive. I winced as she worked on me. She was not the gentlest nurse I had ever encountered.

"I lived in America over twenty years ago," she finally said. "One day as I was leaving the supermarket, I had a flat tire. I was stranded on the side of the road when three men stopped to help me, or so I thought. They walked over to my car. Before I knew it, one of them hit me over the head. Luckily for me, an off-duty policeman drove by and saw this. He turned around to come and help me. He should have waited for help to arrive, but he didn't. He acted bravely, and I owe my life to him, I'm sure. You are right, too. You Americans have many enemies here in Russia. You're lucky you stopped at my cabin."

So the actions of a good cop I would never meet, someone who had just been doing his job, had saved my life here in Russia two decades later. I didn't believe in fate or karma, but if I had, this would be it times two.

"Well, again, thank you," I said sincerely. "What about the bodies?"

"I will brush your tracks from the snow after you leave. I will tell them when they come—and they will—that I was sleeping and woke to the sound of gunshots. I know nothing more."

She finished patching me up, and I geared up to leave. Before I left the cabin, I pulled my notepad from my pocket and awkwardly scribbled a note. She didn't ask me what I was doing. I grasped it in my fingers as I stepped from the door, which closed firmly behind me. Before I left the yard, I tucked the message for Prodinov into one of the dead men's jacket pockets. I left it sticking out a little so that he could see it. It read:

One day soon this will be you.

I slowly made my way back to the highway, circling

wide around the warehouse where I'd had my run-in with Prodinov. Good thing hitchhiking was as common in Russia as back home. When a compact car pulled over to pick me up, I climbed in. The driver said something about where I was headed. I relied again on my limited knowledge of Russian and muttered, "Airport."

It took a while and several rides, but I eventually made it within walking distance of the airport as the sun slowly rose from the east. I was near frozen, but anxious to get the hell out of the godforsaken country. As I walked down the street that would take me into the warm terminal, I pulled my phone from my jacket pocket. I had a text message from Cap. I accessed it.

Have to cut your vacay short. Child killer here has everyone up in arms.

Vacation? Yeah, right. He knew damn well why I was in Russia. I would have to put my personal battle on hold for now.

I had allowed my anger to control my thinking and underestimated what it would take to kill Prodinov, especially here in Russia. Revenge had clouded my judgment. It might take me two months or two years, but I would regroup and replan. I had the patience and the determination. One day, I would return to Russia or wherever my hunt for Alexander Prodinov took me. One day we would meet face to face, and I would kill him.

1

I sat in my car and watched the officers working the crime scene. Some tried to control the crowd, while others took photographs of the vic. Even though we were all trained professionals, this murder was horrible. Channels 2, 11 and 13 were here covering the story. Their news vans lined the street.

Captain Wilcrest had already warned me that this would be one of the saddest things I had ever seen. I had seen some pretty bad ones over the years, so I was mentally prepared for anything. This vic, Emily Miller, age eight, had been kidnapped, raped, cut up, and left in the park like a piece of animal meat. Wilcrest was probably right, and I was not looking forward to it.

I forced myself out of my squad car and headed across the street to MacGregor Park, where her body had been discovered. Boy was this becoming quite the mess. Little Emily was the second kid killed here this month. We definitely had a serial on our hands, or so it appeared. In a city the size of Houston, narrowing down a suspect was never easy. I had left Prodinov behind in Russia, so I was sure it wasn't him, but that was all I was really sure about.

From their width and depth, the set of tire marks appeared to come from some sort of van. The tracks were a little wider than those left by your typical SUV.

"Cap, have someone run a report on rented vans and cross that with people with medical training. Start off with a hundred-mile radius and let's see what we get," I said as I walked up behind him.

"Good idea, David. Whoever did this has definitely had medical training."

I figured as much before I even saw her body. I was pretty sure the MO would be exactly the same as the first, which was good and bad. Maybe now we could take suspects in this case and compare them to the list created from the first killing. If we found a match—anything—we'd catch our first break. Lord knows we could use one.

"Porter, it's bad. We gotta catch this son of a bitch," a patrolman said as he passed.

As Captain Wilcrest and I strode closer to the vic, I smelled an unusual, putrid odor. The smell was so strong, it almost made my stomach heave, and I have a strong stomach. I tried to breathe through my mouth.

"It's the body," Wilcrest commented. "Whoever did this poured something all over her little body."

"Has the lab finished taking photos?" I said. "If so, let's get her covered up, please."

This murder was horrific. Whoever did this didn't need a trial, not in my book. Probably explained why I was a cop and not a judge. Criminals wouldn't like me as a judge. They would be armless, handless, dead . . . or worse. This perp had spared nothing. He had even cut on her genitals. I slipped on a pair of latex gloves, crouched down, and carefully turned her onto her side so I could see the back of her body. It also had been mutilated.

"What do we got?" I asked, glancing up at the captain. "You got anything I can use yet?"

"No, not much." He shrugged. "A note was left for you—by the killer, I presume. It said, 'More to come, Porter. Blame yourself.' That was it."

"I don't know what the hell that's supposed to mean," I said, frustrated and angry.

"Well, hopefully you'll figure it out, 'cause that's our only chance here, I think. Someone's calling you out. You get any serious threats lately? Prodinov, maybe?"

"No. He's a killer, no doubt about that, but this isn't his style. Something about this is different. It's too complex for Prodinov."

Maybe Prodinov was paying someone else, I thought. Maybe I had underestimated what he was capable of. That was the worst part of it all. People were dying for no apparent reason. It was a game to these sick assholes, and this was probably just another. So far, I was eighteen and zero. No serial had ever called me out and won. None. Prodinov was the only one I had yet to bag. Till now.

We kept a close eye on web traffic, because there was always lots of chatter there. Hell, Vegas even had a line going on whether anyone could elude me for more than five years. Prodinov was two years in so far. I had recently been exposed to recruitment efforts by the FBI and CIA, but staying home and around my girls was important to me— even more so than upping my arrest record or enhancing the prestige surrounding my name. I knew I could take some office job, do it well, and probably enjoy the hell out of it. But I also knew watching my girls grow up would only happen once. Maybe after it was just my wife and me, I would consider a change of scenery.

This was the only aspect of my job I hated. I didn't

want to be playing games with killers, but that's exactly what everyone else had made it out to be. A cat and mouse game with people's lives. At this point, I didn't see a way out. Hell, deep down, maybe it was a game to me, too.

I looked at the note through the Ziploc evidence bag and tried to read it again. It may have been our best piece of evidence. I needed to run a handwriting analysis as soon as possible. I was grasping at straws but would take a break any way I could get it.

"Whoever did this went out of his way to make sure these two murders were different than anything I've ever seen," I said. "He wanted my attention. He wanted me to know what he was capable of. I'm sure he knows I have a daughter around this age, too, and that probably influenced his choice of victims. The attention to detail, the precision of the cuts, the placement of the body . . . My mind was already churning.

"You leave for vacation tomorrow, right? Real vacation?" Wilcrest said with a smirk.

"Yeah I'm supposed to, but I think I'll have to send the girls by themselves and stay here to work on this case. Not much else I can do here tonight, but we need to get a jump on it first thing in the morning."

"I think you should go, David," Wilcrest said. "Me and the boys will get started here. I'll keep you updated to the minute. Besides, it's only a week, and you owe it to your family. You've been putting in a lot of hours, kid. I don't want to have to tell Miranda you aren't going. I know how much your family means to you. They need this. You need this."

Wilcrest was right. I had been working insane hours. Even more after the first kid was killed several weeks ago. Like him, I sure as hell didn't want to tell Miranda I wasn't going on vacation with them. I sighed, nodded, and left the crime scene. I took the long way home, feeling like I needed to stop in at Joe's Diner, a small coffee shop on the outskirts of town. A few of my old friends owned the joint, and they always took good care of me.

They had the restaurant set up like an old sixties malt shoppe: black-and-white checkered floors, red plastic booths with chrome trim, and even an old juke box. The best part was they never made me pay. I would still come here if they did, but what the heck, I figured. Take advantage when you can. I walked in and Judy, Joe's wife, nodded at me.

"Hey, David. I assume you just came from the park where that kid got killed, huh?" Judy said as she walked over with my usual cup of coffee.

"Yeah."

"I heard they cut this kid all up, too?"

If anything went on in this town, Judy Ballatip, was all over it. I loved her to death, but nothing got past her well-tuned ears. Sometimes I wondered if we shouldn't bring her on the force, as she always found out everything anyway.

Judy was a throwback from the sixties era the diner portrayed. She had long red hair, always wore a floral sundress and an apron. Hard to even imagine she and I were the same age. I loved her and Joe like family. Joe and I had played high school football together, and I'd probably kill a man for him without hesitation. Not probably, I would. He was the brother I'd never had. There were things about me that nobody knew but Joe. I'd gotten offers to play college ball, as did Joe, but he gave it all up and married Judy instead. I didn't understand that until I met Miranda years later. I turned my attention back to Judy.

"Yeah, it was pretty bad. Can't say too much else about it, though."

"Well you've always caught them before." She offered

an encouraging smile. "I'm sure this will be over soon."

"I sure hope so, Judy."

Judy left to take care of other customers, and I drank my black coffee in silence. I looked around at all the Elvis photos in the shop. Guess I had never paid much attention before. I tried to think of anything about the crime scene I might have missed. There was one thing, one indisputable fact I believed about crime scenes: there was always evidence. Whether I found it or not, well, that was a different story, but there was always evidence.

After forty-five minutes of vegging, I figured I should head home. "I'll see you next time, Judy," I said as I left.

I jumped on I-45 South and took the long way home. I tried to put myself in the shoes of the parents who lost their kids so suddenly and violently. The pain had to be unbearable. There was not much you could do for a grieving parent, either, especially if you hadn't felt the pain firsthand. The parents I gave the "your kid is dead" speech to wouldn't hear a thing past those four words. I could be singing the ABCs and they wouldn't know the difference.

When I got home, I eased my keys onto the kitchen table. I found myself still wanting something to nibble on, even after my coffee stop. I opened the fridge but didn't find much, and cereal didn't sound too appealing at the moment. I gave up and closed the door.

I had a strong urge to check on my daughters, especially after the night I'd just had. I crept up the staircase, trying not to wake them. I cracked the door to Hilary's room. She slept hard, not moving a muscle. I walked over to Karen's room, opened the door, and stepped inside. I squeezed my body into one of her Dora chairs. I just wanted to watch her sleep. She was a perfect kid. For some reason, Karen and I bonded on more levels than I did with Hilary. People always said parents had favorites even if they didn't tell anybody. I guess, in part, that was true for me also.

I sat in Karen's room for two hours as my mind wandered back to what I'd seen earlier. If I ever caught the person who did this, someone better have a video camera out. It was the only thing that would prevent me from ripping his head off right there on the spot. And it wasn't a guarantee. Finally, I sighed and rose. I needed sleep. I gave Karen a kiss on the forehead and headed for my room. Miranda was a beauty, even in her sleep. I cuddled up next to her and thanked God for how lucky I was to have her. Then, I tried unsuccessfully to fall asleep.

**

"David, honey, are you going to lay there and watch *Sports Center* all morning?"

"You got something better for me to watch? Are you suggesting that I watch you instead?"

"I think you can answer that for yourself." She pointed down at her torso. "This is called my bra and panties outfit. You like it?"

"You are the most beautiful woman I ever laid eyes on," I said, meaning every word. "Why did you stop modeling again? The world travel, the big pay checks, the lunch dates with celebs? All that too much for you?"

"Aww . . . you're sweet. I'm the most beautiful woman you've ever seen, huh? How many times have you used that line? I've told you before. I always wanted to be a news anchor, even as a little girl. All that other stuff is nice, but maybe I don't want to rely on these to get what I want." She gestured toward her breasts.

"Excuse me, but I kind of like those, personally," I laughed. "Come over here and let me inspect them again for quality."

My wife, Miranda, had the typical model body. She was tall—almost six foot —with long, toned legs and even longer blonde, silky hair. Miranda had graduated college with a BA in broadcasting and a minor in criminology. She was so humble that when she mentioned being a former runway model, most people couldn't believe it.

"I do think you are amazingly gorgeous, and you know I'd do anything for you right? I would cut the heart right out of my body and give it to you. I only ask one thing." I grinned. "Just stay away from those male models today. Can you do that for me?"

"I know you would, and that's why I love you," she said with a smile. "And FYI, all the traveling and stuff doesn't compare to having a beautiful family. I love my family and being a mom. It's the most wonderful, beautiful thing in the world."

"Sometimes I like to put my hand on your chest while you're sleeping, just to feel your heart beating. I know you like being a mom, and you're the best. You certainly get my vote."

Our relationship wasn't perfect, but it was probably as close to fairytale as you could get in this crazy world. I couldn't even remember the last time we'd had a fight or a disagreement. We'd been together so long, even our thoughts had begun to mesh.

"Hey, don't act like you're just a no-good couch potato, Mr. Big Time College Football Player," she said as she slowly twirled her hair. Hmmm . . . now I'm certain you used the 'you're the most beautiful thing I've ever seen, baby' line before."

"Nope. Never. I didn't have the perks of being a superstar," I said with a wink and a smile.

"Okay, superstar, I have to get ready for work. I'll need

you to remove your hands from my breasts now, officer."

"Don't remind me." I laughed. "Speaking of which, I can't believe we've been on vacation for a week, and they haven't called one time. Wilcrest was supposed to keep me up-to-date."

Miranda and I had met innocently enough. She was a grad student earning credits for her criminology degree, and I was a rookie cop fresh out of the police academy. Luckily for me, I was assigned a two-week stint with the "hot college chick" who later became my hot wife. When the assignment came from the chief, everyone ran from it. Since I was the new kid on the block, it was handed to me. About ten seconds after Miranda walked in, everyone knew they had made a mistake.

"Honey, you need to get up," Miranda said. "The girls will be waiting on you."

"I know, I know, but this is the last day of our vacation, and I don't want it to end."

"Vacation? For you, maybe. I have to do this photo shoot. That's why we're here, remember?"

Miranda had been chosen for a magazine spread featuring the most beautiful newscasters in the nation. The photo shoot was in Florida, where we had never been, so we were taking full advantage of it. Just as I was about to respond, the phone rang. I grabbed my phone from the bedside table and glanced at the display.

"Are you kidding me? Captain Wilcrest?" I looked at my wife. "I think I just jinxed myself."

"Be careful what you wish for, lover boy."

"What's up, Cap? Your ears must have been burning. I was just telling Miranda—"

"Hey, Porter, got some bad news. We got another one, third one in the last two months. People don't even want to take their kids to school anymore. They don't want to go outside. We've got to catch this bastard, and I mean fast!"

"That's what this asshole wants," I replied, sitting up in bed, my heart pounding. "He wants everyone to fear him. 'Hey look at me; look what I can do!' He wants to make the headlines. His fifteen minutes of fame."

"He came to the right place to get his fifteen minutes and then some," Wilcrest said. "Same MO too—severed body parts, possible . . . well, probable rape. I guess this is his version of 'see no evil.' This time he plucked the kid's eyes out."

I swore as Miranda looked at me with concern. "Just get as much forensic information as you can. I'll be back in town late tomorrow afternoon." I clicked off the phone.

"You think you guys are going to catch him?" Miranda asked.

"I don't know," I admitted for the first time. "I try to say the right things, put on my mean-cop, tough-guy suit, but the thought of something like this happening to one of our girls scares me to no end." I shook my head. "I don't know if we'll catch this one. So far, we've got nothing."

"I have faith in you," Miranda said. "If anyone can catch this maniac, you can. I believe that."

"Thanks. I'll do my best; that much is certain. The girls and I are going to the beach while you do your shoot. We can catch up after that. Sound good?"

"Sure. Wish me luck." she said, turning to leave the room. "And I'll try to stay away from the male models."

I dressed and headed to the girls' room next door. To my surprise, they were both up, in bathing suits, and ready to go.

"Took you long enough to get up, sleepy head," Karen said.

"Hey, why is everyone rushing me this morning?" I griped playfully. "I'm on vacation. It's our last day, and I'm trying to enjoy it. Besides, you're five years old. You don't know what tired is yet."

"Yeah, yeah. Whatever," Hilary broke in. "Let's just get to the beach, can we? I'm not five, and I'm not tired either, old man."

"Yeah, you're fifteen. You should be full of youthful energy too!"

"Really, Dad? Can we just go please?"

I grabbed a book, my keys, and my cell phone and locked the door. The three of us made our way over to the beach. As we walked, I swear, every male under the age of twenty eyed Hilary. Some even did a double take as we walked by. They apparently didn't notice the glowers I sent their way.

"Did you see that? What's the matter with these boys?" I said, shaking my head.

"Dad, I'm a beautiful young woman with curves in all the right places. What do you expect them to do? You were young once. Didn't you do the same thing?"

"Give me your towel," I said, only half joking. "I don't understand that bathing suit anyway. And I'm still quite young, thank you very much."

"You're not supposed to understand it. It's called a bikini, and you don't wear them, thank God. And I hate to break it to you, but yeah, you are old."

I found a spot with mostly older people and decided it worked for me. Maybe the old guys wouldn't stare so hard at my adolescent daughter. Then again, maybe the old farts would prove to be worse. Hilary noticed my choice of beach.

"Dad, could you have found a place with any more old people?" Hilary whined.

Before I could answer, Karen darted for the water, bucket in hand.   "Karen and I like it just fine," I said with a smile.

"That's because you're over the hill and she's five!" She shook her head, disgusted. "Whatever."

I wasn't listening. I'd already picked up my book and started reading. Hilary probably figured arguing with me was no use. She sat down, turned on her iPod, and cranked up the music.

We'd been on the beach for a couple hours when Miranda called. She had completed her photo shoot and wanted to meet up so we could spend the rest of the day together.

"Just leave the hotel room, walk onto the beach, and head to the left. You can't miss us." I smiled. "Just look for the group of old people."

Less than fifteen minutes later, I glanced in the direction of the hotel and saw Miranda headed our way. *What the hell was she wearing?* She looked great, but she was going to give one of the old men a heart attack. She smiled as she sank down next to me in the sand.

"Hey, is that a new bikini?" I said. "It's stunning."

"Yes, it's new, silly. You really think I look good in it?"

"Well, let's do a test." Before she could stop me, I turned to a man who sat in a foldout chair nearby. He looked to be at least in his 70s. "Excuse me, sir." The old man turned to look at me, squinting against the sunlight. "Do you think my wife looks hot in that bikini?"

"Uhhh . . ."

He glanced at me and then my wife, his eyes lingering before he replied. "Sonny, I would have to agree. You should take her home before I steal her away from you!"

"I'm not letting that happen, trust me." I grinned. "No one is going to take this beautiful flower away from me. Not today Not tomorrow. Never. She's mine!"

Miranda blushed and turned her attention to her

oldest daughter. "Hi, Hilary."

A mumbled greeting is all she got in return.

My wife turned to me and cocked an eyebrow. "She's quiet today, huh?"

"Not even. She's mad because we set up shop with the old folks instead of the teenyboppers."

"Where's Karen?"

"She's down by the water with a bucket, in her own little world," I said as I rolled over and planted a kiss on Miranda's neck.

"Stop it now! I'm serious," she laughed. "There are too many people out here for her to be that far away from us."

For the first time, I noticed the distance. I turned to my older daughter. "Hilary, walk down and ask your sister to come check in with us, please."

"As if I wasn't doing something," Hilary grumbled.

A few weeks earlier, Karen had been approached by a stranger—a woman—at her school. My little girl had been gone for thirty minutes before anyone even noticed she was missing. The teachers thought she was sick in the bathroom. Miranda had been on high alert ever since. She hated to think it might have been the person responsible for the recent murders, but how could she really be sure? Someone had finally spotted the pair on the playground. The woman ran off when campus security approached. Karen described her as "special," and that was enough for me. We were looking for a highly intelligent psychopath with years of training in the medical field. It eased our minds, but just a little.

"She's fine, Mom," Hilary reported back several minutes later. "She's down there playing in the water." She made a face. "If anyone took her, they'd bring her back fast. Trust me."

Miranda finally caught a glimpse of Karen. "Who's she

talking to?"

"Where? I don't see anyone." I stood to get a better view.

"Right there, David, that blonde woman," Miranda said, jumping to her feet and breaking into a run. "I told you she was too far away!" she shouted over her shoulder as she raced to the shoreline.

As Miranda screamed and pointed, I noticed the woman, now about thirty yards away. She seemed to be pulling Karen along by her wrist, though my little girl was trying to dig her heels into the sand. *Who was this woman? Was she the same one from the school?* I surged forward in an all-out sprint, gun in hand. I couldn't let her get away. Kidnapping cases don't often end happily.

I wove my way through the sunbathers, pushing people out of the way as I ran, fearful my efforts wouldn't be enough, that my Karen would be gone. I tried to swallow, but my mouth was as dry as the Sahara. I heard Karen yelling for help, but everyone on the beach just sat there, stunned into inaction.

The woman reached the parking area. I could tell this was too planned to be random. I was dealing with someone who had done this before. It took her a second to shove Karen into the nondescript vehicle. As the car pulled away, I stopped, lifted my gun, and fired several shots at the back tires. The car swerved, and the woman lost control. I held my breath, panicked that another car would take them out, or they'd slam into a tree or something.

When the car finally slowed to a stop, I was about twenty yards away. The woman scrambled from the vehicle and made a mad dash into the crowd of spectators gathering nearby.

I ran to the passenger-side door, grabbed my little girl, and pulled her from the car. She had a cut on the side of her forehead and seemed a bit dazed. I caught a glimpse of the woman as she ran into the crowd. At that moment, Miranda caught up and snatched Karen from my arms, holding her close.

"Karen, baby, are you okay?" she asked frantically. Her hand smoothed Karen's hair as she quickly cast a glance over her, searching for additional injuries. "Did you know that woman?"

I could see Miranda was terrified. Hilary, too. Tears flooded Miranda's face, and panic made her tone shaky. Karen was calm, all things considered. Adrenaline and anger filled my veins, and the fear of almost losing Karen coursed through my body. I felt light-headed.

I didn't have time to exchange pleasantries. My blood boiling in rage, I ran into the crowd in pursuit of the woman. Beside a dumpster in the parking area, I found the jacket the woman had been wearing. A short distance away, I found a blonde wig. *Damn it!* This pretty much ended my search, since I now had no idea who to look for.

I stood on the curb separating the parking area from the narrow street that followed the coastline. I looked around, gun still drawn, chest heaving with exertion.

"Freeze. Drop your weapon!"

I felt the barrel of a gun press against the back of my head.

"Get on your knees, and give me one good reason why I shouldn't splatter your pathetic brains all over this concrete."

So this was it? Shot dead on a Florida beach in front of a few dozen onlookers?

I did as I was told. There was no way this guy knew I was a cop.

"I'm Detective David Porter, HPD. My ID is in my back pocket, but I'll have to reach into it to get it."

"Okay, but slowly, no funny business, unless you don't mind being shot in the back."

I pulled my ID wallet from my pocket and flipped it open so he could see my shield. "See that? Says detective, doesn't it? No need for any shooting today," I said, perturbed.

"Do you know who that woman was?" the officer asked, lowering his weapon.

I picked up my gun and slid it into my waistband. "No. Were you able to get a good look at her?"

"Not really. Not enough to make an ID."

"Well, we'll need you to come down to the station and make an official statement."

"I know, but first I need to find my wife and daughters. Then we'll head down and take care of that."

The officer holstered his weapon. The crowd remained; the lookie-loos had to get their fill. He handed me a card and told me to phone him when we were headed toward the station. As I made my way through the crowd to find my family, a sense of apprehension took hold of me. I'd dodged a bullet this time. Would I be so lucky if this woman tried to abduct Karen again?

When my family came into view, Karen ran for me, jumping into my arms and holding on tight. Miranda and Hilary stood motionless, their faces creased with worry and fear. I said nothing as I grabbed Miranda's hand and led my frightened family back to the hotel. After a few calls back home, I headed to the station to make my statement. I had to believe this was the same person who had approached Karen at school, but I couldn't be sure. The woman at the school had had half an hour to make off with Karen, if that had been her intention.

I explained it all to the local police and headed back to the hotel. I was sure Karen would be too shaken to answer the millions of questions I wanted to ask her. I opened the door, and stepped into Miranda's embrace.

"Hey there. How's Karen?"

"She's sleeping now, but she'll be okay. Hilary is pretty upset, though." She paused. "You were amazing today. Now I know why you're so highly sought after. It's almost like you were a different person. In an instant you went from husband to super-cop."

"It's my job." I sighed. "Add to it the fact that it involved my baby girl, and I guess you got the perfect storm. Most of the time when you're out there, you don't have time to think. You just react. Thinking gets you killed."

"Well, I think I'm done with Florida," she said. "I'm ready to go home, David. I'm glad we have you on our side. I feel so safe when I'm with you."

I couldn't help but wonder if I was actually keeping them safe or if I was the one putting them in danger to begin with.

"Home sounds good."

2

I drove around listening to adult contemporary on my radio, thinking about nothing at all. I did that often when I focused on following leads. I kind of zoned out and allowed my thoughts to wander. It was my alone time, my quiet time.

I came to a stop sign and looked at the kids playing outside. This was a busy, family-friendly street. Kids and adults engaged in various activities, including flag football and basketball. Others were busy planting flowers or doing other yard work. The radio call ruined the ambience.

"We need all officers to respond to Sam Houston Bridge, possible 187."

Just then, my cell phone rang, and I pulled it from my shirt pocket.

"Porter. What's up, Cap?"

"David, please tell me you're almost here."

"Yeah, Cap. Just heard. I'm on my way."

"Good. We're gonna need your eyes on this. It's pretty bad."

"Aren't they all? I'll be there in five."

When I got to the scene, it was already teeming with cops, paramedics, and the medical examiner. A crowd of spectators had gathered. I'm sure everyone was wondering the same thing I was: were we ever going to catch this guy? I directed one of the cops on the scene to control the crowd and get everyone but medical and law enforcement back. I really needed everyone out of the way—cops and EMTs included; they were doing more harm than good and risked trampling evidence.

I was a stickler when it came to the possible contamination of a crime scene—my crime scene. I was the best crime scene investigator in the state—in the nation, if you asked me. I took pride in being the best. If you aimed for second place, you shouldn't be playing the game. At least that's what I told myself. It was also what had attracted the "best" of the worst to challenge me. My motto was simple: you might not make mistakes, but everyone leaves a trail. The captain saw me approach and waved me over.

"Hey, David," Captain Wilcrest said. "It's a damn kid, David, another one. Looks like she's been beaten, maybe even raped. The bastard severed her hands and her ears. A 'hear no evil' this time, I guess. Get in there and see what you can find."

Wilcrest cleared the stragglers back, and I began looking for clues. Wilcrest followed me, taking notes. He and I had worked well together over the years. We'd had our run-ins from time to time, but we respected each other's work. He knew he could always count on me. I'd heard Wilcrest wasn't too fond of black officers, but never once in all our years of working together had I ever suspected or felt anything like that from him. At this point, I believed the rumors that preceded him were unfounded nonsense. I loved Wilcrest as much as my own father.

Sadly, it was growing easier to work these horrific murder scenes, almost like the victims weren't people anymore. To me they had become cases, numbers, and evidence. A sad state of affairs, true, but I couldn't allow my emotions to get involved at a crime scene. Wilcrest had been right—this one was pretty bad.

I looked up into the crowd. Maybe my killer was somewhere close admiring his work. That'd happened once on another case a few years back. Turned out to be our big break in the case, too. I shook my head.

"With so many footprints, it's hard to tell what's going on here. But from what I can tell, you got one perp. Indention depth of the shoes says possible female, but whatever was done to this girl was done somewhere else. The scene is too controlled for it to have happened here. She was placed here to be found. The cuts on her are surgical. So, again, it's probably someone with medical training. This is our killer, for sure. Make sure we interview all the people who live in those houses," I said, jerking my head toward a section of houses across the street.

"David, we're already on that. I almost forgot; there was another note," Wilcrest commented.

"Who moved it? Where is it now?"

The captain sent one of the officers to retrieve the note, which had already been bagged and tagged. I took the plastic evidence bag from him and held it up. The note read:

Hello, David. We meet again, and all of this is to show you what I am capable of. This blood is on your hands. It could have been your girl. Maybe next time it will be. Good luck solving this case, superstar. You always have to be the best, don't you? Until you beat me, kids will keep dying.

This wasn't the first perp trying to prove he was better than me, and after I caught this one, it wouldn't be the last. I didn't even allow it to affect me on a personal level anymore. In some sick way, I almost took it as a compliment.

Could this be the same person who had been seen talking to Karen at her school a few months earlier? The redhead? Or the blonde? The same person who'd almost made away with her in Florida? I had to believe the woman in both locations had been the same person. Her special-needs act in the playground had been just that—an act.

"All right, Cap," I said with a sigh. "I'm not sure if there's much else for me to get out of this. Make sure I get the reports from the rape kit and forensics."

I left the scene without waiting for a response and drove to the diner. It was my place to unwind and ponder. As I entered, Judy called to me.

"Hey, David. Two sugars, two creams, honey?"

I nodded. I slid into a booth, weary, as the crime scene played over and over in my mind. What kind of creep could do that to a child? What had happened to the perp to make him so insensitive, turn him into such a cruel human being? I had a gut feeling I had a woman serial on my hands, but I'd keep my options open.

One thing being a cop had taught me over the years was that perps justified a lot. They really made themselves believe whatever crooked, diabolical scheme they'd hatched was somehow okay and the victims deserved what happened to them. Whatever pain or cruelty had been dealt out to the perps in their past gave them a golden ticket to hurt others.

"I heard there was a pretty ugly scene down at the bridge," Judy said, placing the steaming cup of coffee on the table. "Something about another dead kid?"

"Yeah, something like that," I said without looking up. "Pretty bad. Nothing I wanted to see tonight—or any night, mind you."

"They cut this one up too?"

"Yeah," I said. My tone made it clear I was done with the questions.

"Well, I hope y'all catch the bastard."

"Makes two of us."

I sat for another half hour, staring at the walls before deciding to head home. As I left the coffee shop, my eyes caught an elderly couple, probably in their early seventies. How did they make it so long, living what appeared to be a normal, healthy life? If they could do it, why couldn't everyone else?

I took the scenic route back to my house, which consisted of driving through a few more neighborhoods. As I crossed the bridge near the crime scene, an uneasy feeling crept into my stomach. I pulled my car over and puked it up over the railing.

When I made it home, I laid my keys on the table and tiptoed upstairs. All was fine, both girls sleeping. I headed toward my bedroom, slowly undressed, and eased into bed next to a sleeping Miranda. I turned on the TV and pushed the mute button. Miranda would have to be up soon anyway, but I didn't want to wake her.

"Hey there," Miranda whispered. "You been to sleep yet?"

"No," I whispered back. "Rough night. Tell you about it later."

"David, honey, you should try to get some sleep.".

I nodded in the shadowy darkness. I had recently been

promoted from Detective Sergeant to Detective Lieutenant and felt an obligation to put in more time as an example to the younger cops. Plus, it was what I loved doing. It was a special distinction. That was still sort of funny to me, especially since my stint in the PD had started out as a job I'd taken to help pay the bills after leaving the army. I'd always had an interest in forensics even going to school for it. I still wasn't sold on policing. Had I hit the ground running, I could have made captain by now. I'd done my time before being accepted for Homicide, but I kept telling myself each year was my last. Now here I was, fifteen years deep.

"I will," I told Miranda. "I just have to wind down first. Last night was extremely difficult, and this new case could be troublesome for us. I don't know how we earned it, but it seems we've got a serial killer on our hands." I flipped through the channels. "And here's another one targeting me, calling me out."

As I spoke, Miranda, in her ever-so-seductive way, snuggled closer.

"This certainly won't help me fall asleep," I whispered in her ear as she perched on top of me, her breasts at eye level.

"I know; blondes drive you wild."

Then she kissed me.

"Mommy! Mommy!" A voice squeaked as the door flew open.

"Party's over," I mumbled as Miranda rolled off me and reached for her daughter.

"Hey, Karen, sweetie," Miranda said, pulling the frightened child into our bed. "Time to get up anyway." She reached for her dressing gown. "Why don't you spend a few minutes with your father while Mommy makes you something to eat?"

"Okay, Mommy."

"Don't leave," I whined as Miranda walked away. She turned in the doorway and smiled seductively. I took it as a raincheck—one I definitely intended to cash in soon.

I immediately turned my attention to my little angel. I never thought I would love being a parent as much as I did. I was constantly amazed by Karen. It seemed there was nothing she couldn't do, no task too big or too difficult for her to tackle. She loved gymnastics and promised to be an Olympian one day. She was good at everything she put her little hands on. She had even mentioned dabbling in softball. Basketball, too.

"How was work, Daddy?"

"Work was work, sugar, nothing too exciting," I told her.

"Did you get to chase anybody last night?"

"Nope. It was actually quite boring last night."

"Daddy, can you tell me an old army story?"

"Well, honey, I think I've told you most of them already. Let's see . . . I probably can come up with one more."

"Karen, honey, come on down," Miranda called from the kitchen.

"I love you, Daddy," Karen said, scrambling off the bed. "You can think about it and tell me your story later."

"I love you too, honey." I smiled. "Go eat and then get dressed for school. I promise I'll tell you that story later."

I watched as my little one scampered out of the room. Time to wake my other sleeping beauty. I sighed as I climbed back out of bed and made my way down the hallway in my robe. I opened Hilary's door to find her out like a light, as was the norm. I walked over to the stereo system, and reached to turn it off.

"Don't touch it, Dad," she murmured, eyes still closed.

Like most teenagers, music was a big part of Hilary's life. Music and boys and not much else. We had become "old" and "out of touch." All she really wanted to do was hang out with friends. The radio, although on low, was somewhat of a distraction to me.

"Time to get up, Hil."

"Dad, I'm not a kid anymore," she muttered. "I know I have to get up and go to school. I know I need to clean my room. I know I need to make good—"

"Whoa! Easy, tiger. I'm just trying to get you up. We'll deal with the other stuff later. Let's take it slow here."

Hilary, as she managed to do at least three out of five school days each week, had overslept. She was fifteen years old now and really beginning to come into her own. I sighed and moved to her window, opening the blinds.

She moaned. "Why did you have to open the blinds?"

"I open them every day, Hil. Nothing new. Rise and shine, kiddo." I said as I walked out of her room.

The summer before, Miranda and Karen and I had taken a family vacation. Hilary had some school and club sports obligations and was given the option to stay behind. While we were gone, some of her friends decided to throw a house party and convinced Hilary we would never find out. We probably wouldn't have, except for the fact that the police were called to a fellow officer's residence. My residence.

After they arrived, alcohol was found, as were a few drugs. Weed mostly, nothing major, but drugs nonetheless. Arrests were made and MIP citations were handed out. I caught hell from my fellow officers. Jokes mostly, but I didn't find them funny at all. No one likes being the butt of a joke.

Our relationship suffered a severe strain because of the party and had never fully recovered. Hilary swore she'd learned her lesson. They were just having fun, she'd said at the time, so what was the big deal? I countered with a litany of complaints: how she couldn't even wake up on time for school, wouldn't clean her room, often missed curfew, and a host of other things. I was a little harsh at times, maybe, but I was right. I didn't like where our relationship was at the moment, but it seemed every attempt I made to make it better only made it worse.

3

As I headed downstairs, I heard Miranda and Karen discussing the pros and cons of packing a lunch for school. Karen, as she did every day, sped through her bowl of Captain Crunch, rushed upstairs to throw on her school clothes, and flopped on the couch to watch *Dora the Explorer*. I sat at the kitchen table, staring aimlessly out the window, trying to figure out how I was going to catch the maniac. The case consumed my thoughts.

"I thought you were turning in, David." Miranda said.

"Yeah, I am soon. Just trying to put all this stuff together, that's all."

I had not been fully honest with Karen earlier when she'd asked how my night went. That bothered me too. I was not about to tell my five-year-old I'd discovered the body of an eight-year-old girl lying naked in a field near the bridge. Or that she had the trauma signs of rape. Or any of the other gruesome details. I didn't like to lie to my family, but at the time I felt it was the best move.

This was certainly not the first dead child I'd seen on the job, but, for some reason, this one was different. It really struck a chord in me, as had this killer. He—or she— was probably out there right now watching me, planning and plotting.

"David." Miranda sat down next to me. "I am sorry. You have a tough job, and you do it well. I definitely know I couldn't handle it. Why don't you try to get some rest? You'll never be able to figure out why people behave the way they do. Most of the time, the criminals can't even explain it themselves. You, of all people, should know that."

"I have to figure out who this guy is and why he's messing with me. This asshole has made it personal—more personal than other perps in the past."

I reached for my wife and held her in my arms for a long time. Then I quietly told her what I'd found the night before, which also explained my despondence. Miranda was deeply saddened and troubled by the news. We both looked over at our little girl, probably thinking the same thing.

"If that ever happened to us . . ." She couldn't bear to say the words.

It had already struck way too close to home.

"Ohhh! Mommy and Daddy are kissing," Karen said with a laugh as she stared at us.

"Ewww. Totally gross." Hilary echoed the sentiment as she came down the stairs.

"We're not kissing, you clowns," I said. "This is kissing." With that, I gave my wife a heartfelt kiss right on the chops. Then I got up from the table and hugged the girls. Well, I hugged Karen and tried to hug Hilary, who brushed me aside. Then I headed upstairs to get some sleep. I thought about how much I loved my family, and how I'd almost lost one of them. Sleep? Not likely, but I had to try.

4

Miranda hurried the girls to gather their belongings for school. She gave a slow-moving Karen a nudge toward the door and called for Hilary to meet them at the car. Three minutes later, Hilary emerged from the house, unconcerned that they were running late. Miranda sighed.

"Come on, Hil, hurry up. I have to get down to the station."

Being in the news business, Miranda often listened to news radio. She clicked it on.

"Last night the body of an eight-year-old girl was discovered in a field near the Sam Houston Bridge. The remains of the body have yet to be—"

"Mommy, Daddy said last night was boring and nothing happened," Karen said from the backseat.

Miranda turned down the radio. "Well, sweetie, maybe your dad didn't respond to this case last night," she said as Hilary slid into the front passenger seat, a nasty scowl on her face.

"Mommy, who is picking me up from school today?" Karen asked.

Miranda had been working on a special for the past few months, and her schedule had been erratic. She felt relieved it was nearing completion. "I'm not sure, dear, but Mommy may have to work late the next few nights. I have a big project at work and I have to finish it by the end of this week."

"Aw, man! I like it better when you pick me up."

"I'll try my best," Miranda promised.

The rest of the journey passed peacefully. She navigated through the crowded elementary school parking lot and pulled in beside the curb.

"All right, little lady. We're here. The mommy train is ready to unload."

"Whatever," Hilary grumbled as she rolled her eyes. "Mommy train?"

Miranda wished Karen a good day and watched as she darted off into the crowd.

"So why did you guys lie to her, Mom?"

Miranda took a deep breath as she navigated her way out of the parking lot. "I think you already know the answer to that question, Hilary."

"Yeah, I do, Mom. It's because you guys always baby her."

"One day, Hilary, you'll have kids, and it will be your job to protect them. Would it have made you feel better if I had told her the person who killed that little girl was probably the same one who tried to take her in Florida? Or could be the same person? Or that she could be next?"

Hilary heaved a heavy sigh. "Never having kids, so I won't have to protect anyone but me."

"Maybe that's true, but you might change your mind

one day."

"So what little white lies are you and Dad telling me?" she said in a raised voice.

"Am I adopted? Is Karen?"

"That's enough, young lady!" Miranda frowned, glancing at her daughter. "Your dad and I protect you in other ways. You're growing into adulthood, Hilary, and your father and I don't need to protect you in the same way we do your little sister. I hope you can understand and appreciate that."

Hilary rolled her eyes.

The car pulled into the high school parking lot, but Miranda had barely crept to a stop at the curb before Hilary flung open the door and dashed out of the car. She slammed the door behind her and flounced away without a backward glance.

"God, why does this have to be so hard?" Miranda muttered.

5

Miranda walked through the busy newsroom and headed toward her office. Everything was always so crazy, especially the final thirty minutes before a broadcast. Cameramen, audio crew, anchors, producers—everyone scrambling to make sure their part of the process was ready to go. It was controlled chaos, and she loved every minute of it.

After the newscast, Miranda hurried back to her office to work on cutting and editing footage for her special. She had done a good job keeping the details of the program under wraps. It was a huge story that would probably get a few people fired and might even result in jail time for some of them. She focused on her task until she heard her cell phone ringing in her purse. She grabbed for her phone and eyed the display.

"David? You're supposed to be asleep."

"I was . . . for a while. You know I only need four to five hours of sleep, and I'm ready to go."   He paused. "Are you working late tonight?"

"Yeah, I am, honey." She sighed. "I'm almost finished with this special."

"You do remember the early morning tease you gave me, right?"

She laughed. "Don't try to guilt me."

"Why don't you come home for lunch today?"

Miranda heard the grin in his voice, and without much hesitance, she agreed.

The kids were at school for several more hours, and she and David would have the entire house to themselves. She quickly shut down her computer and hurried out of the station.

**

Twenty minutes later, Miranda was home, shedding clothes as she headed up the staircase. I watched from the landing with a pleased smile. After our lovemaking session, we lay in bed in silence for a long time.

"How did I get so lucky?" I finally said, my thumb caressing her shoulder as she lay by my side, my arm wrapped around her. Her response was one I hardly expected, but given her quick-wittedness, it didn't surprise me.

"I don't know, David," she whispered. "I've been asking myself the same question. How did you get so darn lucky?"

We laughed as we looked into each other's eyes. Then I kissed her again.

"Okay, Casanova," she said, pulling away. "Enough already. I have to go back to work."

She smiled at me as she slipped from the bed. "I'm

almost finished with the story I've been working on. I'm so close, but I need to tell you . . . well, I've asked a lot of questions and probably raised a lot of suspicion. You think anyone would ever . . . you know . . . try to come after me? Do people do that?"

"Hey, don't talk like that," I said. "You're doing your job. Reporters cover cases like this all the time. Why should this one be any different?"

"I guess you're right, but you know I'm a scaredy-cat." She leaned down to kiss me. "That's why I got you to protect me, Officer Porter."

"Well, at least people will finally know John Carter is a piece of shit when this is all said and done," I said. "I've been telling anyone who'd listen, but no one gave me the time of day. Maybe now they'll agree with me. You gonna give me any idea what might be brought to light? A hint? A clue? Anything?"

"Now tell me how you really feel!" She laughed. "But yes, you'll find out the dirty details with the rest of the world, and our Mayor, Mr. Carter, and his cronies will have lots of questions to answer."

"Good! He's a snake. What you do in the dark always comes to light. I believe that."

"Soon enough, my dear. Soon enough."

I admired her well-toned backside as she walked to the closet to grab a new outfit. She glanced over her shoulder at me.

"Stop ogling. Can you get Karen from school today?"

I told her it would be no problem. She thanked me and told me not to wait up for her.

"Don't be too late," I said. "I worry, you know." I grinned. "Maybe we can go another round tonight."

"If I'm later than nine o'clock, I'll call you. And we'll see about that other round."

Miranda kissed me one last time and told me to go back to sleep. I listened as she headed downstairs and out the door. I lay there for a while, thinking about what she'd said. I hadn't really given much thought to her story before, but now I wondered exactly what she'd been working on and what scandal, or scandals, her exposé would uncover.

6

I woke to the sound of my alarm clock: 3:28 p.m. Time for me to get dressed and pick Karen up from school. Hilary was "too big" to be picked up nowadays, so she typically had a friend drop her off at home. I must have been more tired than I thought.

I turned on the news and caught the last minute of the broadcast. I smiled when I saw Miranda's face on the air. She was doing what she loved, and it made me happy. I quickly grabbed my jacket and keys. When I got to the front door, I found a note from Miranda:

Make sure you're well rested for tonight!

I smiled and breathed a sigh of relief that I'd found the note instead of Karen or—God forbid—Hilary.

I was still thinking about the little girl I found the other day. I took a glance down into the channel that snaked alongside the road as I drove over to Karen's school. *Why hadn't the killer just dumped her body into the channel?* I went with my initial hunch that the victim had been killed elsewhere and purposely placed in the park to be found. I couldn't think of a better reason.

I pulled into the school parking lot and saw Karen standing beside her teacher on the front lawn, students and parents milling around. She saw my squad car, said something to the teacher, and then ran toward the car as I pulled it up next to the curb.

"Hey, Daddy!" Karen said as she pulled open the front passenger door.

"Hey, sugar!"

Karen always talked a mile a minute after school, relating her entire day's worth of activities in a condensed, CliffsNotes-style version that took about three minutes. I loved it, though.

"I'm glad your day went well, honey."

"How was your day, Daddy?"

I smiled, thinking back to the romantic rendezvous with my wife just a few hours earlier.

"Pretty good, dear."

Karen asked me how long her mother had to work that night and if she would be home before she had to go to bed. She hated it when her mother worked late.

"Your mother has a big story she's trying to finish, otherwise you know she'd be home with us. We'll give her a call later so you can tell her goodnight. You have any dinner requests for me?" I asked, trying to take her mind off her mother's absence.

I was an okay cook, but Miranda's culinary skills were unmatched. She had learned at a young age and had taken several cooking classes in the past. She'd even thought about becoming a chef and having her own TV show. I could cook well enough to get by, but I could make it on cereal alone if I had to.

"Well, I know I have to keep it simple for you," Karen said with a laugh.

"How about mac and cheese?"

"Simple enough," she said. "Mac and cheese it is."

When we got home, Karen settled at the kitchen table to do her homework while I tackled the mac and cheese. I felt her eyes on me as I read the directions on the box. "Did you forget how to make it from last time, Dad?"

"Do your homework, young lady. I'll be fine. I promise not to burn it this time."

She grinned, but didn't say a word. She didn't have to.

I placed the box on the counter and grabbed my phone. I thought it would be a flirty gesture to text Miranda and let her know I'd found her note earlier.

Superman is waiting for Lois Lane to return.

Catchy. Not too over the top, but it would get the point across. I placed my phone on the counter and went back to preparing dinner. A few minutes later, I heard a car outside, loud music blaring. *Hilary must be home.* A few seconds later, voilà, Hilary opened the door. It had barely closed before she made it to the staircase.

"Good afternoon!" I called to her.

"Hey, Dad," she grumbled. "Mom working?"

"Yes. She'll be home later. Dinner will be ready soon."

"Mac and cheese again? No thanks, I'll pass."

She disappeared up the stairs. I didn't know what else I needed to do to connect with my daughter. Maybe all father-daughter relationships were like this after they hit fifteen. I was unsure. I thought back to a time when Hilary was my little angel. Boy, had times changed.

7

I sat down to eat chicken nuggets and mac and cheese with Karen. I'd called for Hilary to come down, but I wasn't holding my breath.

"Dad, did you hear about that little girl last night?" Karen asked.

"Well, sweetie, I may have heard a little something about it," I said cautiously. "Not much, though."

"Do you guys know who did it?"

I told her I didn't have many details on the case, and we had no suspects yet. It was pretty much the truth, all in all.

"We don't know who did this yet, Karen, but we'll find them."

My phone buzzed as I received a text from Miranda.

Glancing up at the clock on the wall, I noted it was 5:31.

Lois Lane may need a Tarzan. Superman not adventurous enough. Can you help? lol

I laughed out loud and tried to think up a clever response for my wife.

"Daddy, I'm finished. Going up to my room to play on the computer."

"Okay, sweetie, have fun," I said, still distracted by Miranda's text. "I'll be up soon to get your bath started. We'll call Mommy then, too."

As Karen took off up the stairs, a witty response came to me. I texted:

21st century Tarzan here, equipped with handcuffs and nightstick. Superman's loss, Tarzan's gain.

I turned my attention to the kitchen and the mess I'd made. I knew Miranda would be tired, and no one liked coming home to a kitchen full of dirty dishes. I decided I might as well tackle a few loads of clothes, too.

I took the time to make a few calls on some leads I had. I'd start with Marty Filner. When I needed the best ME on a nasty crime scene, he's the guy I wanted. I took out my phone and hit three on speed dial.

"Marty it's Porter. Where are we on the little girl?"

"Hey, Porter. It's early still, but we know a few things. Her name is Emily Risen. Her bruises and cuts go hand in hand with our other cases. Same blade and everything. We found some smudged fingerprints—small, possibly a female perp. She'd been there about an hour before she was found, not much longer."

"Well, our killer didn't try to hide her; he wanted the body to be found. Hell, I could find a million places in Houston to hide a body. We found her in an hour. That wasn't a mistake, Marty. Keep digging. Let me know if you come up with anything else I can use."

It was nearly 7:00 when I decided to call Miranda to see how things were going. She picked up on the second ring.

"Hey, honey," she said.

"How's the story coming along?"

"That's what Cliff just asked me," she said. "He wanted to know how much longer I'd be here."

I'd met the security guard a couple times. I was glad someone was in the building while Miranda worked. You could never be too careful.

"You think you'll be done soon?"

She sighed. "I'm trying to learn this new editing software and looking for some recorded footage I know is here somewhere. So all in all, it's going slower than I hoped, honey."

My hopes for a hookup later that night were quickly fading. I handed the phone to Karen so she could say hello. Karen and Miranda talked for a few minutes before I told Karen to say goodnight to her mommy.

"Wow, she's a talker isn't she?" Miranda laughed.

"She learned from the best."

"Okay, I know I'll be after nine now, David, but I'll call you when I leave the office. I love you."

"Love you, too."

I disconnected the call and went to Karen's room to say prayers and tuck her in. Hilary still had her music turned up way too loud, even though she knew her sister's bedtime.

I banged lightly on the door. "Turn it down, Hil," I said.

I waited until she did as she was told—barely—and walked back downstairs. I grabbed the TV remote and found a baseball game on ESPN2. The Yankees were playing Boston, and it was still in the second inning. *Should be a good one,* I thought.

As I sat watching the game, I grew tired and dozed off. I

woke up around 9:15 to the sounds of rain and a baseball game now in the eighth inning. I checked my cell phone to see if I had any messages from Miranda, but there were none. She'd told me she would probably be later than nine, and it appeared she was right.

I rose from my chair and went upstairs to see if Hilary was still awake. I opened her door and peeked in to find her asleep. I turned off her radio and adjusted her blanket. She looked so peaceful when she slept. I knelt beside her bed and said a quick prayer. After I left Hilary's room, I walked down the hall and peeked in on Karen. She was out cold. I decided to finish watching the ballgame in my bedroom. Just as I lay down, at 9:30 sharp, my cell phone buzzed with a text from Miranda.

Leaving now, Tarzan. I hope you're still awake!

I smiled and responded.

Barely awake. Fell asleep watching baseball game— girls asleep too. Cya soon.

8

I rolled over and sat up quickly in bed. I had a gut feeling I'd overslept my alarm, that sick feeling you get in your stomach when you know you're late for something important. I looked over at the television, still tuned to ESPN2 but no baseball game. It was a rebroadcast of an earlier recap show. I looked at the alarm clock on my dresser: 1:15 a.m. I had fallen asleep on Miranda. I hoped she wasn't too upset with me.

Then I realized Miranda was not in bed beside me. I got up, put on my robe, and headed for the living room, thinking Miranda might have gone to sleep on the couch so she wouldn't wake me. Or maybe she was mad at me for sleeping through our scheduled romp. I was going to have to do something really nice to make up for this one. When I reached the living room, there was no sign of her. I frowned, my heart racing. I took a quick glance outside and didn't see her car in the driveway either. I ran back upstairs to our bedroom and grabbed my cell phone. No missed calls. No missed text messages. I had just begun to punch in Miranda's number when my phone rang.

"Hello?" I said in a panic.

"David, it's Wilcrest. We just found Miranda's car crashed into the barricades by the Ship Channel, but there's no sign of Miranda." He paused. "We found another note, written in blood and left on the driver's seat. This one reads, 'More blood on your hands, Porter, this time your own.'"

Before I could respond, I heard someone pounding on the door downstairs. I disconnected from Wilcrest and hurried toward the stairs. Karen stood in the hallway, wide-eyed and disheveled. I guess the banging woke her; I didn't take time to ask. I took the stairs two at a time, Karen in close pursuit.

"Daddy, what's going on? I want Mommy!"

I didn't answer but quickly opened the door. Two officers from the station stood there.

"David, we're looking," one of them said. "But we haven't found anything, and with this rain . . ."

"Save it!" I snapped, my voice high pitched and quivering. "Find her!"

I heard a noise and glanced around. Hilary and Karen stood behind me.

"Dad, what's going on?" Hilary asked, her voice tinged with alarm. "And don't lie to us. What's happening? Where's Mom?"

I squeezed my eyes shut, praying the terror I felt inside wasn't showing on my face. I had to be strong in front of my girls and my men, but the emotions threatening to overwhelm me left me stunned.

"Dad!" Hilary screamed at me again.

I pulled myself together as best I could and turned to my girls. "It looks like Mommy had an accident," I told them. "Her car ran into a barricade, but she's not in her car. They're looking for her now."

"Dad, what do you mean?" Hilary frowned, her voice rising. "Where is she?"

"Your mother sent me a text earlier tonight, saying she was on her way home . . ."

"It's after one o'clock in the morning! Why are you just now looking for her?"

"I was watching a game on TV when I got your mother's text," I explained. "I must have . . . I don't know. I guess I fell asleep." I felt the guilt and also saw it in Hilary's eyes as she glared at me.

"So you fell asleep, knowing Mom was out there and on her way home? Maybe if you'd gotten worried sooner, we would know where Mom is!" Hilary spun around and dashed up the stairs.

"Hilary!" I called after her, but she didn't stop. A moment later, I heard her bedroom door slam behind her.

The mood was somber as I stood holding Karen, wondering where my wife was and if she was even alive. I couldn't help but wonder if the same maniac from the previous days had struck again. This time he had made it personal. I should have seen this coming. Somehow I should have known. The killer had been taunting me, but I hadn't put two and two together.

As the officers moved toward the door, I set Karen down and stepped onto the porch with them.

"Is there anything we can do, David?" one of them asked.

I stood in shock as the officers looked at me, expecting an answer. They didn't get one. I stood there for a minute until their taillights disappeared. I was soaked from the rain, which still had not let up. Suddenly, Karen stepped onto the porch and hugged my leg.

"It's okay, Daddy," she said. "It's not your fault. We're going to find Mommy, and everything will be okay."

My daughter's comforting words were pleasing to my ears. I was hopeful, but I knew if my wife wasn't found soon, there was only a slim chance I'd ever see her alive again. I was also burdened with a massive amount of guilt. Hilary was right. If only I'd stayed awake. Maybe I could have started looking sooner. This was my fault. It had to be. Even the killer blamed me. Now the game had been taken to another level, a personal one.

I looked down into my daughter's big blue eyes. She stood looking at me with a sorrowful expression that stabbed deep into my heart. She too was soaked from the rain, which seemed to be coming down harder now. I picked her up and carried her inside. I called for Hilary to come down, but she was either ignoring me or had her radio blaring too loudly to hear me. I slowly walked up the stairs to her room.

Still holding Karen, I opened the door to Hilary's room and sat down next to her on the bed. I explained that it was okay if she was mad at me, as I was mad at myself. But I also told her it was not my fault. I promised to do everything in my power to find their mother.

"Stay here with your sister," I said. "You're in charge. I'm going out to look for your mom. I promise, Hil, I'm coming back with her."

2

After I finished talking to Hilary, I carried Karen to her room and set her on the bed. "Karen, honey, I'm going to find your mother, don't you worry. I'll find her if it's the last thing I do." I paused and hugged my daughter tightly. "Hilary will be here with you."

"No, Daddy, don't leave," she pleaded.

"It's all right," I assured her. "Hilary will be here, and there are a couple officers from the station outside. I have to help look for Mommy, Karen."

Karen didn't want to let me go, but she understood why I had to leave. She told me to be extra careful and to come back with her mother. As I left the room, I took one slow look back at my daughter.

"I promise," I whispered as I disappeared from the doorway.

As I stepped outside my front door, I saw Wilcrest and a few others waiting outside. I told him to leave the suits behind to stay with my girls and then requested that he ride with me down to the channel. He held out his hand for the car keys, and I gave them to him, realizing I was too shaken to drive myself.

Being a fifteen-year-veteran officer, I had worked hundreds of accidents, but I'd never approached one knowing it involved one of my loved ones. It gave me an odd, eerie feeling that made me sick to my stomach.

"Are you sure you can handle this, David?"

"Just drive," I snapped back. "I don't have a choice."

The uneasiness in my stomach grew more intense. My head rang and hundreds of thoughts clouded my mind. As we approached the crashed vehicle, I held my emotions in check. I couldn't fall prey to my fear or I'd be useless. It took me a second to get out of the vehicle, and when I finally did, I had to force down the trembling that sought to overcome me. Wilcrest stood by my side, but I remained stoic, tough as it was. I wanted to wail in anguish, to shout my fury into the night, but I couldn't. When the officers and emergency crew noticed my presence, a somber mood fell over the rain-soaked group. No one spoke.

Captain Wilcrest had never had a reason to think I might do something irrational, but he watched me cautiously. I knew what he was thinking. I had never been in this position before. He knew stress affected people differently, and I had to be emotionally drained; he was right. Usually, I was the one assessing people in this manner.

Captain Wilcrest spoke to me. "David, we're doing everything we can and then some."

He placed a hand on my shoulder in assurance, but I didn't respond. I just looked at the railing, bent and battered where Miranda's car had crashed into it. Then I started diagnosing the scene as a police officer rather than a husband.

"We'll probably be able to get a clearer picture of what happened when we get some daylight behind us," the captain continued. "You know how these things work, David."

As calmly as I could, I spoke. "I know who's behind this. He would do anything to protect his reputation. My initial hunch back at the house had been to pin this on our child killer. But he'd have no reason to kidnap Miranda, other than to terrorize me. Carter, on the other hand . . . . If he'd found out about Miranda's report, he had every reason to want—to need—her gone."

"Everyone loves her; you know that," the captain said. "Use your head. We're proceeding to process the scene, but it may take some time."

I just stared at him. "Captain, do we have divers in the channel?" My voice sounded wooden, even to me. I could tell Captain Wilcrest didn't want to say anything to upset me any further. He thought long and hard before he responded.

"David, as your boss, I can't let you do anything that would put your life or the lives of other officers in jeopardy. As your friend, I understand your wanting to dive right in with a flashlight and begin looking around. But I think deep down we both know there's not much we can do down there right now."

"There is plenty I can do right now," I disagreed. "I'm going to find that asshole Carter and put two in his head."

"Carter? The mayor?" Wilcrest said in surprise. "David, be reasonable. I know you two have your differences, but to suggest that he'd murder . . . I don't like the man either, but I doubt he's capable—"

"Miranda was doing a special. This stays between me and you. She was almost done with it, and she said heads would roll. Guess whose name was at the top of the list?"

"What kind of investigation? I mean, on what grounds? What do you know?"

"Nothing. I don't know anything specific. She wanted it to be a surprise to me and everyone else, but I know he was the head honcho. I also know she was finishing it up tonight, and it was due to air tomorrow."

"David, don't hold out on me here. If you know something, spill it!" He frowned. "If Carter was behind this, how do you explain the note?"

"Like I said, Cap, I don't have anything concrete, but she'd spent a year on this and said jobs would be lost and jail time might be issued. Other than that, I don't know. I asked her several times for a hint, but she wouldn't budge. Carter is smart. He watches the news; he hears the chatter. This would be a perfect chance to get rid of her and make it look like this child killer is behind it. Remember our serial has been targeting kids."

The other officers were diagnosing the scene as we talked, measuring the length of the skid marks leading toward the railing. I glared at those telltale black marks. What had made Miranda lose control? They had already searched her car, looking for anything that might have fallen from her hands and caused her to take her eyes off the road. They'd found nothing.

As I turned my attention back to the captain, an officer approached us.

"David, we have reason to believe there may have been another car here. We've spotted a second set of fresh skid marks about twenty feet down the road. Maybe somebody stopped to help and then left. Maybe they took Miranda to a hospital or something. So far, we've not located any Jane Does at nearby hospitals, but we're still checking."

"Cap, you know what I need right now," I said. "Get these guys back so I can work."

A few minutes later, Wilcrest and I stood alone on the scene, just as I liked and needed. I turned to the captain. "Let's do it."

"David, are you sure?"

Without validating his question, I began. "Tire skids indicate the vehicle came in fast after the crash. Anticipatory. Small car, probably a four-door. The rain has washed away the tire tracks, or I'd be able to tell you what kind. I don't know how this asshole planned it so perfectly, but the rain has effectively obliterated most of the evidence."

Minutes turned into hours. With each second, I grew increasingly impatient and less hopeful of finding Miranda alive somewhere below the crash site. People had survived this kind of thing before, but the condition of Miranda's car meant she had been traveling at a high rate of speed. Probably hurrying home to see me after the late night at work. I'd made her feel guilty by saying I might fall asleep waiting for her. Now, as fate would have it, I was wide awake, still waiting for her arrival.

<u>10</u>

As daylight approached, additional officers flooded the scene in an increased effort to find my wife. She was well liked and respected by my colleagues. Several had left for the night, but once word got around, they returned. I could tell they were pouring everything they had into finding Miranda.

I sat down on a rock, took my cell phone from my pocket, and decided to call my daughters to reassure them that the entire force was out looking for their mother. The house phone rang and rang—a hundred times, it seemed—before my youngest daughter answered the phone.

"Karen?"

"Daddy, did you find Mommy yet?"

"No, sugar, not yet. Daddy is still looking. I just wanted to check in on you guys."

A long silence ensued. Then I heard a dull thud as the receiver dropped to the hardwood floor. I listened to the heart-wrenching sounds of my daughter's sobs. I had never felt so helpless in my entire life. I could do nothing but listen to her cries and wait until she'd recovered enough to pick up the phone again. My heart pounded in my chest as I waited. Finally, I heard her scratchy voice.

"Daddy . . . are you still there, Daddy?"

Swallowing hard, I choked back my emotions and forced myself to sound calm. "Karen, honey, please tell your sister I called. Don't give up. I promised you I would find Mommy and I will. I love you."

"I love you too, Daddy," she whispered. She sounded like she was about to cry again.

"I have to go back to work now, honey. You be a good girl for Daddy, okay?"

"Yes, Daddy. You go look for Mommy."

I stuffed my phone back in my pocket and looked around. Daylight had arrived. It was supposed to be in the low seventies today with no wind. It would be a gorgeous Texas morning, boasting an orange-sherbet sunrise, but for the fact that my wife was out there somewhere. I had to find her.

The scene overflowed with officers and the media. Some of Miranda's coworkers had also arrived, including her boss, who offered to help in any way possible.

As we talked, I spotted Wilcrest walking in my direction. I thanked Miranda's boss and met the captain half way.

"David, we need to talk."

I followed my boss a short distance away. He pointed toward a cluster of smeared footprints near the side of the road.

"It looks like a car could have been here on the side of

the road before Miranda approached. We can now see a trail of spots where traffic cones had been placed. Maybe someone was faking car trouble and put out the cones to divert her attention. Maybe a light was flashed at her car, or maybe someone stepped out in front of her to flag her down. We don't know. Miranda has the biggest heart in the world. You know she would have stopped if she thought someone needed help. What we do know is the cones are gone. We checked with the city, and they said no work was being done on this section of road last night. We've been scanning the lake all morning. Nothing. No jewelry, no clothing, no reason for us to believe she went into the water. We're treating this as a kidnapping now, David. We definitely believe foul play was involved. Is there anyone—?"

I knew where Wilcrest's next words were going. "No. No one. She has no enemies." The harshness of my tone registered on Wilcrest's face.

"Obviously she does."

I frowned. He was right. "Only John Carter would have done this," I said, my calm voice belying my raging emotions.

"You mean the investigation we talked about last night? Do you really believe Carter is behind this?"

"Like I said, I have nothing concrete," I told him. "As far as I know, the story was still under wraps, but I suppose she'd been snooping around and asking questions. Still, I don't think anyone had put it all together. She was careful not to let that happen. That's one reason why the project took so long. She spaced out interviews and file searches weeks apart to try to keep suspicion down."

Wilcrest nodded. "You may have something there. But be careful and tread lightly. If Carter is behind this and thinks we're on to him, any trail you might have picked up will vanish."

I had to think like a cop now and not a husband. I wondered about the details of the story Miranda was working on.   Maybe someone had caught wind of her investigation, and Carter indeed wanted to silence her.

Wilcrest told me I should go home and be with my girls; there was nothing else I could do at the scene. I hated to agree with him, but he was right. My adrenaline drained, I felt fatigued from head to toe, both mentally and physically.

Wilcrest signaled for an officer to drive me home. I rode the entire way in silence. As we pulled up to the house, I saw Karen sitting in the living room window, her elbows perched on the sill. She flung open the front door and raced toward me as I scrambled from the police car.

We were all devastated, and I knew my little girl didn't understand what was happening. Neither of us said a word. I held my crying daughter close and tried my best to comfort her. I happened to look at the upstairs windows and caught a glimpse of Hilary staring down at us. When I made eye contact with her, I was stunned by what I saw in her gaze. It wasn't the pain or sorrow I expected, but a look of anger and hatred. Then Hilary stepped away from the window, and the curtains fluttered back into place.

I knew the coming days and weeks would be tough, especially if Miranda wasn't found. Or worse . . .

11

I lifted Karen into my arms and headed inside. The officer who'd dropped me off had asked if he could do anything for me, but I'd waved him off. I sat Karen down on the living room couch and told her to stay put while I went upstairs to get her sister. I knew Hilary was angry and upset, but we needed to talk. I knocked once and opened the door without waiting for her reply. Her room gave me an eerie feeling. Her posters of Madonna, Kid Rock, and various other musicians almost came to life—like they were staring at me, ashamed of me. As usual it was a pigsty, with books, magazines, and clothes strewn everywhere. She sat on the edge of her bed, her back to the door. I walked over to her and sat down on the bed—not too close, but close enough to reach out to her if she wished it. I watched a tear trickle down her cheek.

I had offered many words of condolence to hurting families. I had attended funerals, been beside family members as their loves ones died, and yet I found myself at a loss for words for my daughter in her own time of need. I reached out, gently clasped Hilary's hand, and tugged her off the bed. Then I guided her downstairs. She took a seat beside Karen without saying a word. I sighed and offered them an update.

"So far, we've come up empty-handed. They're still looking for her, but beyond that, there's not much I can tell you."

I told them where her car had been found. "We really don't know what happened. Something made her swerve from the road, or maybe she was tired and fell asleep." I paused. "There's no sign of her being injured, but there would be no logical reason for her to walk away from the scene." I shook my head. "We just don't know."

The girls digested what I told them. The awful reality was sinking in; I could see it on their faces. Karen asked me if the lake had been searched. I glanced at her, thinking it was terrible that such a young child could make the connection between the location of her mother's car and the lake below. I calmly assured her it had also been checked.

Hilary placed a comforting arm around her little sister's shoulders while I sat on the coffee table in front of them. I fought back tears as I spoke quietly to my daughters. I had to be strong for them. Anything less was unacceptable.

When my cell phone rang, my heart leapt with hope. I pulled it from my pocket and glanced at the number. It was Wilcrest. With staggering disappointment, I answered.

"David, it's Wilcrest. We did some research on those cones. The city was out here yesterday doing some road work after all. They mentioned leaving a cone behind. That leads us to believe someone or something forced her off the road. We haven't found anything, but we're still dragging the lake."

I waited for Wilcrest to continue, while my girls stared at me with hope in their eyes. I shook my head.

"Miranda could have traveled a long way during the night. We have a big search area, David, you know that. You've been involved in such searches before, and you know what we're up against. In the meantime, don't do anything stupid."

"Like what?" I asked. He didn't reply. I knew what he meant, though. He meant for me to stay away from the mayor. He didn't have to worry. I wasn't going to go off half-cocked. I told the captain to keep me updated and ended the call.

"Did they find her, Daddy?"

"No, Karen, not yet. They think your mother might have lost control of her car and then walked off."

I knew I wasn't being completely up-front with them. They seemed to know it too—or at least Hilary did. I could tell by the way she looked at me. I knew foul play had been involved, but I wasn't ready to tell them I suspected she'd been run off the road and maybe dumped into the lake.

Karen sagged against her big sister, and I moved from the coffee table to sit beside them. With Karen cushioned between us, I sang softly, as Miranda had when both girls were tiny babies:

"Hush little baby, don't you cry. Daddy's gonna sing you a lullaby."

Eventually, the girls fell asleep right there on the couch, huddled together. They had been up the entire night before, hoping and waiting for good news, and they were exhausted.

I finally left them to their slumber, and stepped into

the kitchen. I needed to eat, but my appetite was nonexistent. I stood there, staring blankly into the refrigerator when my phone rang.

Again, my heart went into overdrive. Again, I felt crushing disappointment when I saw the call came from my father-in-law, Tom.

Earlier, I'd asked Captain Wilcrest to call Miranda's parents to tell them what had happened and to ask if they knew anything about the project Miranda had been working on. I hadn't wanted to alarm her parents, but we were grasping at straws, and any lead, from any source, would be vital.

My father-in-law and I had never gotten along. Tom thought his daughter could do better than me. Much better, as he bluntly put it. Miranda had told her father I was the one, and she was in love. I wasn't ready to hear the words I expected to spew from Tom's mouth.

Tom Pete was a successful business man, a Princeton graduate, and a good friend of many local politicians, including John Carter. Miranda's mother, Grace, had been a housewife her entire life. Rosa, Miranda's former nanny, did all the real work, as Grace spent much of her time shopping and gossiping with the other ladies from the country club.

"Hello, Tom," I said, my voice subdued.

"David, I just want you to know we don't blame you for any of this. Captain Wilcrest called us last night and told us what happened. Unfortunately, Miranda didn't tell us what she's been working on these past few months. Apparently it was very hush-hush. I just wanted to let you know we're leaving now and should arrive later this evening to help with the girls."

I felt relieved that they had not found fault with me for Miranda's accident or disappearance. I blamed myself enough and really didn't need it from anyone else.

I thanked Tom and left it at that. I said nothing of my fears regarding who she'd been researching. After all, Tom knew Carter well. And I didn't mention the scenarios running through my head: Maybe the cone left in the road had caused her to swerve. Maybe it had been placed in her way on purpose. Maybe the nut-job serial had come at me directly, hitting where it would hurt me most. Or maybe Carter had planned the whole thing. Right now there were more questions than answers.

We wrapped up the conversation with Tom's promise to see me in a few hours. I barely made it back to the fridge before my phone rang again.

"David, we're pretty certain now that something went down here," Wilcrest said, getting straight to the point. "We found some blood off the side of the road, near the drainage ditch about twenty yards from the front of Miranda's car."

My heart pounded as I waited with bated breath for him to continue.

"Looks like a dragging pattern. It's already begun to seep through the drying soil. There are tire tracks nearby. Maybe she was placed into another vehicle. We've already made more calls. Still no Jane Does at any hospitals. Not yet. That doesn't tell us if she was alive or dea . . . It doesn't tell us what state she was in, but you know as well as I do we have to move fast."

I knew Wilcrest was right. If we didn't find Miranda soon, we would probably never see her alive again. My girls needed their mother, and I needed my wife. A wave of grief washed over me, followed by overwhelming guilt and frustration. Who had taken Miranda? I should have been able to find more clues at the scene. Was this guy better than me, or had he done his homework and simply avoided the mistakes other perps had made?

12

I knew what I had to do. The clock was ticking, and if I hoped to find Miranda before it was too late, I had to act now. It was after midnight, and I knew no one would be at the city's office downtown. It was highly unlikely any records of wrongdoing would be there, but that's where I had to begin.

I alerted the security detail out front, pulled my car from the garage, and sped away. Once downtown, I parked in an alley behind the city building so I could get in and out without being seen. I knew if I got caught, regardless of the circumstances, I risked losing everything I'd worked so hard for. Still, I knew I had to press forward; it was all I had. I sighed, reached into the glove compartment, and shuffled through the papers. I grabbed the small leather case I'd been searching for and slipped it into my back pocket as I climbed from the car. I opened the trunk and reached for the disposable surgical-type gloves we always wore at crime scenes. I slipped on a pair and, with resolve, moved toward the building.

I approached the back door of City Hall, which I knew was not currently equipped with an alarm system. Being a cop, I was privy to such information. John Carter liked to cut corners; I found myself thanking the man, for a change. I pulled the kit from my pants pocket and picked the lock without any trouble.

With a quick glance over my shoulder, I stepped into the hallway. The horrid, black-and-yellow-diamond-patterned linoleum probably dated back to the forties, perhaps even earlier.

I went straight for Carter's office and picked my way in within seconds. I was looking for an inconspicuous file cabinet; anything of importance wouldn't be easily visible. I quickly scanned the room but found nothing. I heard a noise outside the office and froze in place. Had someone seen me enter the building? Had I been followed?

I eased my gun from the holster at my waist and made sure it was ready to fire. I knew if I were caught there would be no talking my way out of breaking and entering. That's what it would be. Unlawful search. I didn't have a warrant. Maybe claiming temporary insanity would work, given the circumstances. Criminals were certainly using that defense just fine.

I crept from Carter's office and tiptoed down the hall in the direction from which I thought the noise had come. My heart throbbed so hard, I was certain whoever followed me could hear it. It was dark and I couldn't see a thing. Who was watching me? Carter? I nearly swore out loud when I saw a stray alley cat that had obviously wandered in through the door I'd left ajar.

I went back into Carter's office to continue my search. I figured I'd try his computer next but, to my dismay, found only a docking station. Carter had a laptop. I grew increasingly frustrated. My chances of finding Miranda dwindled with every passing second. I knew I had to make the boldest move I'd ever made as an officer, possibly a career-ending move, but I had no choice.

I left Carter's office and City Hall. I climbed back into my car, peeled off the gloves, and tossed them in a dumpster at the end of the street. Determined, I drove to Carter's estate with one thing in mind—finding answers.

I parked about a mile away from Carter's gated community. I knew I wouldn't be able to just drive in. I walked along the fence line until I found a blind spot the security cameras couldn't see. I was still in fairly decent shape and had always been an above average athlete – the fence wouldn't be a problem. As soon as I touched down on the other side I noticed a car approaching. I quickly ducked behind a row of bushes narrowly escaping being noticed. As it turned out it was a security car. This clearly wasn't one of my best plans but I was desperate. About the time I got to the driveway of Carter's home, something happened. I snapped. I had never been a rogue cop, but this was different. My plan to get in and find the laptop had gone out the window. I wanted answers, and I wanted them now. I banged on the front door like a madman until Carter appeared. I could hear him on the other side of the door. I figured he was staring thru the peephole trying to figure out who the mad man was banging at his house in the middle of the night. Finally he slowly opened the door.

Carter stood in the doorway wiping the sleep from his eyes. He peered at me and nodded in recognition. Before he could speak, I grabbed him by the throat, drove him backward into the foyer, and slammed him against the wall.

"Where is she?" I demanded . "What did you do to her, you asshole?"

I'd been trained in criminal interrogation strategies as a police officer and in the military. I was skipping a few steps, but, nonetheless, I would find out what I needed to know. Carter wiggled and squirmed and tried to free himself, but I was too strong for him. "Where is my wife, you piece of shit?"

"I don't know what you're talking about," Carter blustered.

"You know exactly what I'm talking about! What the hell did you do to her?"

"Take your hands off me!" Carter demanded.

The guy had some nerve. It was after two o'clock in the morning; he was being manhandled in his own house, and still had a pompous attitude.

"I'm going to ask you one more time," I said, pressing against his neck with my forearm as a warning. I could choke him or snap his neck instantly, thanks to my military training, but I struggled to remain in control. For Miranda.

"Where is Miranda? I don't have time to play games with you!"

Carter coughed harshly, eyes wide with fear as he tried, without success, to pull my arm away from his neck. He obviously noted my fury and tried to placate me.

"Look, Porter," he gasped. "I know we've had our differences, but I can see you're reacting on pure . . . emotion. You're not thinking clearly."

"That's not what I want to hear," I said. "You have two seconds to tell me where my wife is, or we won't have differences anymore. I don't differ with dead men, and you'd just be one less headache for me."

Carter swallowed hard. He had no reason to think I would hesitate to kill him right there on the spot.

"Okay, okay," he sputtered. "I heard about what happened to Miranda, and I'm sorry, but I swear on my life I don't know anything about it. I'm the mayor! Why would I be involved in a murder?"

Had I mentioned murder? I didn't think so.

Just then, Carter's wife walked down the stairs, tying a robe around her waist.

"John, what's going on?" she asked, her voice shrill with panic.

"Nothing, Jill." Carter choked out the words. "Go back upstairs. Now!" "Detective Porter!" Jill's face blanched as she caught sight of me. "What are you doing here?"

"Go back upstairs, Mrs. Carter. This is between John and me."

"I'm calling the police!" she shouted over her shoulder as she scurried back up the stairs.

I didn't care. I'd probably lose my job, but I had to know. I refocused my attention on Carter, who stared at me with dismay.

"Where is she?" Spittle flew from my lips and landed on his cheek as I yelled.

"David, I'm telling you the truth. I don't know anything about what happened to Miranda. Some of my people told me she'd been asking questions, but I haven't done anything wrong. I have no reason to want to kill her or anyone else. I may be a lot of things, but I'm not a murderer."

He paused to catch his breath. His fear was real, and I had a feeling he was speaking the truth. My hold on him loosened, but only slightly.

"I know you're hurting right now, which you have

every right to be. On top of that, you hate me . . . which is okay, too. But please don't hurt my wife."

Carter displayed none of the outward signs of lying or deceit. I looked up to find Jill standing near the top of the stairs, eyes wide, one hand clasping the handrail so tightly her fingers turned white. I snapped again, this time back to reality. I released Carter and headed toward the door.

"David?" Carter said, rubbing his throat. "I'm sorry about Miranda. Really."

I walked through the foyer without a backward glance and slammed the door shut behind me. I didn't worry about him telling anyone, though for some reason I doubted he would. Carter was guilty of many things, and keeping a low profile was high on his priority list.

I got in the car and drove, hoping to sort my thoughts. I had nowhere to go, no leads, nothing to go on. I knew John Carter was up to something. Maybe not murder, but something. Something big. If that weren't the case, Miranda wouldn't have been investigating him or his staff. Still, I had no proof. Not one shred of evidence.

<u>13</u>

I walked into the house and collapsed on the couch, exhausted beyond belief. I stared at the ceiling for several moments, too tired to even attempt to choke back my emotions. Tears pooled in my eyes, and before I knew it, my shoulders were shaking with my pain. I was filled with fear, despair, and an overwhelming sense of uncertainty. Not knowing was the worst. Unfortunately, I could now relate to those who often asked me that all-consuming question: Why?

**

"Anything different, Dad?" I heard Hilary ask.

I cracked open my eyes and saw her staring down at me as I sprawled on the couch. I quickly sat up and rubbed my face.

"Not much, Hilary. The investigators believe someone took her." I decided it was time to be brutally honest. "It looks like she was moved. That could be good or bad. Maybe someone stopped to help her, and she'll turn up at one of the hospitals."

"Okay. Why were you sleeping on the couch?"

"Long story."

She looked uncomfortable, nervous. "What's wrong, Hilary? I mean, besides the obvious? Are you holding up okay?"

She nodded and then sat down next to me.

"I need you to know I don't blame you, Dad," she admitted. "You couldn't have stopped this from happening, and I just said all that stuff without thinking."

I wrapped my arms around my daughter, relief flooding through me.

"I know, honey. It's okay."

"I just miss her so much. I hope she's okay . . . but deep down, I don't think she is." She buried her face in her hands as she burst into tears.

"Don't say that, Hilary," I said, though I'd thought the same thing more than once. "We're going to keep looking for her."

"I'm just scared I'll never see her again."

As I sat helplessly listening to my daughter's mournful weeping, my eyes filled with tears. I tightened my grasp around Hilary and held her close.

After a time, her tears subsided. Hilary told me she'd spoken to both sets of her grandparents. I knew Miranda's parents were on their way, but apparently mine were coming as well. She said she'd needed someone to talk to while I'd been out looking for Miranda, and I was glad her grandparents had been there for her in her time of need.

As Hilary and I talked, Karen came downstairs. One look at our faces and she knew her mother had not yet been found. I reached for her just as we heard a knock on the door.

As Karen crumpled into Hilary's embrace, I rose from the couch and opened the door to find my parents standing on the porch, their faces awash with sympathy.

My parents were both hardworking, small town people who owned a modest cattle farm on the outskirts of Rosharon, where I grew up. My dad, Roger, had dropped out of school after eighth grade. He only knew one way to live—work hard or die trying. My mother, Sara, didn't do much better in school, dropping out midway through her tenth grade year. Still, they managed to raise a family and make ends meet through grit and determination. I had grown up happy and loved which, in the end, was all that really mattered.

"David, how you holding up, son?" my mother asked. "I know that's a stupid question.

She wrapped her arms around me, like she used to do when I was little. I appreciated the comfort. "I'm doing the best I can in the spot I'm in." I stepped back and gestured for them to come inside. "I'm more worried about the girls."

Karen and Hilary hurried into the foyer to hug their grandparents. I realized my kids couldn't be in better hands right now. I glanced at my dad.

"Since you guys are here, I'm going back out. I may head to the station or back out to the accident scene, but I can't just sit here and do nothing."

Dad offered to go with me, and at first I declined. I wanted to be alone. I always worked better that way, although this case was certainly different. In the end, my dad came with me. As I backed down the driveway, I hated to see the faces of my daughters as they stared out the window at me, fear and confusion clouding what should have been youthful joy—or teenage indifference, in Hilary's case. I'd take teenage angst any day over this. I could deal with my pain, but watching my children suffer was another matter.

My dad and I rode for several minutes with neither of us saying much. Finally, my dad broke the silence.

"David, what do you guys know?"

I sighed. "We don't know much. It looks like she was dragged from her car. Not sure by whom or for what reason." I glanced at my dad as I navigated the streets. "The girls don't know any of this, so let's keep it to ourselves, shall we?" Dad nodded and I continued. "Our best guess would be something went wrong, either with a kidnapping or a hit. We're almost at twenty-four hours, and no Jane Does have shown up anywhere."

I had resisted uttering the words, but I knew I couldn't avoid them much longer.

"I don't know if I can do it without her, Dad—the girls . . . life."

"David, don't give up. There's a chance she's still alive."

I gripped the wheel hard, determined to keep my emotions in check. "I can't help but think somehow I could have . . . should have stopped this from happening. This is not just a simple accident. I mean, I'm always out here trying to protect and save everyone else, but I couldn't even protect my own wife."

"David, whether this was an accident or not, there was nothing you could have done. No way you could have known this would happen or you would have stopped it."

Growing up, I'd rarely shown much emotion. I was a quiet kid who kept everything bottled up inside. My dad was the same way. It was easier that way. But this pain . . . this was too much. It was as if a boulder rested where my heart had been. I ached inside—for me, my girls, and Miranda, wherever she was. I swiped away the lone tear that escaped down my cheek.

We approached the accident scene, and I was surprised to find no one there. Not one single squad car. No investigators, no patrol, no one. Even the crime scene tape was gone. My pulse raced with anger as I dug into my pockets and hurriedly dialed up my captain. At the same time, Dad got out of the car and walked toward the damaged railing where Miranda's car had crashed. I followed as the captain answered my call.

"Captain, why isn't anyone at the crime scene?" I demanded.

"David, the crime scene has been processed. We've combed every inch of it. We're waiting on a few lab results, but that's about it. We do have a dive team headed out to search the far side of the lake this morning." He sighed, frustration and sadness in his voice. "You know there's just not much else we can do, David. It's a waiting game now."

I didn't respond but angrily disconnected. I knew he spoke the truth, but I didn't want to hear the truth right now. I walked over to my dad and looked over the railing with him.

"Is there any chance she could have been . . . she could be in there somewhere?"

"I suppose it's possible," I said. "We just don't know. We've searched the shallows of the lake in the vicinity of the bridge here, but they're sending the dive team over to search the far side in a little while."

We spent nearly an hour looking, searching, hoping for anything. Finally, Dad suggested we go back to the house to check on the girls. The look I gave him was angry and ugly. Desperate. I regretted it immediately and softened my stance, suggesting we look for a few more minutes. Something might have been missed by the other officers who'd already spent half the night and into the morning doing the same thing.

As my dad wandered back toward the car, I scanned the rocks below the bridge and, to my surprise, saw something glisten in the deepening sunlight. I climbed down the slope at one side of the bridge, knelt down, and pushed the rocks and dirt aside.   A ruby earring. Miranda's birthstone. I recognized it as something she'd picked out a few years earlier as a birthday present. I looked up and realized I was about two feet from the edge of the railing.

I looked around some more, but saw no blood or other signs of her presence there. *Miranda, where are you?*

I put the earring in my pocket. I would tell no one what I'd found. I didn't have a good reason not to share the evidence, but this earring and where I'd found it—so close to the water—suggested. . . . I tried hard not to think it, but it was impossible. Something bad had happened here. The earring might be further confirmation, but it still provided no answers. Besides, I really didn't want to part with it. Not right now.   It was clear, at least in my mind, that John Carter and his men were responsible for whatever had happened to Miranda, and the motive was her report. Somehow I had to prove that.

I climbed the slope to the pavement and headed for the car. Dad leaned against the back bumper, staring off into the distance.

"Let's go, Dad. I think I'm done here."

Dad told me he was sorry we hadn't found anything and had reached a dead end. I nodded as I blinked back the warmth again flooding my eyes. I felt so helpless. Hopeless. Finding the earring by the railing almost nailed the coffin shut. I knew it in my heart, but I wasn't ready to give up.

"David, I hate to ask, but how long do you usually suggest families wait in situations like this? You know, before making arrangements and such? How long before your team updates you on what they think happened?"

I didn't answer him right away. I just kept driving. When I pulled into the driveway, I spoke my only words of the trip back.

"We'll wait a while. Give my guys time to come up with something more conclusive either way. Maybe we'll get a break in the case or a tip or something. I know it doesn't look good, but until there's definitive proof . . ."

Dad reached over and laid his hand on my shoulder. No words were needed.

Hilary and Karen knelt on the couch, peering out the window as the car pulled in. They watched as the two of us got out and headed for the door. The pain on their faces hurt me to my bones.

14

"Hello! Can anyone hear me? Help me! Please!"

Miranda waited, but no one responded. She lay on her back on a hard surface, her arms and legs tied down tight. She raised her head, blinked hard to clear her vision, and strained to survey her surroundings. The room was dark, except for a few milky strands of light that filtered in through one dirty, partially covered window. She saw tables, clutter atop them, though she couldn't tell what any of it was. The air felt damp and had a rotten smell to it. She coughed, hoping to clear the dry, chalky feeling from her throat. A solitary fan oscillated in a corner; its slow, steady headshake issuing a warning but doing little to move the air around the room.

Where was she? She tried to move her hands again, tugging hard against the bindings. A sharp, numbing pain in her right hand rewarded her movement. Overcome with emotion, she sobbed as she desperately sought to free herself.

"Help! Help! Somebody help me!" She screamed until her voice grew hoarse.

She sagged with weariness, and then lifted her head again to inspect her body. Her right hand appeared to be wrapped in some type of cloth, and it throbbed with every movement. Other than that, nothing seemed amiss. At least nothing she could tell at the moment.

Who had done this to her? Why? Had someone found out about her story? Was this a way to punish her, to keep her from talking? *Surely my boss will run the story anyway,* she thought. She had saved the final draft before she left her office, intending to send the file via email to her boss.

She heard a noise and strained to listen. Was someone coming? She heard footsteps. Then a door opened and closed. Someone approached.

"Hello there, pretty Miranda. I see you finally woke up."

She felt startled to realize the voice belonged to a woman.

"What? Who's there? Who are you?" Miranda said, voice trembling.

"Don't you go worrying about that. I know who you are. Perfect little life. Good job, good-looking husband, beautiful kids. Don't worry; I'll make sure they're all well taken care of. You just start getting adjusted to your new home here."

"Don't you screw with my family, you bitch! You better not hurt them."

"You like that word don't you?" the woman asked. "We've only spoken twice now, and both times that's what you called me. Why, you don't even know me, Miranda, but your family will. That, my friend, is a promise." The woman laughed. "Now make yourself comfortable, and let me know if you need anything. Oh, and this whole thing . . . it's nothing personal. Sadly, I may even come to like you. But I have a score to settle with that husband of yours. I'm going to destroy his family and let him watch you die. Then, after I've broken him down, I'll kill him too!"

She laughed again.

"By the way, do your daughters use such language? I hope *bitch* isn't what they decide to call me. Well maybe your oldest one will; she seems a little high strung."

The woman headed for the door.

"Wait, no! Don't leave!" Miranda yelled. Her plea fell on deaf ears. As quickly as the mystery woman came, she disappeared.

Miranda had no idea who this woman was or why she was doing this to her. She worried for her family's safety. Surely David would find her. She knew he would be looking. The entire police department was probably looking.

The door opened again.

"Oh, one more thing. I'm sorry about chopping off that finger, but I needed something to use as solid identification. Hope it doesn't hurt too bad. If they find the little clues I left behind, they'll think you're lost to them and will eventually stop looking for you. That's an awfully deep lake. They'll try, but they won't find your body. Such a shame." She laughed again and slammed the door behind her as Miranda's screams echoed in the musky darkness.

15

I lay alone in my bed—our bed—looking up at the ceiling. Karen lay next to me, sleeping an exhausted, restless slumber. I hadn't eaten in two days, nor could I sleep. My in-laws had finally made it in; I heard them stirring downstairs. I knew they'd stay in a motel since Miranda wasn't here, but having them around during the day would be good for the girls. A fresh pot of coffee brewed, and the smell of bacon had made its way up the stairs.

And then it hit me again: my wife is missing. A wave of fresh agony swept over me. Could I have done anything to prevent this? Where was Miranda? More importantly, was she dead or alive? I refused to give up hope. Maybe we'd get a break today.

My cell phone rang, and I rolled over to answer it. It was Captain Wilcrest.

"David, we spoke to Miranda's boss. He did acknowledge that she was working on a story, but even he had not been aware of the details. He checked her office. Her laptop and the video and audio footage she'd gathered are gone. It must have been in the car with her when she wrecked at the lake."

"What? " I asked, confused. "Why the hell are we just finding this out now? Why didn't someone tell us items were missing from her office?"

"Her door was locked, and her boss was out of town for a couple days. He checked her office the minute he got back," the captain explained.

"That definitely confirms foul play! Why else would they have needed to keep her laptop?"

Captain Wilcrest said nothing as I ranted. Karen stirred, looking up at me with fear in her eyes. I calmed myself.

"David, we're doing everything we can. You know that. The divers have been out dragging the lake for the past three days and . . ."

The captain hesitated, which was strange. I've never known the man to be at a loss for words.

"David, they found a shoe. It might belong to Miranda. We'll need you to come in and identify it."

I sat silent and stunned. They'd found a shoe?

"At this point, it doesn't look good, David. But I don't have to tell you that, do I? If the shoe is Miranda's . . ."

Wilcrest paused, giving me a chance to comment, but I couldn't.

"I know what you told me about her story and the mayor," the captain continued. "But, David, we have nothing concrete to go on, and we can't exactly storm into his office and make him talk. No judge in his right mind would sign off on a search warrant on such sketchy grounds."

" Thank you, Captain. I know the boys put in more time than they usually do on a missing person's case. I appreciate it. I'll come down there as soon as I get the girls off to school."

I strained to keep my emotions in check.

"David, I can't imagine what you're going through. Take all the time you need."

"Thanks, Captain," I muttered.

"And since I'm the only one who knows the report was about the mayor, I'll keep the fact that it was you who broke into his office to myself."

I bypassed the comment, not wanting to incriminate myself or deny the accusation, either.

"Can you get someone from HR to get some counseling sessions lined up for the girls?" I asked instead.

"David—"

I disconnected.

"What's wrong, Daddy?" Karen said. "Did they say they found Mommy?"

I hugged my daughter without saying a word.

"We'll be okay, Daddy," she said. "I'll take care of you until Mommy comes home."

Hearing my daughter say this brought the lump back into my throat again. A knock on the bedroom door brought my thoughts back into focus. It was Hilary.

"Dad, I'm going to hang out with some friends," Hilary announced. "I've been here for three, almost four, days. I have to get my mind on something else." Her eyes filled with tears. "I need to go, Dad."

"Okay, okay," I said. I understood completely. "Just be careful, and be sure to call me every few hours, will you?"

"Call you? Why? You couldn't protect Mom—"

"Hilary, that's not fair," Grandmother Sara said as she appeared behind her. "And besides, you shouldn't talk to your father like that, especially in front of Karen. What kind of example are you setting, young lady?"

Hilary, her face reddening, bolted out of the doorway.

"It's okay, Mom," I said. "It's to be expected. Sometimes people just need someone to blame. Right now that someone is me."

"She shouldn't talk to you that way," she insisted. "Would you have spoken to me or your father that way?"

"Times have changed, Mom, but you're right; I probably wouldn't have. But Hilary and I have had a strained relationship for a long time. That's no secret. Miranda has been the glue between us. I don't know what's going to happen now."

"Yes, times have changed, David. Parents are too lenient with their children, and it leads to this." She held out her arms to Karen. "I'm going to take Karen into town and make sure she's got something to wear for the vigil tonight. Do you need anything?"

A candlelight vigil had been planned for the community after word of Miranda's disappearance spread. Our church was hosting. I shook my head. As they left the room, I mouthed a thank you to my mother. She nodded and closed the door behind her.

I sat down on the bed again. The only word I could think of to describe myself at the moment was lost. Lost. Without Miranda, I am—we are—lost.

16

I stared at the ceiling. My head ached and I couldn't stop shivering. I felt like I had the worst case of the flu—ever. It had been five full days since my wife disappeared. The only thing I had consumed was a few sips of water.

"Daddy, you don't look good."

I glanced at Karen as she walked into my bedroom. "I don't feel good, honey. Not sure what's come over me."

I knew all too well. I didn't want to be here anymore. I was ready to give up. Life without Miranda didn't sound like something I wanted to experience. The only thing keeping my heart beating was my daughters. I felt a sick sense of despair and guilt over her disappearance. It threatened to engulf me. If only I'd stayed awake the night she disappeared!

"Is there anything I can do to help?"

"No, I don't think so, sweetie. Daddy just has an

upset tummy and a headache. I'll be okay. I promise."

She was about to reply when my phone rang. I groped for it on the bedside table and opened it without looking at the display.

"Porter here."

"This David Porter?"

"Yeah, who is this?" I asked, watching my daughter climb onto the bed and sit cross-legged beside me, staring intently.

"Listen, I have information for you. You want to know about your wife, don't you?"

"Who is this?" I sat up, fully attentive.

"Meet me in one hour at Mills's old feed store. Come alone. If I see anyone else, I'll leave and you'll never hear from me again."

The call disconnected, but I suddenly felt better—much better. I forgot all about my flu-like symptoms as hope surged in my chest. But I didn't want Karen to see the excitement in me and start to ask questions I couldn't answer yet. Calmly as I could, I turned to her.

"Karen, why don't we get you some Captain Crunch? You've got to be hungry. Daddy has a quick errand he has to run."

We headed downstairs, and I sat her at the kitchen table, prepared a bowl of cereal for her, and then hurried back upstairs to dress. Then I peeked into Hilary's room to tell her I'd be out for a few hours. As I turned to leave, Hilary stopped me.

"Dad, you promised us you'd find Mom."

As she turned to me, I could see she'd been crying. I stepped inside, and sat next to her on the bed. I wanted to hug her, but decided not to press my luck.

"I'm trying, Hil, believe me. I've run myself into the ground looking for her, trying to find solid leads. I'm not giving up. I actually have a new lead I'm working now. Keep your fingers crossed—mine are."

I kissed her forehead and left the room.

After letting my parents know I'd be out for a while, I hurried out the door to meet my mystery informant. On my drive to the designated location, I had to wonder if it was a setup. Maybe I was driving right into the middle of John Carter's plan to get rid of me. I had been snooping, after all. Still, it was a chance I had to take. I reached down to feel the comforting weight of my gun at my waist.

I ran a few red lights, driving recklessly in an effort to hasten my trip. After a short drive, I pulled into the decrepit parking lot of the old feed store on the outskirts of our neighborhood. There wasn't a soul in sight, no other cars nearby. My senses on high alert, I stepped out of my car and moved toward the building. A side door hung crookedly on its hinges. I pulled it aside and stepped into the darkened structure.

"Hello?" I called out, gun drawn.

I saw a rat scurry away at the sound of my footsteps. Could this informant have picked a worse place for this meeting of the minds? For the predicament I found myself in, I was being as cautious as I could. With gun in hand, whoever was here would at least know I wasn't going to go down without a fight.

"Don't turn around."

A male voice. I froze.

"And lower your weapon. Now!"

At that moment, I felt the first trickle of fear. I had made a mistake. In my eagerness to find out what had happened to Miranda, I had stepped into a trap, no backup. I never should have come here alone or at least without telling someone where I was going. I was afraid my life was about to end.

Before I could reply, a sharp retort caused me to hunch down. A bullet whizzed past my ear.

"What the hell are you doing?" I yelled.

"Just wanted to give you some incentive to make sure you don't try something stupid. I know how you John Wayne cops are."

I tried to place the voice, but couldn't. My back tensed, awaiting the impact of a bullet.

"I used to work for Carter," the man said. "I was low man in his entourage. I know why he made your wife disappear. What I don't have is proof. I can tell you where to dig and what to look for, but you'll have to do the legwork yourself, super cop. And by the way, I don't like you. Let's get that out of the way now. I'm not doing this for you. I hate Carter even more than I hate you."

"Okay, I'm okay with you not liking me," I said, turning slightly.

"Don't do it, Porter, I told you not to turn around. You turn around and I stop talking."

"Okay," I said, freezing again. My heart pounded in my chest, waiting for him to tell me about Miranda.

"I did everything I could for Carter. I lied when I needed to lie, covered up what I needed to cover up. Whatever it took. I picked up his damn kids from school, bought flowers for his stuck-up ass of a wife when he forgot his anniversary. First chance that prick had to get rid of me, I was out. I have a family too, ya know. He ain't the only one who needs money. So one day I overheard him say I was replaceable and useless. On top of that, he blackballed me."

I wondered how long he would continue to whine about his sorry life. I kept my mouth shut.

"Now I can't get work anywhere, and over a mistake I didn't make. We'll see about that; we'll see how useless I am. I'm going to enjoy watching him rot in jail."

This guy was obviously bitter and hurt, but it would be interesting to see how much he could help me.

"I get it," I said. "But why did he let you live if you know something that will get him thrown in jail?"

"Hey, I'll do the talking here. He threatened my family. I have three kids, Porter. Plus, he doesn't think I have the balls to do it or the proof. Which, like I told you, I don't have."

"We'll protect your family," I said. "Don't worry about that."

"Shut up!" he shouted. "You couldn't protect your own wife. How the hell are you going to protect mine?"

My blood boiled but I tamped it down. "In all fairness, mister, I didn't know my wife was in danger or I would have, trust me!"

"Playing the I-didn't-know card? Being a super cop and all, how could you *not* know, with all the digging she'd been doing?"

"She didn't tell me the details of her investigation. Actually, she didn't want my help. She wanted to do it alone, so I let her."

"Well, this is what I know. For starters, Carter has a laptop detailing all of this business hidden in a safe in his wine cellar. He doesn't know I know about the laptop or where it is. I have a few secrets of my own. I don't have to tell you that besides being the mayor, his family left him with more wealth than he could ever spend."

He paused, but I remained standing where I was, waiting impatiently for him to continue. What the hell did he know about Miranda's disappearance?

"I always felt that if a man had too much money, he'd eventually do something bad with it. Carter went on a trip to Dubai early last year, minus his wife. There were five of us on that trip. By the way, you'll be glad to know your tax dollars paid for it." He laughed. "Carter told the media he fronted the bill. He has money tied up in several businesses there, and that was the nature of our trip. While we were there, he met with a man named Abu Da Hussein. Remember that name. He was offered a piece of Hussein's business to be a partner."

"What kind of business?" I asked.

"International sex slave trade."

"What?" My heart skipped a beat. The mayor was involved in trafficking human sex slaves? "Is this what Miranda found out about?"

"I'm getting there," the man replied. "We're almost out of time. Let me finish. Several of us advised it was a bad move that would only end in scandal, but Abu made it clear there would be no ties back to Carter. He detailed how his money would be covered and moved from company to company and bank to bank to avoid suspicion. Hundreds of businessmen travel to Dubai every year for this very reason. It's a popular and lucrative business, Mr. Porter. Carter has even visited the boutiques on more than one occasion. He fit Abu's investor profile, which is why he approached him with the offer. The five of us who traveled to Dubai are the only ones who know about the deal. I was never approached, talked to, or asked about it again after that day. Actually, I tried my best to forget it."

"I doubt that only you five know," I said. "I mean, there's too big a chance that someone would talk. It just doesn't make sense. Why would he take that kind of risk?"

"Why do evil men do what they do, Porter? Pick a public scandal and then ask yourself why the person did it. Why do serial killers kill seemingly innocent people? Look, I don't have time to play these games with you. I shouldn't be here in the first place. And like I said earlier, you can't protect me or my family. If I went into protective custody, wouldn't that tell Carter I talked?" He spat. "You know, for a cop, you're pretty stupid. Aren't you like some big renowned crime scene expert? They should really make you guys take some sort of aptitude test or something. We're on his payroll. Money *is* the root of all evil. Surely you've heard that before, right super cop?"

I shrugged, still with my back to him. "I guess I'm smart enough not to get involved in something that would eventually ruin my life and my career, especially something so highly immoral and stupid. I have daughters. With that said, it's hard for me to understand someone who can or does. So you're saying if I can get to Carter's laptop, I'll have everything I need to find my wife?"

"Here we go again with the stupid questions. Yes. Like I told you, I hate Carter for what he did to me. I hope you're as good as they say you are. So far you haven't impressed me much. But I'd like to be able to visit Carter in prison one day. Good luck and I hope you find your wife."

"Any special info?" I asked before he left the building. "Like a good time to try to get this laptop or whether the safe requires a key or a combination? Can you tell me where it is in the wine cellar? Is the cellar locked?" I stopped spewing questions and waited for a response but heard nothing. "Are you thinking or waiting for me to ask a more intelligent question?"

Nothing. I turned around. He was gone. I ran out the door and around the back of the old feed store, but saw no trace of him.

"Damn it!"

I hurried back to my car, armed for the first time with something I could run with. I decided I couldn't trust anyone with this information, not even Wilcrest. My next challenge would be getting inside Carter's wine cellar and putting my hands on the laptop. Maybe I would find out what had happened to my wife. Maybe, just maybe, I would find her still alive.

One thing did trouble me. How had Miranda stumbled onto this? I might never find out, but it did explain why they took her laptop. It didn't, however, explain why they'd left the note blaming me. Maybe it was to throw me off the trail. It had worked . . . till now.

17

I knew the first thing I had to do in order to stack up a case against Carter was get a tap on his phones. But to do that, I'd need a warrant, which would mean I needed probable cause. Not to mention everyone in the department would know. What if Carter had someone working on the inside? I couldn't risk it. Time to call in a favor from a friend.

"Tracy, it's Porter."

"Hey, David. What's up, sweetie?"

"I need a huge favor, and I'll owe you big-time. I already know that."

"Just tell me what you need, honey."

"I need trace and tap put on a few phone lines."

"That's it? Way too easy. Okay then, who's the future inmate?"

"John Carter."

"You mean like Mayor John Carter?"

"Yes."

"Come on, David, I'll do anything for you. You know that. But this could be big trouble."

"I know, I know, but I have no choice. You've got to trust me on this one. I'm flying solo here. Just sit back and watch the skeletons fly out of the closet. I promise you I'll be revealing some pretty nasty ones in the next few days."

"You know I hate you, right, David?"

"Yeah, I know you do." I smiled. "Let me know when it's a go. And remember, I'm on my own on this one. I'll get you a plane ticket somewhere nice when this is over."

"Yeah, yeah, but this better be good," she said with a sigh. "This is a ball you can't afford to swing and miss on."

I knew I could count on Tracy to get the taps quickly and stay quiet about it. Next, I needed to call the girls and check in on them, as the day had turned into much more than I had originally anticipated. My oldest daughter answered the phone.

"Hilary, I got some info I have to run with. I'm going to be out later than I expected. Let your grandparents know, okay? And keep an eye on your sister for me. Everything okay there?"

"Yeah, Dad. Just do what you promised. I love you."

I drove downtown and parked on a side street within view of city hall. I sat in my car, waiting, my laptop on the passenger seat. Some time ago, I'd downloaded the software I needed to monitor communications I otherwise wouldn't have been able to tap into. Tracy had come through with the tap and hooked me into the system, so now it was just a waiting game. After an hour, I finally got something. Someone from Carter's office was making an international call. I perked up and listened in.

"Abu, we have a problem."

It was the mayor! My heart pounded as I adjusted my earpiece, not wanting to miss a syllable.

"Hello, my American friend. We were never to talk on the phone, so why are you calling me?"

Abu's accent was thick, but his intent was quite clear.

"I wouldn't have called you unless it was urgent," Carter said. "A reporter here found out what's going on. She's out of the picture now, but I don't know if she had backups to her report or who she might have told."

"Friend, you are obviously looking for the wrong person. I mistake you for someone else," Abu said. "I am bad with names and voices. Unless you travel to Dubai so I might see your face, I am afraid I don't know who you are. Have a good evening."

I heard Carter slam down his phone. Less than two minutes passed before he made the first of several calls requesting an emergency meeting with his private staff. Within an hour, Carter left his office and headed down the street to a popular local bar. I followed a discreet distance behind. I had no ears inside, so I just watched and waited, trying to sort out what I'd learned so far. Carter's phone call to Abu confirmed at least some of what the man had told me at the old feed store. Miranda's disappearance, it seemed, was a direct result of her report; I was certain of that now, too. With the information I had, including Carter's partial admission to being involved in Miranda's disappearance, I felt I could bring Wilcrest in.

An hour later, I learned Carter and his crew had booked flights to Dubai and would be in transit soon. Because I'd flown worldwide speaking at forensics and crime scene seminars, my international flight status and passport information were already in place. Still, I knew I could not simply fly to Dubai without telling my boss. I would indeed have to bring Wilcrest up to speed.

I grabbed my phone to call Wilcrest.

"Cap? Porter here. I need you to meet me in an hour at the park." I didn't wait for a response, but simply hung up.

I drove to the park and waited. I'd changed my mind about getting my hands on Carter's laptop—for now. He'd probably take it with him anyway. Plus, I needed to be in Dubai when Carter arrived. It'd be much harder to track him otherwise. I needed to stay one step ahead of him. I sat in my car on the east side of the park, waiting for Wilcrest. In no time at all, he pulled his car up behind mine and slid into the passenger seat next to me.

"David, what's going—?"

"Cap, listen. I don't have much time. I got a call from someone who wants to remain nameless. I don't even know his name. I met him in . . . well, it doesn't matter right now. He told me Carter was involved in Miranda's disappearance."

"David? Everyone knows you don't like Carter. You got a vendetta against the guy or what? What do you have? Don't tell me you called me out for this."

"Just listen, please. I told you I don't have much time." I placed the laptop on the console, opened the audio file, and hit the play button.

I watched the captain's face as he listened to the conversation I'd recorded between the mayor and Abu. He was a hard man to read, but I could tell he was soaking in every word.

"That enough for you?" I asked when the recording ended.

Cap frowned. "Where did you get that?"

"I don't have time to explain all that now. I have to go home and grab a few things and fly out to Dubai tonight."

"Dubai?" Cap said, his voice rising an octave. "Why

Dubai, Porter?"

"That's where the money is going, and that's where Carter is going next."

"I don't know how you do it, Porter, but I guess you're the best for a reason. What else do you need from me? I don't like being left out of the loop, but I suppose you had your reasons. Go get him."

"I need a warrant for his house. I need access to everything he has access to. I'll definitely need Fingers on this. I know where Carter's private laptop is kept. I'll have to get it, but this has to be on a need-to-know basis. The judge and the DA are both on that short list. I gotta ride solo on this a little longer, at least until I know who I can trust. I don't need word getting out about this yet. Like I always say, sometimes it's good to be the best, but being lucky sure don't hurt."

"You didn't get a tap on John Carter's phone by luck, David. I'll work on those warrants for you. You have Fingers' number, so call him. Now get outta here."

I sped home to tell the girls I needed to leave for a few days. I wasn't sure how I'd break it to them.

As luck would have it, I found both girls and my parents gathered in the kitchen, a batch of freshly baked brownies cooling on the counter. Karen came running the minute she spotted me.

"I may have a break in Mommy's case," I said, untangling myself from my youngest daughter's embrace. "I'm not saying I know where she is, but I think I'm getting closer. The break in the case won't come from here. I'll have to go and get it, so I'll be gone for a few days. Your grandparents will be here while I'm gone."

"Dad, do you have to go?" Hilary asked.

It had been a long time since I'd seen my oldest looking so vulnerable.

"Yes. It's the only way to get what I need."

I hugged them both. Then, I went to my room, threw Miranda's Nikon, a change of clothes, and my laptop into my backpack, and headed out.

.

<u>18</u>

"Fingers, Porter here," I told him over the phone. "Got something good for you to work on; it's right up your alley."

"Hey, my friend! I was just breaking into the World Bank," a gruff voice replied. "I was, like, fifteen digits away. Thank you for keeping me down again. What's up?"

"You better be behaving yourself, before I have to run you back in."

"You wouldn't do that, 'cause then you couldn't use me for shit like this!"

"You got me there. Listen, I have reason to believe John Carter is helping to fund an illegal sex slave business in Dubai. I'm nearly one hundred percent sure of it. I already have some decent evidence, but what I need is damning evidence. Air tight, you know?"

"So what exactly do you want from me?"

"What I need from you is his itinerary, which is

probably on his city computer," I explained. "He's a public official, so I'm sure it's detailed so he can be tracked down in case of emergency. I need to know what hotel he's staying in, who he's meeting, where, and what time. Everyone worries about being followed, so I'm going to be in front of him. I'm just about to board a plane headed for Dubai now, so I'll beat him there. I need the information as soon as you get it. I have a plan, but I can't work it until I get that info from you."

"I'm on it, Porter," Fingers replied, his voice tinged with excitement. "Now I get to do some legal hacking. Well, more legal than what I'd be doing otherwise."

"Okay, just hurry."

I disconnected and went over my plan in my head yet again. I had worked it out down to the very last detail. I needed this trip to tie Carter and his goons to Dubai— something other than computer records, which could be falsified. I wanted something concrete enough that twelve jurors would have no choice but to send him away for a very long time.

The flight to Dubai took just over sixteen hours. I traveled so much doing seminars that I always had enough frequent flyer miles to upgrade to first class, which was nice. Though I had napped a bit on the plane, my plans and thoughts of Miranda had constantly played through my mind. After we landed, it didn't take me long to shake off the cobwebs and get going. I had a mission awaiting me. I gathered my backpack and disembarked. After going through customs at Dubai International Airport, I found a café advertising free Wi-Fi, ordered a cup of coffee, and powered up my laptop. I nearly shouted in relief when I saw the email from Fingers.

He'd done it again. Now I could take the coordinates he provided from Carter's itinerary and plan his route a step ahead of him. I nearly laughed when I saw what hotel he had booked. I downed my coffee and headed outside to get a taxi.

"Take me to the Ritz-Carlton," I told the cabdriver. At this point, I didn't care what this trip would cost me. I had Carter's schedule. Now I knew his every move.

Carter had a room reserved on the second floor. I even had the room number. He had arranged for a private car to take him on his appointed rounds; I did the same. I called the car fleet and arranged for a private vehicle for twenty-four hours, starting tomorrow morning at six a.m.

When we arrived at the Ritz, I paid the driver and walked inside the contemporary structure with its limestone façade, exquisitely tiled floors, modern furniture, and classy décor. After registering and parting with a good deal of money—thank you, credit card—I walked to the elevator bank and pushed the button that would take me to the seventh floor. I had requested a room on that floor so the chances of the two of us crossing paths were reduced. I used a computer program Fingers had told me about to reprogram my room key to allow me access to the room on the second floor.

Carter was not due to arrive at the hotel for several more hours, so I left my room, returned to the elevator, and made my way to his room. The hallway was empty, so I swiped the card, waited for the click and green light, and let myself in. Next came the task of setting up audio and video surveillance. I ran a tap from the phone line and set up my recording devices, all linking back to my computer. After a thorough double check, I headed back upstairs to my room.

Now I would wait.

I watched from my room window as Carter's vehicle pulled up to the hotel. With Miranda's long-lens camera, I snapped photographs of the crew getting out and walking into the hotel. I knew it would take a few minutes for him to check in and take the elevator to the second floor. I moved to my computer, laying open on the bed, and activated the audio mikes I had placed in his room. Carter's meeting with Abu was scheduled for that evening. This was a short trip for Carter, right to the point. From the looks of his itinerary, he had scheduled to meet with Abu in his hotel room. Moments later, I was able to listen to what was happening in Carter's room.

"Hey, boss, want me to meet Abu down in the lobby when he arrives?"

"No, he can meet us here. I don't want anyone to see us meeting Abu," I heard Carter reply.

I listened to Carter talk, hoping to get something I could use to help bury him. If Wilcrest had secured the warrants, everything would stand in court. If he hadn't, the public outcry from the evidence, conveniently leaked to the press, would force him out of office anyway.

"We have less than an hour until Abu arrives," Carter said. "Let's go downstairs and get some food."

I knew this might be the only chance I had to get my hands on Carter's laptop. I waited ten minutes, listening carefully to be certain no one had remained behind. Then I hurried down to Carter's room, swiped my keycard again, and slipped inside. As I scanned the room for the laptop, I heard a keycard in the door. I dashed into the bathroom and stepped into the tub, drawing the shower curtain closed behind me. I unholstered my gun, my heart beating wildly as I clicked off the safety.

I held my breath as someone rolled open the closet door and rummaged about, hangers clanking. Just as quickly, the person retreated. When I heard the click of the room door, I climbed from the bathtub, took one last look around, and made my escape. I headed to the stairs and exited on the third floor. From there, I took the elevator back to my floor.

I didn't have time to search thoroughly for Carter's laptop, which was likely password protected anyway. That would be yet another job for Fingers when I returned to the States. Maybe he could hack into Carter's laptop from a remote location.

I listened in as Carter and his men returned to their room less than fifteen minutes later, one of the crew complaining about the dinner hours.

"Who wants to wait until nine o'clock to eat dinner?" one of them asked.

"Shut up," Carter snapped. "Let's get ready. Abu is coming through the lobby now."

I listened with rapt attention and heard the double knock on the door.

"Don't ever call me on a cell phone again," Abu said as he stormed into the room.

"I told you we had a serious issue. What was I supposed to do, email you?" Carter replied.

"How did this American reporter find out about this? What is her story?"

My heart thumped in my chest. It was true. Miranda had uncovered a scandal.

"Like I said, Abu, she's been taken care of. She's dead now, so she's not a problem."

Dead? Miranda was dead?

"She was working on an expose," Carter continued. "I don't know who she told or if her files are on a flash drive somewhere."

"It seems you do have a problem then," Abu growled. "I am not certain what I can do to help or why you are even involving me. Where is your other man? You came with four the last time."

"I fired him. Had to cut back my staff."

"You American idiot! What makes you think he won't talk?" Abu hissed.

"He won't talk. It'd mean jail time for him too," Carter replied. "Plus, I threatened his family. Trust me, we don't have to worry about Tony Strat."

Now I had a name for my informant.

"Have you searched the home of this reporter?" Abu asked. "How can you be sure you are not being followed?"

"No, we haven't searched her home. Her husband is one of the best detectives on the planet. And no, it's not possible I was followed. No one even knows I left the country except my office staff. Even if someone knew I was leaving, I'd have no reason to be followed, Abu."

"Your stupidity is incredible!" Abu said. "So do you not think this cop is going to figure out you idiots had his wife killed? You think he is going to let it go? This meeting is over, as is our business with you.

"Abu—"

"I cannot do business in this matter. My boutiques have run without problems for ten years, and you threaten everything I do in only a couple."

"Abu, don't be hasty," Carter implored. "I just need some time to sort this out. Don't worry, friend, this will all blow over soon."

"You play this game like an amateur," Abu said. "Was this room scanned for bugs?"

"Bugs?" Carter asked.

I heard shuffling. "Look what I have here a scanning device, you fool!"

A moment later, I heard a high-pitched alarm.

"You idiots!" Abu yelled.

"Porter! It must be Porter," Carter said. "He won't

be too hard to find."

"You Americans never cease to amaze me. If he is the one who set up this equipment, he knows we're on to him," Abu said.

Abu was right. My mission had now changed. I had gotten the photographs and the audio recordings. The laptop would have to wait. My next goal was to make it out of Dubai alive.

19

"Go quickly to the front desk," Carter ordered one of his men. "Find out what room David Porter is in. Now!"

"You must find and kill this man!" Abu said. "I do not want my name associated with this foul play."

Time to leave. I closed the laptop, shoved everything into my backpack, and quickly left the room. I walked past the stairs and the guest elevator bank, and headed for the service elevator at the end of the hall. I pressed the button for the basement. When I reached the bottom, I stepped out cautiously, hugging the wall that led from the elevator to the laundry area. I spied a cement ramp that led to street level and sprinted up. With a quick glance both ways, I headed across the street, hailing a cab as I ran. One of Carter's men spotted me as a taxi pulled to the curb.

"I got Porter getting into a cab! I'm going after him!" I heard a man yell.

I leapt into the cab, glancing out the back window. Carter's man was dodging traffic in his effort to get across the street.

"Go! Go!" I yelled. "Don't stop at the light."

Just then, two rounds came through the back window of the cab. One of the bullets caught the driver in the shoulder. He yelped and lost control of the car. It jumped a curb near a corner.

I jumped out of the car as it sideswiped a lamppost, stumbling to get my feet under me just before the cab crashed into two parked cars. Seconds later, it exploded into a fireball. I ducked instinctively, feeling the sting as shards of flying glass nicked my face and arms. Fortunately, I was far enough away from the cab to avoid being struck by any major debris.

I looked behind me; one of Carter's men was still giving chase. Dusk was approaching, and I hoped I could avoid them and use the cover of darkness for protection as I tried to make my way back to the airport. I couldn't go to the cops, because I was certain a billionaire like Abu would have several of them, if not the entire force, under his control.

I ducked into an alley and ran to the nearest doorway. I stood ramrod straight against the building, blending into the shadows as I pulled my gun. My pursuer followed me into the alley and came charging in my direction. As he ran by me, I put one dead center. He dropped instantly.

I looked down at the dead man and noticed a walkie-talkie attached to his belt. I grabbed it and thumbed the tab.

"Carter? One down. If you tell them to turn back now, maybe they'll live. If not, I'll kill them all."

"Shit!" Carter said.

I laughed. "Abu, leave now and I'll keep your name out of this. I have no beef with you. I didn't come here for you."

I knew making this deal was the only way I could escape the wrath of the entire Dubai police force.

"You fools have created a mess." Abu's voice crackled over the walkie-talkie. "Porter, my business with this man is finished."

I had shifted the odds and created a chance to make it out of Dubai. I had already taken one of Carter's bodyguards out and was confident the others would pose the same level of incompetence. Carter apparently didn't realize his mike was still activated, as I was able to hear his next words.

"Meet me back in the room now!" Carter told his men. "Porter has audio with us and Abu. We must find him. You know the implications if we don't."

I made my way to the back of the alley, pulled my phone from my pocket, and called Captain Wilcrest, courtesy of international roaming. I quickly filled him in.

"Cap, they found my bugs," I informed him. "They gave chase. I took one down already."

"David, have you gone to the local PD?"

"No. I can't trust any of them. Abu has too many ties. The cops here are probably all in his back pocket."

"David—"

"Cap, listen. Carter said Miranda's dead. I'll send you the audio file as soon as I get to the airport." My voice shook with fury. "He's coming back with me, I promise you that."

"There's actually one man there you can trust," the captain said. "His name is Frank Mitchell. We served together in Vietnam. I'll send his number to your phone. I'm sure he can help you out."

"Okay, Cap. Send over a suit to watch my house. I gotta run."

I ran deeper into an alley and then into what looked like an abandoned store. I needed a mirror and a restroom to clean up some. Couldn't walk into an airport bleeding without arousing suspicion. I hurried to the back of the long-abandoned store—or at least it seemed that way considering the stink and filth laying about—and found the restroom. I opened my backpack and pulled out my clean pair of socks. They would have to do. I turned on the water and looked in the mirror, only to realize that the blood on my shirt had not been caused by flying glass. I'd been shot. The bleeding came from a through-and-through wound in the meat of my upper arm. My heart had been pumping so fast, I hadn't even noticed it.

I had just wiped the blood off my arm and wrapped the other sock around the holes, tying a loose knot with one hand and my teeth, when my cell phone rang. I reached into my pocket with my good hand and answered it.

"This David Porter?" a deep voice asked.

"Who's asking?"

"Must be my guy. Wilcrest gave me your number. Said you were in a heap of trouble here and needed a little help. Any friend of Wilcrest is a friend of mine."

"You're Frank Mitchell?"

"Yeah."

"I'm in an old, abandoned store restroom right now. I took a shot, so I'm trying to clean it up a little."

"Do I need to take you to the hospital?"

"No, I don't have time for that. I've got some cleaning up to do here before I head back to the States."

"I'm coming to pick you up. I'm able to track your location through your number. Stay put. I know where you are."

"You sure you want to get involved?" I asked him. "It could get pretty nasty."

"Son, I served in Nam - if things get nasty, I'm sure I can handle my own."

I made my way to the front and looked out, careful to keep myself hidden from any passersby.

"Hey, let's get outta here."

The voice came from behind me. My heart leapt and I spun around, gun in hand.

"If I was one of them, you'd be dead," the voice said. "And you were worried about me?"

I cursed under my breath. Mitchell had snuck into the building some other way. He'd had an easy kill shot had he wanted to take one. I couldn't afford to be so careless.

"David Porter, I presume. The name's Frank Mitchell. Wilcrest said you were pretty good at what you do." He smiled. "You don't look like much to me, though."

"Yeah, you know you can't judge a book by its cover. C'mon, let's go."

Mitchell had long, dark hair and was pretty muscular for an old guy. He wore dark fatigues and military-issued boots. *Did this guy still think he was in Nam?*

"Where'd you get your training, kid?"

"After college, I did three years with the Army Rangers. Did a few tours in Saudi. Not exactly Nam, but I know my way around. Didn't see myself making a career out of the military, so I joined the PD. Didn't know how that'd work, either, but I'm still there, fifteen years deep."

"Ranger, huh? I was a Marine - Tiger Force. Most exhilarating job in the military, we did shit you cupcake boys only dreamed about. We came to get you guys when the stuff got too deep. And as fate would have it, I'm saving one of you again."

"Pretty impressive," I grunted. "Look, I don't have

119

much time. I need to take these guys down before they decide to head back to the States, and I don't mind having a Marine save my ass."

"Well, you look like shit. Let me get you some food and a few toys, and then you can do what you gotta do. What kind of trouble you in anyways?"

"No trouble I can't handle, just a couple bodyguards. The trouble will be finding their boss. I don't want to kill that one. I need him alive."

We walked four blocks before arriving at a nondescript house. Inside, the place looked as I expected it would—dark, cold, and messy—more like a military barracks than a house. Guns littered the coffee table, and ammo was piled everywhere. As long as he had food and a little firepower for me, I could deal with the mess.

"Come on in. Get some of this grub in you."

Mitchell slapped a bowl of hardened oatmeal in front of me. I was hungry, but when the aroma of the food hit my nose, my stomach churned.

"Thanks, but I'm going to have to pass."

Mitchell shrugged and handed me a military issued assault rifle and some ammo.

"You can set these down and make you a perimeter if you need to," Mitchell said.

"You preparing for war in here or what?"

"I *stay* ready, son. That way I don't have to *get* ready."

"Well, thanks for all this." I picked up the equipment. "I have to get going."

"Good luck, Ranger. Here, take this too."

I caught the grenade he tossed my way.

"Never know when one of these little puppies will come in handy," he said with a grin.

I left Mitchell's and headed back in the direction of

the hotel to see if Carter and his men still lingered there. To my surprise, they did. I saw one of Carter's men standing guard on the sidewalk in front of the hotel, and, unfortunately, he also spotted me.

I dashed into the street, dodging cars as they honked and swerved around me. One crashed into a compact car waiting at the stoplight. It was only a fender bender, so I made my move. I ran to the dented vehicle and tapped on the driver's-side window with the butt of my pistol.

"Get out now!"

I don't know if the driver understood my words, but he took one look at me and scrambled out of the car.

I hopped in and ran the red light, barely avoiding being T-boned by a car crossing the intersection, and sped down the street. I glanced in the rearview mirror and swore. Two of Carter's men reappeared on black racing bikes. *Where the hell had they gotten bikes?* It appeared Carter had found some toys of his own while I hooked up with Mitchell.

I pushed the little foreign car as fast as it would go. *Could I have stolen a slower car?* The bikes closed the distance in a hurry. I slammed on the brakes and turned down a back street. The bikers behind me gave chase. Looking ahead, I saw another bike headed straight toward me from the opposite direction.

I swerved toward the sidewalk, jumped the curb, and took out a row of trash cans, hoping the cans would roll into the street and into the path of the trailing bikers. At the next intersection, I would make my move. I revved the engine and waited until the last second. I pulled up the hand brake, sending the back end of the car spinning around.

The back fender smacked into the oncoming

motorcycle. I heard a cry and the crunch of metal as the bike and rider flipped into the air.

I quickly released the brake and slammed my foot down on the accelerator. I fumbled for the walkie-talkie still in my jacket pocket. I tabbed the switch.

"Two down, Carter. I told you I was going to kill them all."

The two men trailing me opened fire with automatic weapons. At that moment, I realized Carter might try to ditch his men here while he headed back to the States. I pulled my cell phone from my pocket, and with one eye on the street and one on my display panel, I thumbed through my call log.

"Mitchell, Porter here. You want some action?"

"I thought you'd never ask," Mitchell drawled. "Sounds like you got plenty of it going on right now."

"Just some minor gunfire and a high speed chase. That's a little out of your realm, huh, Marine? I got a recon mission for you, though. The Ritz-Carlton, room 202. A man named John Carter." I described him. "I need him alive. I'm picking his men off one by one. I'm sure you'll have a chase on your hands when he realizes I'm coming after him next. Try not to make too much of a mess, okay?"

"Now that's what I'm talking about." Mitchell laughed. "I'll get your man. You stay alive, Ranger."

20

I needed to plan my next move. I still had two of Carter's bodyguards giving chase and bullets whizzing around me. Then, an idea popped into my head. I knew it would be risky, but I had no choice. I decided to use the grenade to take out one of them. If I timed it just right, it would blow right on top of the man. I would have to set him up, though.

I made a sharp right turn on the next street I came to, and the bikes closed in on me. I quickly pulled the hand brake, and the car skidded to a near halt, burning rubber along the way. Both bikes swerved crazily to avoid rear-ending the car and flew by. I disengaged the hand brake and slammed the car in reverse, my foot pressed down on the accelerator. The narrow street I found myself on was relatively empty. I dodged a few parked cars and upended some trash cans, but otherwise my plan to avoid busy streets was paying off. I didn't want to involve innocent pedestrians or occupied vehicles in my ploy.

I knew the bikers would be doing everything they could to catch me, and their guard would be down. I reached into the bag on the passenger seat and pulled out the grenade. I watched closely in my rearview mirror, rolled down the window, pulled the pin, and waited. Just as the bikes drew near, I tossed the grenade at the biker on the driver's side. I watched in my side mirror as it detonated just in front of the bike and rider and sent both flying twenty feet into the air.

I keyed the button on the walkie-talkie. "And then there was one, Carter."

My phone rang. While keeping an eye on the street ahead of me and glancing repeatedly in the rearview mirror to keep track of my lone pursuer, I turned on my phone and cradled it between my shoulder and my ear.

"Porter."

"Porter, I got your guy. " Mitchell laughed. "He came running out of the hotel without any baggage or anything. I almost passed him by while walking up the hotel steps. I did a double-take, and he ran for a cab. No use . . . I yanked him into the alley next to the hotel and Tasered him right in the back. He squirmed like all get-out while I handcuffed him. Then we made our way back to my car and off we went. Why didn't you tell me he was the soft, office type? I thought I was going to have a fight on my hands."

"Good going, Mitchell. I'm almost done here. I'll meet you back at your place."

I flipped off my lights, made a hard turn into the lane the last gunmen was in and slammed on the brakes. The biker slid in an attempt to avoid me and ended up laying his bike down in the street. He flew off his bike and rolled several times until the curb stopped him. I slammed the car in park, leapt out, and ran toward him. He was still alive, but not for long. I stood over him and put one in his head. That quickly, it was done.

I left the newly beat up Mazda where it was and hot-wired a car parked a short distance down the street—another skill I'd learned long ago. In less than ten minutes, I was pounding on Mitchell's front door.

"Where is he?" I said to Mitchell, shouldering my way inside minus any type of formal greeting.

"Took you long enough. C'mon, I'll take you down to him."

I hurried down a narrow set of stairs to Mitchell's basement. There I found a shirtless, bound and gagged John Carter.

"Well, well, what do we have here?" I said.

My blood surged as I stared at the man I believed responsible for the disappearance and probable death of my wife. Without hesitation, I punched Carter in the face, knocking him and the chair over. Mitchell picked them back up, and I hit him again. I didn't like the look in Carter's eyes, so I released a barrage of punches at his face. One of his eyes had swelled shut and his entire face was a bloody mess before I stopped. Mitchell looked way too calm; he just sat there, popping sunflower seeds into his mouth like he was watching a baseball game.

"I guess you know by now that I heard you tell Abu my wife is . . . how did you put it? Out of the way?"

Carter didn't respond.

"Okay, Carter. If that's the way you want to play it. Wanna help me out here, Mitchell?"

"Oh yeah," Mitchell said, popping in another handful of seeds. "I got just the thing to make this asshole squeal like a pig."

I ripped the tape off Carter's mouth while Mitchell

reached for a set of jumper cables. He attached them to a charger.

"Wait!" Carter exclaimed, his bravado gone now. "Porter, I didn't have nothing to do with your wife, I swear!"

"Why the hell would I believe that?" I asked him. "You needed her gone to protect your disgusting sex slave business!"

"No! Well . . . I did, but I didn't kill her! I hadn't even talked to my guys about it. I might have needed her gone eventually, yes, but somebody beat me to it. I didn't even know about her report. I didn't know she was on to me before all this went down."

"Shut up!" I snapped. "Now, I'm going to ask you this one time and one time only, so listen carefully." I stood over him. "What did you do to my wife?"

"Porter, think about what you're doing," Carter blubbered, eyes wide. "Think about your girls."

I shrugged. "Who's here to see? I know exactly what I'm doing. It's you who should have thought about what you were doing before you killed my wife!"

I took the cables and attached the leads, one for each of Carter's nipples. I looked over at Mitchell and nodded. Mitchell flipped the unit on and gave Carter a jolt of electricity.

Carter screamed as his body convulsed. The outer layer of skin burned where the cables were attached. The smell of burned hair and fried skin was both disgusting and gratifying. I gave it a second more for good measure and gestured for Mitchell to stop.

"Porter, I'm warning you. You're playing with fire here!" Carter yelled.

"You're tied to a chair with an electric device strapped to your nipples, in a foreign country, with the man whose wife you killed, and you're threatening me?"

"Okay, okay. You're right. I'm sorry. Let's—"

I nodded to Mitchell to hit him again.

Carter slumped over in the chair. The last hit had definitely weakened him. He tried to speak, but nothing but spittle came out. I walked over and lifted his head.

"You got something you need to say?"

"Porter, there's nothing else I can say," he stammered. "After I found out your wife might be onto us, I needed her out of the picture. But I swear to you, I had nothing to do with it."

I shook my head in disbelief.

"There's no one else on this planet who would want to harm Miranda. You see, Carter, there's this little thing called motive, and you're the only one who had one. I can do this all night; I nod, you get hit. Haven't you figured that out yet? If my wife is dead, tell me as much so I can find her body and start putting the pieces of my life back together. Either way, I'm going to kill you here tonight. You decide if you want to go out with any dignity."

I signaled to Mitchell. Carter screamed as the current shot through him. Seconds later he slumped in the chair again.

The look on Mitchell's face told me he had done this before, probably more than once. He was way too comfortable with it. I acted tough, but this was out of character for me. Deep down, I knew it was wrong, but my anger told me to keep pushing.

"Take the cables off him," I instructed. "What else you got?"

Mitchell walked over to a box in a corner of the room and came back with a blindfold and a bucket. We put the blindfold over Carter's eyes and lay his chair down onto the floor. Mitchell went over to the sink and filled the bucket with cold water.

"Listen, asshole. Thanks to you, I got no wife waiting up for me at home. No curfew, nowhere to be. You're the only thing on my mind right now."

I took the bucket and slowly poured water over Carter's face. *Nothing like a little makeshift waterboarding.* When Carter stopped flailing, I stopped pouring.

"I killed her!" the mayor yelled.

"What did you say?" I choked out the words from between clenched teeth. "Don't whisper, speak up! Say it loud and proud, you piece of shit!"

"I killed her! I killed her, damn you! They forced her off the road. She flew through the windshield into the river and they left. I had to get rid of her! That what you wanted to hear?" Carter wailed, tears streaming down his face.

"You lie!"

Mitchell refilled the bucket, and I began pouring again.

"There was no way she went through the windshield. I was at the crime scene, you moron. I saw the car. They dragged Miranda from the car. The windshield was intact. What did you assholes do to her before you threw her over the railing and into the lake?"

A few seconds went by before Carter could regain enough wits to respond. "We didn't do anything to her, I swear. They . . . they pulled her out and tossed her in the lake. That was it. Please, Porter, I told you what you wanted! Don't kill me."

I dropped the bucket, fury surging through me. Carter was sticking to his story, but I knew the evidence didn't support it. The comment he'd made about the windshield came out too quickly; it wasn't contrived. I knew that. He wouldn't have mentioned it if he'd known the windshield was intact. He simply wasn't that intelligent. I still believed Carter was somehow behind Miranda's death, but I realized I wouldn't get the confession I had sought. I also knew getting it would not make me feel one bit better about Miranda being gone.

I thought seeing Carter crying and begging for his life would make me feel good, but it didn't. It truly only added to my pain.

"Take off the blindfold and sit him up," I said to Mitchell.

I turned back to Carter, water and snot streaming down his face. "As bad as I want to, I'm not going to kill you. I'm taking you back to the States with me, along with all the evidence I have against you. I'm going to turn it over to the DA and watch you serve the rest of your sorry life behind bars. We'll start with kidnapping and murder; I'm sure there'll be more as we go. You'll have plenty of time to think about the choices you've made and the lives you've ruined."

Carter said nothing. With a nod to Mitchell, I trudged up the stairs and out of his basement. I pulled the phone from my pocket and punched in the captain's number. After three rings, he answered.

"Cap, I got him," I said, my voice heavy with weariness. "I'm bringing him back with me. I got all the evidence we need to bury this scumbag."

"What about the rest of his crew?" Wilcrest said.

"They didn't make it. I'll make flight arrangements in the morning," I said. "I have him secured. I'll call you tomorrow with the details."

21

I spent the night at Mitchell's, woke up early, and got ready to head to the airport. I signaled for a cab and tried to keep my head down in case someone had seen me shoot the guy in the street the day before. If that was the case, the cops would be looking for a man who fit my description.

"Where to?" the cabbie said in broken English as he pulled next to me on the curb.

"The airport."

The ride was uneventful, for which I was grateful. I headed for the airport security office and explained that I was a US police officer, and I'd be taking a prisoner back with me later in the day. When the security office personnel called the local police department, they were informed that the prisoner would need to be interviewed by the police before leaving the country. I was afraid of this, and hoped there would be no problems leaving with Carter. I made the necessary flight arrangements and caught a cab back to

Mitchell's place.

I paid the cabbie and stood outside after banging on Mitch's door for what seemed like five minutes.

"Hey, Ranger, c'mon in," Mitchell said looking around to make sure I was alone.

I went down to the basement to check on Carter who was sound asleep. He definitely wasn't going anywhere.

"I'm going to catch a few z's before I have to head out to the airport," I said to Mitch when I returned from the basement.

"Go ahead. I'll keep an eye on Carter."

Mitchell offered me his bedroom, but I opted for the couch instead. I knocked a few things onto the floor and laid my head down. I didn't sleep well, or very long, as it turned out. I sat up, came to my senses, and made a bathroom pit stop before heading back down to the basement to round up my travel partner.

Carter said nothing as I untied him from the chair, stood him up, and pulled the handcuffed bastard up the basement stairs.

"Okay, Mitch. Time for me and this scumbag to head back home. Thanks for everything."

"No problem, Ranger," Mitchell said. "I cleaned him up for you the best I could. If you decide to come back to Dubai for some R & R, you let me know. I know *all* the spots. You find some mean shoot-'em-up action for us to throw down with Mexico, Columbia, Russia . . . hell, I don't care who . . . you can call me then, too. I'm old, but hell, at this point I'd even do a bar fight just for some action. Tell Wilcrest to take care."

"Will do, buddy. Will do."

Mitchell was definitely someone you wanted on your team. I knew if something ever went down, I had a lifetime warrior friend I could call on.

An hour later, I was in the airport security office, waiting to speak to the local police.

"I'm Sergeant David Porter," I said. "I need to speak with Police Chief Amir. I have an appointment."

"Yes, he awaits you." The security officer gestured to the door behind him. He looked at Carter. "Is this your prisoner?"

I nodded, and we followed the officer down a narrow hallway to a closet-sized office, its walls painted institution green and peeling badly. Behind a tiny desk and nearly hidden by mounds of paperwork, a dark-skinned man in a forest-green uniform sat in the single, fold-open metal chair. There was barely enough room for us to stand before him.

"Ahh, Mr. Porter," the man said. "I am Amir. You've had an exciting couple of days here in Dubai, eh?"

"Not sure what you're referring to," I replied. "Just apprehended a murderer on the run." I nodded my chin toward Carter. "Figured you'd be appreciative that I took him off the streets for you."

"Appreciative? What about the damage you caused during your little high-speed chase?"

"Again, not sure what you're referring to," I said.

I knew Amir couldn't prove I was responsible, but he wasn't stupid, either. He was simply letting me know he knew what I'd been up to.

"What happened to your prisoner? He looks pretty beat up."

"That's what happens when you attack a police officer who's trying to do his job. Being hit, kicked, and spit on doesn't bode well with me when I'm trying to make a lawful arrest. Wouldn't you agree?"

"I suppose," Amir said with a lazy shrug.

"I simply used the force needed to get the job done—nothing more, nothing less."

"Let's cut the crap, Porter," Amir said. "You know I can't put anything on you, but the next time you decide to visit Dubai, don't."

"If that's all you got, I'd like to get back home . . . sir."

There was a long silence and a bit of a staring match between us. Amir glared at me for a few seconds longer and then got up and left the room. I followed him, Carter still in tow. No one bothered us as we went through security, headed to our gate, and boarded our flight ten minutes before the plane was scheduled to leave.

I sat on the aisle, Carter in the window seat. He stared sullenly out at the tarmac. I watched as an attractive young flight attendant approached.

"Excuse me, sir," the flight attendant said. "The Captain would like to have a word with you."

What now? Another interrogation about my beat-up prisoner? I guess they didn't do that type of thing here. I couldn't figure it out. With a sigh, I nodded. I shot Carter a look of warning as I removed one of his handcuffs and attached it securely to the armrest. He didn't bother to look at me. I followed the attendant to the front of the plane. She knocked once on the door separating the flight control deck from the first-class passenger cabin. The door opened and I stepped inside. The captain turned in his seat and gave me the once-over.

"Officer Porter," he said in near-perfect English. "I understand you have a prisoner with you. This isn't going to be a problem, is it?"

"Not for me. You won't even know he's on board, Captain."

"I hope not," he replied. "I've got a clean record. I'd

kinda like to keep it that way."

"Likewise, sir."

When he dismissed me with a nod, I made my way back to my seat, relieved.

Carter slept most of the way back. I didn't. It was an eighteen-hour flight, and all I could think of was Miranda. As the flight landed and the plane taxied to the gate, I removed Carter's handcuff from the armrest and locked his hands together. We exited the plane to find Captain Wilcrest and two of my peers waiting to take charge of the disgraced mayor.

"Wow, Porter! Looks like Carter tried to evade arrest, eh?" one of the officers said.

"Yep. Scared of going to prison and finding out who his new daddy's going to be. I told him he'd get used to it, though. They all do."

Wilcrest leaned in close to me. "What happened to him, David? His face looks like—"

"Better we don't talk about it," I muttered. "You can't get in trouble for something you don't know."

"Well, actually I can. You're confident Carter is behind Miranda's death?"

I nodded. "One hundred percent. Her report threatened to expose him for the scum he is. You can't be the mayor of Houston and be sending money to help fund an international sex slave operation. I just wish I'd asked more questions while she was working on it."

I paused for a minute, swallowing hard to clear the lump of emotion in my throat.

"Maybe I could've protected her. Some of the stuff she was going to accuse him of is pretty bad. I can only assume she didn't think Carter was capable of murder, in spite of what she was going to pin on him. I still don't have all the pieces. Carter's story didn't completely add up in regard to the crime scene. Or maybe his goons didn't give him all of the details or gave him the wrong details." I sighed with an overwhelming weariness. "I don't know."

"I'm just glad you can get some closure here. You did good work. We'll get those recordings and photos downloaded to the DA's office. Not many of us can say they chased a man halfway across the world to capture them."

"Not many of us can say their wife was murdered either, Cap. It's a bittersweet victory, if that's even what it is."

I handed my laptop to the captain. "I'm going home to be with my girls."

"One down and one to go," the captain said. "We still got this child-killing maniac to bring to justice."

"Don't worry, Cap. Now that this case is solved, that'll be my number one concern. I'm going to nail his ass too."

I retrieved my truck from the short-term parking lot and began the long, lonely drive home. I knew the hardest part was still ahead of me. I would have to tell the girls the truth about what I knew.

Halfway home, it hit me. I pulled my truck to the side of the road as tears warmed my eyes and ran down my face. I banged the steering wheel with a closed fist until the pain was too much. I screamed and yelled. I cursed myself.

Five minutes. Ten minutes. Thirty minutes. I cried till there were no tears left in me. My rollercoaster of emotions had finally hit rock bottom. I was mad, hurt, and tired—mentally and physically. I'd held it all in for as long as I could, and I definitely didn't want to fall apart in front of the girls. They were going to need me now more than ever. I would not return to this place of weakness and despair again.

I wiped my face, took a deep breath, and put the

truck back in gear.

22

My parents and in-laws were both at my house spending time with the girls. I called ahead to let them know I would be home shortly and asked them all to stay till I arrived. I needed to sit down with them and tell them what I knew. Better to hear it from me than read about it on the internet or hear a report on the nightly news. The girls were going to need all the support they could get. They all needed closure, an ending point so they could begin to grieve and move forward with their lives.

Karen and Hilary met me at the door.

"Dad, what's going on?" Hilary said.

Her question came before I entered the house. Her voice sounded unsettled. My oldest daughter surely had an inkling of what I was about to say. I gathered them all in the living room. Six somber, pale faces stared at me. I cleared my throat.

"I'm going to tell you all something very important. I

want to do it with everyone together. I need to clear up some things before you hear differently in the media."

"Daddy?" Karen said, her eyes filling with tears.

I cleared my throat again, and before the first word even came out I began to tear up.

"I've done this at least a hundred times during my career as a cop."

I choked out the words as Hilary's eyes filled with tears. Miranda's parents paled, slumped on the sofa beside me. Karen crawled into my lap.

My heart hurt for what I was about to do to my little girls. It was different this time. This was not delivering the news to a husband or wife I didn't know. This was not walking in, saying what you gotta say and leaving. I don't get to leave this time.

"Take your time, son," my dad said.

He took a step toward me and placed a comforting hand on my shoulder.

"Miranda was working on a story that would have sent John Carter, our mayor, to prison for a long time." I looked down at my youngest. "Karen, do you understand that, honey?"

"Yes, Daddy," she said, her eyes wide and swimming with tears. "The big story Mommy was working so hard on."

"You stop! Stop right now!"

Miranda's mother leapt up from the sofa and stared at me, her face drained of all color.

"There is no way you're going to make this Miranda's fault," she cried.

Tom reached out to his wife and encouraged her to sit back down. "He's not blaming Miranda," he told her. "Let him finish."

"None of this is Miranda's fault," I said. "I want you

to know what happened and why."

I related the story, sharing the facts in a manner I hoped the girls could understand.

"Dad, spare us all these details, please," Hilary demanded. "Did you find Mom? Is she coming home?" She swatted her tears away with the back of her hand.

"No, Hilary, she's not coming home. Your mother is . . . she's gone."

"No!" Hilary cried. "You promised! You swore you would bring her home!"

"I tried, honey, but it was already too late. I did everything I could."

"I hate you!" she said, flinging herself into my mother's open arms.

Karen burrowed herself into my chest as the finality of my news sank in, her tears soaking my shirt. Everyone cried. No pretenses. We hurt, and hurt deeply, but I was determined to hold my emotions in check. The girls needed me. The pain of watching my little girls suffer knifed through me. I felt like an absolute failure.

"You told her to be the best, to work hard!" Hilary exclaimed. "She told me you said that all the time! She was the best . . . so good it got her killed."

She knew better than to blame anyone, but she was angry and lashing out. I understood. I knew I needed to be the fall guy, and I accepted that burden. I deserved it for failing to protect my wife.

"I'll help with the funeral arrangements, David," my father-in-law said. "You have these girls to take care of, so you don't need to worry about that too."

We hadn't always seen eye to eye, but his willingness to help seemed genuine. We'd all lost someone special to us. I figured we could put our differences aside, at least for now.

This was a tragedy for our family. A good person had died doing the right thing— exposing a crooked politician, a criminal. She had paid the ultimate price for it. The lives of two young children, now motherless, had been forever changed. For them, this would not simply be a fork in the road to deal with; this was an ocean to cross. I just hoped I would have the right words to say or know the right things to do when they needed me.

I would have new responsibilities as well. I didn't know if I could handle both roles, being both mother and father to my girls. Hilary had placed the blame for this squarely on my shoulders, and this certainly wouldn't help our already strained relationship.

I pictured Miranda in my head. I missed her deeply—her laugh, her sense of humor, her beauty. The kind words she always had when I needed them. The kick in the butt when I needed one, too. The unconditional love she had shown me, in spite of my shortcomings. The mother she was to my children. All gone forever.

23

I dressed slowly. The memorial service for Miranda was scheduled for eleven a.m. It was already ten. Maybe if I took my time and waited long enough, I would wake up and this horrible nightmare would end. I knew it wouldn't happen, but I played mind games with myself. My heart felt heavy, my breath unsteady, and my hands trembled. I knew I had to hold it together for my kids, but choking back the emotions surging through me was extremely difficult.

After I finished dressing, I looked in on Hilary, already dressed and back on her bed, head down, listening to music. I peeked in on Karen and found her lying on the floor writing in her journal. I sat down beside her and glanced over her shoulder, my hand on her back, offering wordless comfort.

Dear mommy,

I wantid to wayt until I new for sure – but now I am sure daddy says that u are gone. I wish you wood not have left me. I am going to miss you so much. We are having ur fuunerule tuday – I will give u sum flowers. I now u like those red ones. Hilary is mad at daddy – im not tho I don't think it was his fallt. It was the bad man u were doing the story on. I hope he goes to jail daddy said he wood. Pleeze watch over me and Hilary and daddy and keep us safe. I will right to u everee day. I hope u right back. Pleeze pray for Hilary she needs to be nicer to daddy I know he luved u and he misses u. I thing granne is mad at him two so pleeze pray for her two. U r the best mommy a girl culd ever have had. Pleeze help daddy lern how to cook we will need to be abil to eat. I don't want a new mommy ether. I will always think about u and dreem about u everee nite.Luv Karen.

**

I heard footsteps coming up the stairs and looked up to find my mother standing in the doorway. She wore a black dress, and her makeup did little to mask her red, swollen eyes and flushed cheeks.

"Good morning, son. How are you holding up?"

"About as well as possible with what we have to do today, I imagine."

"The girls ready?" She held out her arms, and Karen went to her, tears flowing anew. "Where's Hilary?"

"In her room. We're all moving pretty slow this morning."

I scrambled to my feet and brushed the wrinkles from my pants.

"The limo will be here in about five minutes," my mother said.

I stopped by Hilary's room to get her, and in a matter of moments, we all stood downstairs, silent.

The limo arrived and we stepped outside. It was a beautiful day; the weather was perfect. The contrast between the beauty of the day and the fact that I was soon to bid my wife farewell hit me hard. How could such an awful day be so beautiful? If Miranda was alive, we'd probably go biking with the girls or take a hike together, enjoying each other's company.

I had already asked the preacher to keep the service short and sweet. This would be hard enough on me and the girls as it was. No need to drag it out.

I looked around the church and saw many familiar faces. Miranda's coworkers from the station had shown up, as had a large contingent from the police department. They wore their dress blues and stood in a long row at the back of the church. As my gaze passed over the mourners, my heart gave a jolt. There, in the far back corner, I made out the almost totally shielded face of Carter's wife. She wore a floppy hat and sunglasses, but I recognized her. My heart froze, though I applauded her bravery for showing up. The few choice words I had for her would have to wait.

We sat in the front pew of the church our family had attended for years. As the organist played "Amazing Grace," people walked by, shaking my hand, patting the girls on the head, and murmuring words of condolence. I tried to understand how I had gotten here. My family was in shambles, my wife gone. It was surreal, and it had all happened so quickly. This wasn't the vision I had for my life.

I stopped feeling sorry for myself for a moment and realized it was not the way Miranda had planned it either. All she wanted was to be a good mother and wife. She'd wanted to be a good reporter, too. She'd been ambitious. It had cost her—and us—dearly.

The service began, but it seemed a blur to me. While the preacher spoke, photos of Miranda scrolled on a projection screen behind him. I had gone through all the steps of grieving once. I was now back to the point of being angry. I was angry with God for allowing this to happen. I was angry at myself, angry at Carter and his men, and on some level, even angry at Miranda for doing this investigation. Why couldn't it have been me? I remembered having the conversation with Miranda the day she disappeared, when I wondered how I'd gotten so lucky. Now it seemed my luck had run out.

After the ceremony, I played the role of a good host and reminded the friends and family in attendance that food would be served and everyone was welcome. I faked it well. My mother had finally convinced me I needed to eat.

It had been nearly a week since the night of Miranda's murder. I had lost a lot of weight and knew I looked frail and sickly. I would be no good to anyone if I allowed myself to fall apart. Still, as I went through the serving line, nothing looked good to me. I forced myself to put a few things on my plate and moved to the table where my daughters were nibbling on fried chicken legs. I sat down and stared at my plate.

"Dad, you gotta eat something," Karen said.

"Normally I'm fussing at you about eating," I said, forcing a smile.

As we picked at our food, I noticed a short-haired blonde woman about my age walking our way. She had full, pouty lips, almond-shaped eyes, and delicate features. I couldn't help but notice her well-toned arms and shapely legs. I tried not to pay attention to the fact that the woman was gorgeous, considering I had just endured my wife's memorial service. Her choice of clothing didn't help. A skin-tight, low-cut black dress showed off her ample breasts and every curve, which may have been her goal. I'd seen her type before.

I wasn't the only one who noticed. Hilary looked at the woman and rolled her eyes as she approached the table. Hilary muttered something, but I only caught the word *slut*.

"Excuse me," the woman said. "You probably don't know me, but I went to school with Miranda." She held out her hand. "I'm so sorry to hear about your loss. Do you mind if I sit down?"

I gave her hand a polite shake and glanced at Hilary and Karen. "No, go right ahead. Have we met before?"

"Miranda actually called me a few weeks ago, and we caught up a little," she said. "She told me she had a wonderful husband and two beautiful girls. But no, we never met."

"Hilary and Karen, right?" She extended a hand to each of them as she introduced herself. "Hello, I'm Stacy. Stacy Demornay."

Hilary faked a smile, but I caught the roll of her eyes again. I'm sure Stacy also noticed, but she graciously ignored it.

"She left out the part about her husband being so handsome, though," Stacy said, flashing a mouthful of perfect, cosmetically whitened teeth at me.

I didn't respond and quickly changed the subject.

"So how did you know Miranda again?"

"Can I be excused?" Hilary rudely interrupted.

"Sure Hilary." I nodded. "Don't stray too far."

"College. We went to school together," Stacy said as Hilary gave her one more piercing glare and stomped away in a huff. "I just graduated from nursing school. I'll be working at the new hospital in town."

I began to feel a little uneasy, so I also excused myself from the table, making the excuse that Karen needed to see her grandmother. Stacy merely nodded, a smile playing around the corners of her mouth. The woman had made herself a little too comfortable with me. Real over-the-top flirty. In another setting it might have been okay, but not here and not now.

"Well, it was nice meeting you . . ."

I paused as I rose, momentarily forgetting her name.

"Stacy."

"Stacy. That's right. You'll have to forgive me; I'm terrible with names."

"No problem. I understand. You've been through a lot the last few days. I understand—firsthand, actually. I lost a longtime boyfriend last year. He died in a motorcycle wreck. It's hard to let go. I'll leave you my number. Perhaps we can talk again soon. Feel free to call if you need something. Is that okay with you?"

"Sure." I had to be polite but had no intention of calling her. "Thanks again for coming by, and I'm sorry about your loss, too."

Stacy handed me a card with her number on it. I slipped it into my coat pocket as I walked away.

She seemed like a nice enough lady. I could see how she and Miranda had been friends. As I walked away from the table, I saw Jill Carter heading my way. I knew trouble was brewing when Miranda's mother leapt from her chair and stalked toward her.

"What are you doing here?" Grace demanded.

"I've come to offer my condolences," Jill said.

"Well, you can keep your damn condolences!"

I placed my hand on my mother-in-law's back. The anguish on her face stunned me.

"Please," I said, urging her to return to her husband. "Now's not the time."

"David, can I talk to you for a moment in private?" Jill asked.

I hesitated and then whispered to Miranda's mother, "It's okay. Let me talk to her."

Jill and I walked to a room down the hall from the main room.

"Look, I don't know why I came here," she said in a rush. "I'm just so sorry about what happened, and I feel guilty, in a way. I've heard most of the story. Enough to know John was no doubt the catalyst here, and I'm sorry. We may not have the same background or friends, but none of that matters. What he did was wrong. I'm sorry. I'm sorry for him. I'm sorry for what your family is going through. I love John and I always will, but what he did to you and your family was wrong."

I said nothing for several moments. "It took a lot of guts for you to show up here. I'm sorry for what I did a few days ago as well. I was angry, and I wanted to get even. I should have remembered my roots, though. Vengeance is for the Lord."

"No need for you to apologize. I can imagine how much pain you and yours girls are in. I know you probably think I'm a rich, spoiled little bitch, but I don't condone what my husband did. Maybe one day you'll be able to forgive him."

"You coming here showed me a lot more about your character than I would have given you credit for. And honestly, on different levels, we've both lost a spouse. He took mine and I took yours."

Jill turned to leave. "You take care of those girls. They will need you more than ever now."

After she left, I looked around for Hilary.

People continued to stop me to offer their condolences as they left. I felt a calming sense that everything would eventually be okay. It would be a long process, but it would be okay.

I finally spotted her near the doors that led outside. She stood in the corner, gazing out the window. She heard me as I approached and turned around.

"There were times when I was so mean to her," she said, her voice soft and filled with pain. Tears pooled in her eyes. "All she ever did was try to love me and help me grow up. Even the day she died, when she dropped us off at school, it's like I was always trying to one-up her, to prove her wrong, make her mad."

"It's okay, Hilary," I said.

"I loved her, Dad." Hilary wept, her face crumpling. "I really did."

"She knew that." I wrapped my arms around my daughter. "She loved you, too. Very much. All you can do now is use what she tried to teach you and learn from your own mistakes. No one is perfect. No one does it right all the time. Your mother did love you."

I released her, intending to find my parents and Karen and say our goodbyes to the remaining guests. Hilary had never been one for emotional scenes. I respected that and moved away.

"No, Dad, can you just stay here for a few minutes? Please?"

It was the first time in a long time that Hilary had shown any interest in me. I was shocked—pleased, but shocked. I tried not to let it show on my face. I placed my arm around her shoulders.

"I've been pretty ugly to you, too, Dad. I'm sorry." Hilary buried her face in my shoulder.

"Let's put all that behind us, Hil. Start over. It will be rough, but we'll make it. We can both learn something from it. The teenage years are tough. I'm not too old to remember how trying it can be at times."

Hilary and I held each other for a long time. I knew she didn't need more words of advice or wisdom. She just needed a shoulder to cry on. Shortly, my mother-in-law approached with Karen, who ran to join us.

I wrapped my arms around my daughters and held on for dear life. They were all I had left now.

"Girls," I said, my voice choking up, "I'm sorry I couldn't protect your mother. I loved her so much." I took a deep breath. "But I promise you I'll do everything in my power to be the best dad I can."

The words had barely left my mouth when Hilary spoke.

"Dad, we have each other. We'll make it."

As we rode home in the limo, we passed the spot where Miranda had her accident. I noticed both Hilary and Karen staring over the railing, perhaps hoping—maybe praying—to catch a glimpse of their mother, while knowing all too well it wasn't possible.

When we got home, I told the girls I needed to rest for a few hours. I went to my room—our room—and climbed into bed. The presence of my wife was everywhere. Her bra hung over the shower curtain rod and her clothes filled the closet. Her housecoat draped the chair by the window.

I wondered how many more nights tears would precede my falling asleep. The Miranda- sized hole in my heart would be a long time in mending.

24

"Hello? Who's there?" Miranda called out.

"Oh, it's just me again, Miranda. It's time for you to eat. I was able to bring you some food from your lovely memorial service. That sounds kinda unreal, but it's true. After seeing your daughter again today, the little one, I've decided to stop killing kids. At least for the time being. I've got my prize now anyway."

Miranda felt a frisson of shock surge through her.

"Your husband and kids are nice," the woman continued. "Your honey bunny, David, is already thinking about giving me a chance. I could tell that much. I'm going to keep his number right here in my purse. He's put on some muscle over the years, hasn't he?"

"You leave them alone!" Miranda screamed, tugging on her bindings.

"Well, now, we only met today, but it seems he's taken a liking to me already. How else do you get the phone number of a guy who just lost his wife? Huh? Any guesses? I suppose looking like this doesn't hurt. You think he liked your body? Well, he's going to worship mine. He's going to need me. He's going to want me. He's going to adore me. He'll never even remember you existed."

Miranda cringed as her captor's evil laughter echoed around the room.

"He'll dream about me. He'll father my kids. Your daughters will love me, too, before I get rid of them. If you're a good girl, maybe I'll make you a video or two of our lovemaking sessions."

"David would never do anything with a two-bit skanky bitch like you!" Miranda snapped.

"Miranda, please . . . Bitch? Such an ugly word. We'll see, dear. His eyes didn't call me that today, and a man's eyes never lie. Besides, I always get what I want. I got you, didn't I?"

It took every ounce of strength Miranda had, but she remained silent.

"Well, enough about that. I actually came down to feed you. You do want to eat, don't you? I mean, I'm not going to kill you, if that's what you're thinking. If that were my goal, don't you think you'd be dead already? And since your family thinks you're dead, eventually you and I will have to help them change that perception. We'll toy with them . . . give them a reason to believe you could still be alive. It'll be more fun that way."

Miranda seethed. This skinny bitch had stolen her life and now maybe even her husband and kids. She tried to calm down. After all, David was too good at figuring people out. Certainly he would see right through this ploy. And she was sure the entire Houston Police Department was working hard to find her. She would be rescued in no time.

CHAINED GUILT

25

Several months later . . .

Life goes on; that much is true, though adjusting to life without Miranda was hard on all of us. I still had not captured the child killer who had terrorized our city. The killings had stopped suddenly—almost too suddenly to make any sense. Six months had passed since Miranda's death, but I'd been too preoccupied with my loss to think clearly enough to focus on the case. I strongly believed the killer was still out there, blending in, watching. Pleased with how his work had forever changed the lives of so many. Everyone was still afraid.

We had not officially closed the case due to lack of evidence, but because the killings had stopped and other cases emerged, it had gotten pushed into the background. I scoured the net often for reports of similar killings being committed elsewhere in Texas or surrounding states, but came up empty.

Why had he stopped so suddenly? Did he have a

new goal or objective? Or had he, as Wilcrest hypothesized, died in some unrelated accident or even been incarcerated for some other crime? There was no way to know for sure.

"Run… run! Go, Karen, go!" Hilary yelled as we watched Karen score the go-ahead run for her Little League T-Ball team. It was Karen's first year playing, but she'd quickly picked up the game. Baseball was all Karen could think about now. She had always been fearful of trying the game, even though Miranda had talked to her about playing. Since her mother's death, she had decided she would give it all she had and dedicate her efforts to her mother.

"Dad you should go out with Coach Stacy," Hilary said, sliding beside me in the bleachers. "She really seems like a nice lady. I mean, I know I didn't like her at first, but I do now. She's really good with Karen, too." She glanced up at me to see if I was listening. "And I'm pretty sure she's into you."

"Really?" I glanced over at Stacy, who was offering advice to a batter. She didn't look anything like she had at Miranda's memorial service. Today, she wore tight-fitted skinny jeans and a loose T-shirt. "I don't know, Hilary. It just seems too soon."

"When will it be long enough, Dad? You have to have a life, even if you are old." Hilary laughed as she patted my knee. "Seriously, you should think about it. Mom would have wanted you to move on. She would not have wanted you to be lonely. I know when a girl is into a guy. I'm a girl, Dad, remember?"

I sighed. "Okay, well, maybe you're right." I didn't think so. "I'll think about it."

"Well, she's a beautiful woman, Dad, and she isn't going to wait on you forever."

Cheers erupted from proud parents on the home

side of the bleachers, and I turned to watch a little boy round home base, followed by Karen, for the winning run. I'd thought about the possibility of dating again, even making an attempt with Stacy. Every time I did, images of Miranda flashed in my mind. I watched my girls, pleased that Hilary had seemed to take more interest in her big sister role since Miranda died. Her attitude and demeanor had turned a one-eighty. She was helpful around the house, looked after her little sister when I had to work late, and was once again getting good grades in school. But it had only been six months, which seemed a little too soon to be grazing again.

Behind me, I heard two guys in their late twenties talking about Coach Stacy.

"Man, she is definitely the hottest coach I've ever seen. She could coach me anytime," one of them said with a laugh.

"Yeah, she blows my wife away," the other said. "She looks like a Playboy model or something. Look around out here. You see anything close to that anywhere?" He paused. "I didn't think so."

I was mildly surprised to hear the two fathers speak so openly about Stacy in such a way. Still, I did have to agree she was beautiful. And Hilary was right; Stacy was great with Karen. I frowned. Why was I trying to talk myself into this?

"Hey there, David, you okay?"

I glanced up to find Stacy standing in front of me.

"Hey, Stacy," I replied, sitting straighter. "You're fine . . . I mean, I'm fine."

"You sure?"

I nodded. "Yeah, just letting my mind wander, that's all. You did a good job today, coach." I stood. "In fact, you've done a good job this entire season. It's pretty weird that Karen ended up on your team. Nice coincidence, though. We got the best coach around."

"Hey, the girls did a great job." she said. "I've just been helping out a little."

"We did it, Daddy!" Karen yelled as she raced toward me, Hilary trailing behind.

My youngest jumped into my arms, and I wrapped her up in a congratulatory bear hug.

"Yes, you did. You played real good, Karen. I'm really proud of you."

"Why don't we all take a picture?" Stacy suggested.

"Yeah, sure, why not?" I said.

The three of us lined up as Hilary pulled out her iPhone and snapped a quick pic.

"Hold on, why don't you get into the picture with us, Hilary?" Stacy asked.

"Are you sure?" Hilary said

"Of course! Don't be silly."

Stacy waived one of the other parents over to take the picture while the four of us posed together.

"Are you coming to the team party tonight, David?" Stacy asked.

"We wouldn't miss it for the world."

On the ride home, Karen recounted the game for us, play by play. She was so excited. Hilary told Karen their mother would have been proud of what she had accomplished. The comment noticeably saddened Karen, as any mention of her mother did, but she understood what her sister was saying. I played the proud parent, grinning all the way home.

"Girls, when we get home, I have some yardwork to tackle. After I'm finished, I'll clean up and we can head out to the party, okay?"

As we walked into the house, I heard Hilary talking

to Karen.

"You really think Mom would have been proud of me?" Karen asked.

"Yeah, I really do," Hilary said. "Karen, I need to talk to you about something. I told Dad that he should go out on a date with Stacy. How do you feel about that?"

The question must have caught the usually quick-tongued Karen off guard, because she didn't answer right away. I closed the front door behind us and watched her gaze around the living room at the family pictures on the walls.

"It's kind of strange to think of Daddy being friends with another lady," Karen admitted. "But I think Mommy would like Coach Stacy. I think she'd want Daddy to be happy, too."

"Wow, that's a big girl answer," Hilary whispered to her little sister. "But I totally agree, and that's what I told Dad."

"So what did he say?"

"I think he's going to talk to her tonight and see what happens."

With that, the girls climbed the stairs and went to their rooms to change. Moments later, Hilary's radio blasted. I smiled and went out to start my yardwork. I mowed the front lawn, trimmed and swept up the clippings on the shrubs out back, and hosed down the driveway.

After I finished with the yard, I went back inside to wash up. Karen was in the kitchen with Hilary, eating a light snack. As I passed her room, I saw the uniform she'd dumped on the floor. When I bent to pick it up, I noticed the piece of paper on her bed.

It wasn't the first letter she'd written her mother since her passing. For the last six months, she'd been writing letters and putting them in a special box. She was keeping them to give to her mother so she would know everything that happened after she died.

Dear mommy,
Tuday my baseball team won the city ternament. I was picked as MVP of the game. Tonight we have a team party to celbrate – at Encreduble Pizza. Coach Stacy (the one I have been telling you about) likes daddy I think. I think daddy likes her too. I hope that you are not mad. I think that you woud be happy if daddy was happy. Me to – I think? I do like Coach Stacy but I wish that you were here insted. Maybe one day they will get maried and she will be my new mommy. I don't want a new mommy but I want daddy to be happy. I miss you so much. All of the other little girls at school have mommies. I get sad when I think about you being gone. I never told you this but I loved getting tikkles from you (daddy is to ruff shhhh don't tell him I said that). I wood always tell you to stop but I loved it. I think that is all for now – I love you mommy.
Karen

<u>26</u>

"Girls, let's go! I don't want to be late," I yelled up the stairs.

I checked my hair and clothes in the hallway mirror. It felt like I was in high school again. I couldn't help but laugh at myself.

"You look great, Dad," Hilary said as she came down the stairs, Karen following close behind. "Stop worrying. It's just Incredible Pizza anyway. Give it fifteen minutes, and I'm sure some little kid will have spilled soda on you or touched you with her messy little pizza hands."

"I was just looking. Promise."

I grinned as the three of us headed out the door and climbed into the car. I was looking forward to seeing Stacy and hoped to find the right time to bring up the idea of us seeing each other. Hilary and I had talked about it a little, but I knew it was a really big step for our newly restructured family. As we drove to the party, Karen solved the problem for me.

"Dad, I think it's cool that you and Coach Stacy are dating."

"We're not—"

"Are you going to marry her?" Karen said.

I glanced in the rearview mirror. "Hey, slow down some. I was going to talk to you guys about that."

"What's there to talk about?" Hilary said. "She likes you. You'd be stupid not to like her, so what's left?"

"Well how do you feel about that?" I asked. "Besides, I'm not sure what makes you think she likes me anyway."

"I guess I'm okay with it," Karen mused. "Mommy would be okay with it, so I'm okay with it." Karen folded her arms, a smug look on her face.

"Okay. I guess I don't get a say in this?"

"Nope," Karen said with a satisfied grin. "Hilary and I have decided for you."

"And make sure you're in at a decent hour," Hilary ordered. "You pay for all meals. Open the door for her and pull out her chair for her, too. Got it?"

When we arrived at Incredible Pizza, Stacy waved to us from a table by the window. My thoughts raced. I wasn't exactly sure what I would say to her. I hadn't dated since I met Miranda. That had been so long ago. I'd been a college kid then. I'd been allowed a stupid comment or two. Now I was a thirty-something widowed father of two—and at a complete loss for words.

As we walked toward Stacy's table, I was bombarded by the racket. Leftover pizza crust littered the tables and floor. There were a million kids, it seemed—up high, down low, everywhere. Hilary had been right about the probability of messy pizza hands landing on me. The noise rivaled that of the jet engines I'd flown in while I was in the service. It was deafening, to say the least. The sounds of children having the time of their lives. Everywhere I looked parents tagged along, trying to keep up with their kids as they led the way to the next game. What appeared to me to be utter chaos was nothing of the sort to the children as smiles, joy, and laughter radiated from each of them. This made me think back to the child killer we'd had here months earlier. Why in the hell would someone want to do harm to one of these precious gifts?

"Hey, Karen," Stacy said. "Here are some gaming tokens. Let me know when you're ready for pizza."

Karen thanked Coach Stacy for the tickets and ran off to find her teammates.

"David, some of the parents are sitting at tables in the back. Would you like to join them?"

"Actually, no," I said. I glanced at Hilary, who nodded at me in encouragement. "There's something I wanted to talk with you about." I thought I saw Stacy grin.

Hilary obviously knew where the conversation was headed and excused herself to go in search of two classmates she'd spied a few minutes earlier.

"Stacy, I haven't done this in almost twenty years," I said. "I'm not sure…"

"Done what in twenty years, David?"

"Well, I know you don't have a boyfriend, and the girls really like you, and—"

"And you? How do you feel about me?" Stacy interrupted with a smile.

"I . . . I think you're great."

Stacy attempted to stifle a giggle.

"Why are you laughing at me?" I asked, smiling myself.

"It's cute, that's all. Watching you stammer for words."

As Stacy spoke, she moved closer to me. It made me

uncomfortable, and I took a step backward. I was up against a wall . . . in more ways than one. No more backing up.

Stacy looked around to make sure we weren't being watched too closely by anyone. Then she leaned close enough to kiss me. She placed one hand on my chest and slowly, ever so slowly, trailed her fingers down my body.

"You need to relax, David. No need to be nervous with me. We're both adults. I've noticed you looking at me when you didn't think I could see you. And yes −"

She stopped her hand right at my belt line.

"Yes, I feel the same way about you."

I didn't know what to make of this. While I felt relieved that Stacy was receptive to my words, I wasn't quite sure what to make of her straightforwardness. Apparently my mixed feelings were noticeable on my face.

"Don't look at me like that, David. I'm a big girl." She grinned. "I know what I want. I've known for a long time."

I tried to squirm my way around her. As I backed up, the chain I was wearing got caught on a button on Stacy's blouse.

"Man, see what I mean? I'm terrible at this," I said, trying to free the chain and myself.

"It's okay," Stacy said, laughing, obviously enjoying the moment. "Do you ever take this thing off? Every time I see you, you have it on."

"My mother had me when she was in high school. I spent most of the first two years of my life with my grandmother. She died from breast cancer when I was five, and this chain was the last thing she gave me. I added the locket a few years later; there's a picture of her in it. So yes, it's dear to me. Honestly, I can't remember the last time I took it off."

"Daddy! Look how many tickets I have!" Karen yelled as she ran toward me. She waved her ticket-filled fists in my direction, and flew right by me. Stacy acted as if the interruption never occurred.

"Look, David, we're not getting any younger. I know what I'm getting into with you. You have two beautiful girls, and you're a great guy. We both know what it feels like to lose a partner. We can probably help each other on so many levels."

"Do I get a say in this?" I couldn't help but chuckle at myself, and she looked confused. "Sorry, it's just the second time I've asked that exact same question today. To be honest, it sounds like we both feel the same way, but we can take it slow, right?"

"Sure we can. I just want you to know I'm committed to you and your family. I love watching you guys together, and I want to be a part of it." She straightened and stepped back. "Well, I think *you* have taken enough of my time, Mr. Porter. I'm going to mingle with some of the other parents."

"Yeah, sure." I took a deep breath, somewhat flustered. "Thanks for the pep talk, coach."

I felt exhausted and relieved and even a little confused . . . and happy, all rolled into one moment. I was excited about her interest in me. I also had an inkling that Stacy had been prepared for the conversation. It seemed almost calculated on her part. It bothered me. I wasn't really sure where we stood. Did this make her my girlfriend? Are we dating? Is it exclusive? I had the feeling she was thinking long term, but I wasn't ready to go there yet.

The encounter over, I meandered my way through the games and kids. I enjoyed watching the happiness and excitement on the children's faces as they dropped in tokens and played games without a care in the world.

Suddenly, someone tapped me on the shoulder.

"So?" Hilary stood behind me, an eyebrow raised in question.

"What?"

"You know what." She prodded me with a smile.

I sighed. "A gentleman never kisses and tells."

Hilary glared at me, arms folded across her chest.

"Oh okay. I think we may have a chance. We'll take it slow and see what happens. Nosy Rosy!"

Hilary squealed in delight and then quickly changed the subject.

"Can we get outta here, Dad? Kids eating boogers and then using the same hand to eat pizza has me all grossed out."

I had to agree. I'd had about all the excitement I could take for one day.

27

Miranda looked around the room, wishing she could figure a way out of the hell hole. She had already lost about twenty pounds, she figured, and grew weaker by the day. She was slowly starving. She only ate once a day, if that, and showered once a week—a "hose down," her captor called it.

She cringed as the door clicked open.

"Good morning, Miranda."

Miranda refused to answer.

"Not talking today? That's okay. And to think I actually came with a gift for you."

She walked toward the chair where Miranda sat, bound hand and foot, and slapped her across the cheek.

"I have something for you."

She opened a folder and pulled out a photograph. She turned the picture so Miranda could see it. It was a picture of the woman with Karen, Hilary, and David. As

Miranda stared at the picture, she was both happy and heartbroken at the same time.

She was glad her kids and husband were okay, but deeply saddened that, somehow, this woman had managed to weave her way into their lives. They all looked so happy, happiness that had once been hers. Miranda struggled to remain emotionless when all she really wanted to do was cry.

"Do you like it?" the woman asked. "It's a good picture of us, isn't it? It's so rewarding to totally fuck up someone else's world. Someone you hardly even know. I must admit, it does feel pretty good."

It grew harder for Miranda to hide her pain.

"So what are some things David likes? Any insider tips you can give me?" She chuckled. "Here's a question for you . . . is he passive or aggressive in the sack? Huh? Come on, at least tell me that much."

Miranda stared at her, her captor. *If only looks could kill*, she thought.

"Nothing? Well aren't you just a killjoy today, Miranda. You know what? I like surprises. So I'll just have to find out these things on my own. How about that?"

"Yeah, you'll have to find out for yourself. Your day will come soon, you evil little—" She stopped short of calling her a name. She refused to give her the pleasure of knowing how much pain she was in.

"Okay, Miranda. It's time for me to go now. I have a date with a handsome detective to get ready for. Should I wear black or red panties tonight? Or should I be a bad girl and wear none at all? Decisions, decisions. I'm sure I'll figure something out. Bye-bye now."

Miranda closed her eyes, refusing to shed tears as her captor headed for the door. Then, the footsteps stopped and the woman turned around.

"Oh, Miranda, one more thing."

She returned to Miranda's chair and pulled a roll of duct tape from her jacket pocket. She pulled off a piece and secured it around Miranda's mouth and the back of her head. Miranda tried to twist her head to avoid the tape but it was useless.

"I need you quiet tonight, dear. Got big plans!" She laughed. "Oh, and in case you're wondering after all this time, my name is Stacy. I don't think I formally introduced myself to you."

With that, she was gone. Miranda sat in frustrated confusion. Stacy? She'd never known a Stacy. Why was the woman torturing her this way? What had she ever done to her? And the picture. She'd left it behind. *On purpose?* Miranda didn't know, but if she couldn't be with her family, she'd settle for seeing their smiling faces in the photograph. It was all she had left.

28

It was early, a typical Sunday morning for me: quiet and lonely, but not in a bad way. I enjoyed working Sunday mornings; it felt more laid-back. While pursuing leads or on stakeouts, I got to spend time thinking. I'd just pulled out of Myrna's Coffee Shop when my cell phone rang. I wondered who could be calling so early.

"Detective Porter here."

"Hey, David. It's me, Stacy. Detective Porter, huh? You sounded so official."

"Stacy," I stammered, surprised.

Stacy and I exchanged small talk for a few minutes. I'd just seen her the night before at the party, and she was already calling me? It seemed kind of strange, but I decided to play along. I was headed back to the station to pick up a rookie officer the department had just hired. She would ride around with me today and learn more about the town.

"Hang on one second, Stacy; I'm turning into the

station lot to pick up an officer."

"Oh, okay."

Officer De Luca was waiting at the curb for me. I waived for her to get into the car. Pretty little thing, I noticed.

"Good morning," she said, climbing into the passenger seat.

"Good morning to you, Officer De Luca." I nodded, holding my open cell phone face down on my thigh. "Give me a minute; I'm on a call."

She nodded and looked out the window. I lifted the phone to my ear.

"Stacy, you there?"

Nothing.

"Stacy? Hello? Can you hear me?"

"De Luca?" Stacy said.

Her voice sounded hard. I frowned.

"Sounds Italian. Is she?"

"Not sure. Just met her a few days ago." I turned to the rookie and shrugged. "Hadn't really had the chance to delve into her family tree," I said, laughing.

Stacy was not amused.

"Okay, well, I'll talk to you later, David," she said. "I know you're busy. Enjoy your day."

She disconnected the call, and I wondered what had just happened. Was Stacy jealous? Of someone she had never even seen or met? And we weren't boyfriend and girlfriend yet anyway. "What the hell was that all about?" I muttered.

"Everything okay, sir?" De Luca asked. "Sounds like your girlfriend is curious about me."

I gave her a serious look before I answered. "Everything is fine, Officer De Luca, and I don't have a girlfriend. *Capiche*?" I smiled, using my severely limited

Italian.

Officer De Luca laughed, too, and informed me that she was indeed Italian.

"Glad we're able to get your lineage out of the way. Anything else I need to know?"

"Let's see," she said. "I'm twenty-nine, single, and I'm not a rookie cop. I'm only new to your department. It seems like that fact was misstated somewhere along the way. I was a detective in New Valley before I transferred here. I've been a cop for eight years." She shrugged. "I know what I want, and I usually get it. I have family back east tied to the mob, so that helps. Oh, and I don't have lots of women friends, particularly blondes. Just something about them. And yes, I think we dark-haired women are sexier. That enough for now?"

I drove out of the lot with a grin. "Thanks for the bio. I don't think I'd be bragging about the whole mob thing, though."

"It was a joke," she said with a grin. "But everything else was true. You're a good-looking guy, but not my type. Let's just get that out of the way from the get-go. I don't date cops, so please be sure to pass that along to your friend, as you put it."

I laughed, pulling the car onto the highway.

"What about you?" she said. "What skeletons you got chained up in your closet?

I frowned, not sure what she meant. "Skeletons? Nothing you don't know already, probably, and anything I did before I turned eighteen doesn't count."

Her laughter was rich and genuine. I liked her.

"On a more serious note, I have two daughters, and I've been a cop for fifteen years. This job has kind of grown on me, even though I wasn't in it for the long haul at first. Oh, and I like blondes."

"Natural or artificial?"

She was good, I acknowledged with another grin. I paused for a moment before answering. A mental match for me, maybe. A person more quick witted than myself? No way.

"Touché. Never really thought about it, actually," I admitted. "Does it matter?"

"Nope." She shook her head, her eyes on the highway. "Doesn't matter to me if it doesn't to you. Guess that's something you should consider, though, Porter. Your girl—I mean, friend—does she happen to be a blonde? By the way, *touché* is French, not Italian. Good try, though."

"Coincidentally, yes, my *friend* is a blonde."

"Imagine that! Or should I say *Immaginare che*?"

29

Detective De Luca and I talked the entire shift. She was a different kind of bird, no doubt, and I enjoyed her company. She was also a knowledgeable detective and took her job seriously.

I drove back to the station at the end of our shift and stared in surprise. Stacy was waiting by my truck.

"Your girlfriend is waiting for you," De Luca mumbled as she climbed out of the car.

I peered over at Stacy and smiled, but she walked right past me and introduced herself to Detective De Luca.

"Hi there," she said, not the least bit shy. "I'm Stacy, David's girlfriend. Detective De Lucha, right?"

"Hello there yourself. Nice to meet you," De Luca replied. "And the name's De Luca. It's Italian."

The two ladies looked each other over. *What in the hell was going on?*

"Stacy, surprised to see you here," I said. "I told

you I'd call after I made it home this afternoon."

"Oh, it's no problem," she said, flashing a brilliant smile at me. "I'm full of surprises. I just thought we could start our date a little early."

De Luca snickered under her breath, but it didn't go unnoticed by Stacy or me.

"I'll see you tomorrow, Porter," she said. "I'm going to review some of the department's paperwork procedures and then head home. What time are we riding tomorrow?"

De Luca knew full well that I had already given her a time to meet me at the station. I guessed this was her way of getting back at Stacy for her obvious cattiness. Also a sly way to let her know we'd be riding again tomorrow.

"Tomorrow at nine a.m., detective."

"You okay, David?" Stacy asked, watching De Luca head into the station.

"I'm fine."

"Are you upset with me because I showed up here?"

"No, no. Just unexpected that's all. I wanted to go home and clean up some first before our date tonight."

"Do you have a change of clothes with you? You could come by my house and clean up there."

I kindly rejected her offer and reminded Stacy that the girls needed me to make dinner and visit with them for a bit before I was off for the night.

"Single parent here, remember?" I said with a smile.

"Of course I remember. How could I forget your beautiful girls?" Stacy said as she reached out and tapped my chest. "But hurry."

I headed for my truck, surprised to see Stacy still watching me as I backed from my parking space. She smiled seductively and blew me a kiss as I drove away.

To be honest, I had mixed emotions about Stacy

showing up. Part of me was flattered by her need to see me. But on the other hand, it seemed she'd shown up to check out Detective De Luca for herself, which would be kind of strange, considering we weren't even officially dating yet. Then again, Stacy had just introduced herself as my girlfriend.

<u>30</u>

I pulled into the driveway, and suddenly my mind flashed back. I put the truck in park. The memories flooded over me, thoughts so real it felt like my brain was about to explode. It was fifteen years ago, maybe sixteen. Miranda and I had just left a movie and were parked in a driveway. I remembered looking into Miranda's eyes—hoping, wanting, and waiting for her to give me a sign so I could make a move.

Before that point, we'd taken it slow, holding hands from time to time and sharing the perfunctory good night kiss. So when she gave me the sign I was looking for, I seized the moment without hesitation.

At the time, I was a lonely bachelor living in a huge house. I'd purchased the home for next to nothing and spent many months remodeling it. Miranda had always refused to go inside. That night, as I vividly remembered, would be different.

I took her in and spent almost an hour proudly showing Miranda every detail of every upgrade I had installed—every wall I had removed and every cabinet I'd rebuilt. Miranda had marveled at my carpentry and seemed impressed that I had managed to make so many beautiful changes without the help of a woman. It was a point she reiterated to me more than once.

As I recaptured the moment, my hands began to sweat. I could almost feel my nervousness all over again. And then Miranda gave me "the look," the one that said, "okay, enough with the talking—"

A hand slapped hard against the driver's-side window, jolting me out of my reverie. "What the . . . ?" I jumped. It was the girls. As my heart rate returned to normal, I opened the door and slid from my truck. "You have fun startling your dad?"

"We were just wondering what you were doing out here for so long," Hilary said.

"Nothing. Just thinking."

"Thinking about Stacy?" Hilary said, laughing.

"Actually, no." I chose not to explain.

I picked Karen up and asked her about her day as we followed Hilary inside. She filled me in and asked if I was ready for my big date. I didn't understand why they were so preoccupied with my date with Stacy. Maybe because this was my first date since Miranda died. I couldn't be sure.

"Don't make too much of this, guys," I said as we gathered in the kitchen. "We're going to take it slow. It's just a date. We may not even hit it off, or maybe she'll decide she doesn't like me any more after she spends some time with me."

I tried to make light of it. I liked Stacy, but I didn't know if I was ready to give my heart away to another woman.

"Have you girls eaten?"

I placed my keys and cell phone on the counter and turned to wash my hands at the sink.

"We had Sonic," Karen replied.

"Sonic sounds good. Better than my mac and cheese! Listen up. About tonight . . . I want you girls to behave while I'm gone. You're in charge, Hilary. No boys, no parties. I won't be out too late, but don't wait up for me. We're going to have dinner in town and maybe catch a performance at the theater."

"Ohhh! The theater! Don't show her all your moves at once, Dad," Hilary said.

"Ha ha. Some people really enjoy a good narrative, young lady. It doesn't have to be a blow-your-eardrums-out concert in order for it to be enjoyable."

Karen, who had been pretty quiet up to now, spoke softly. "Didn't you used to take Mommy to that same theater?"

"Karen?" Hilary tried to cut her off.

I walked over to Karen and put my arm around her.

"No, Hil, it's okay." I looked down into Karen's sad eyes. "Yes, Karen, I did. Do you want me to take Stacy somewhere else? Actually, I could stay home with you girls."

"No, it's okay, Daddy." Karen said. "Please go."

Hilary grabbed my coat and helped me into it. They both nudged me out the door. As I climbed into my truck, I got a text message from Stacy.

Change of plans. Why don't you come by my house now and drop off your truck? We'll take my car.

I had planned on meeting her at the restaurant, within walking distance of the theatre. Not wanting to start our date on a bad note, I responded and agreed to do it her way.

31

Miranda woke suddenly to the sound of voices from somewhere above her.

"David, I thought we could take my car. Is that okay with you?"

Miranda's screams were muffled by the tape across her mouth. *David!* He was here! It had taken Miranda a while to realize she was being kept in the woman's basement. Now it appeared her captor had been telling the truth the entire time. She had infiltrated Miranda's family with the intent to take it over. Miranda was horrified beyond belief, and all at once, everything made sense. Tied to her chair, she struggled to make a noise—anything that might capture David's attention.

"Yeah, Stacy, no problem," David said. "You're kinda out in the boonies, aren't you?"

Miranda felt a myriad of emotions running through her, followed by an agonizing pain in her chest. She could barely breathe. How could David have fallen for such an evil person? How long had he waited before he simply moved on? Tears warmed her eyes.

For a while, Miranda had been able to keep track of the days and months, but that time had long passed. *Maybe it's been a year*, Miranda thought. If David had no reason to believe she was still alive, certainly he could be expected to move on eventually.

Miranda knew Stacy had intended on bringing David here all along to torture her. That's why she'd taped her mouth earlier that day. She knew Miranda would be in agony, listening to David's voice only a few feet away. It might as well have been miles. They talked for a few moments more, and then Miranda heard the front door close.

Miranda realized the anger she once felt was slowly turning into hopelessness and despair. She missed David and the girls, and as bittersweet as it had been, she was glad to at least hear his voice once again.

32

"So tell me, David, why did you want to be a cop to begin with? I mean, had you always wanted to be one?"

I thought for a second. I could give some macho answer that wasn't the truth, or I could start off this relationship with some honesty.

"Honestly, it kind of happened. I mean, I know that sounds cliché and all, but it really did. I'd been bouncing around dead-end jobs after the army, and someone told me to give it a shot. I never thought I'd be doing this for fifteen years." I paused. "I probably owe much of that to Miranda. Lord knows I thought about quitting more times than I can remember."

"She must have been a really special girl," Stacy said.

"Yes, she was . . . but what about you?" I asked, wanting to change the subject. "Why nursing? Not to be rude, but it seems like with a little more schooling you could be a full-fledged doctor."

"I don't think it's rude. And to be perfectly honest with you, I have no idea. But I can tell you this—the thought of more school right now is out of the question. As a nurse, I already have more medical training than most of the people on this planet."

"Well, I guess you do," I said. "That's a good point."

I knew if I allowed my mind to wander, it would drift back to Miranda. She was dead, and I had accepted that, but I still missed her dearly. I never thought dating again would be this tough on me emotionally. I felt a sense of guilt for trying to fancy another woman.

A few minutes later, we pulled up at Papadeuax. I got out and moved around the car to open Stacy's door. I was a perfect gentleman.

"Thank you, sir." She smiled.

I returned her smile, my heart pounding. I felt like a high school boy on his first date.

I escorted Stacy inside and gave the hostess Stacy's last name for the reservation. She had asked for a secluded spot at the back of the restaurant. I was surprised. She'd gone all out.

"So what do you think, David?" she asked as we sat down.

"This place is incredible . . . and you look incredible."

Stacy leaned closer. "I look even better in my tight, little night-night shirt," she said with a seductive smile.

Then she kissed me.

33

Hilary lay in her bed and looked around her room. She opened the nightstand drawer and felt around for her iPod. Music—her escape. She knew her dad really liked Coach Stacy, though she secretly had some reservations of her own. She would continue to hide her concerns, though. After all, she'd encouraged her dad to go out with Stacy. How could she explain that lately she thought something just wasn't quite right with the lady.

Since the first encounter with her at her mother's funeral, something about Stacy made her uneasy. She'd tried to ignore it. After all, Stacy was a pretty woman, and she knew her dad was lonely. Sometimes, when no one else was looking, she thought she caught Stacy peering at her from the corner of her eye. It was creepy.

Hilary also needed to decide what she was going to

do about her boyfriend, Rodney. Rodney and Hilary had met at a house party right after her mom went missing. Fireworks had shot between them from the beginning, even though they were very different creatures indeed. Rodney was a computer geek, hacking into anything and everything he could find. Hilary hated computers almost as much as she hated school. She majored in partying and rock music.

Unfortunately, a night of drinking games had left them naked, drunk, and lusting for each other. They had gone up to one of the bedrooms and began making out. Something—perhaps the memory of her mom's nagging voice in her head—gave Hilary enough willpower to avoid having sex with him. Ever since that night, Rodney had been pressuring her to go all the way.

Sure, she wanted him to like her, but she didn't want to feel like a piece of meat. Suddenly, her thoughts were interrupted by the ding of her phone. She picked it up and answered, knowing who it would be.

"Hello," Hilary said.

"Hey good lookin'. Wanna see me tonight?"

"Rodney, I don't know. Right now I'm home watching my little sister. My dad is out with Stacy."

"Yeah? Well, why don't I just come over there then? I'll be good. I promise. C'mon, Hil. You know you wanna see me. Hey, did you finally tell your dad Stacy gives you the creeps?"

"No. I told you my dad really likes her, and she may be good for him even if she's not good for me. Look, I'll call you after my sister goes to sleep. My dad won't be in 'til late, I'm sure, but you have to be gone before he gets here or he'll kill me!"

After the phone call, Hilary went to check on her sister. She found Karen in her room, writing in her diary, as she often did. She sat down on the floor next to her little sister and read over her shoulder.

Hi mommy me again,
Tonight daddy finily went out with Coach Stacy. I hope you are not mad. I was right about them liking each other—they do. Will I ever see you agin? Maybe in heven I will. I sure hope so you ment so much to me. Hilary has been sneaking boys in when daddy is gone. She dusnt think I know but I do. When I get older I wont do that don't wurry.
Bye for now.
Love
Karen

**

Stacy and I seemed to be enjoying each other's company. We laughed and shared stories about our pasts as we finished our dinner at a local restaurant. It wasn't nearly as fancy as our first dinner, which I preferred. I was more comfortable with diner-type fare than fancy dishes I could barely pronounce.

"I really like you, David," Stacy said. "I don't need to go on fifteen more dates to know you're the man I want. Actually I don't need another date. I want to be a part of your life and the girls lives . . . permanently."

I didn't see this one coming, and it must have been plainly written on my face. No hiding this one.

"I'm not asking you to marry me, silly, but I would like to move in with you and the girls and make our relationship feel more real."

She looked at me with expectation. I didn't know what to say. She was moving kind of fast, but I knew a lot of things had changed since I'd first dated Miranda. Still . . .

"This is a surprise," I admitted. "Not in a bad way, but a definite surprise. I mean, I thought we had a connection, possibly, but—"

"Talk it over with the girls," she suggested. "Think about it, David. I want you, the girls, us. Our own little family. Maybe even a kid of our own one day."

I pushed myself away from the table. The "one day" relieved me a little. I breathed a sigh of relief.

"I'm on not one, but two types of birth control right now. Mainly for some problems I've been having," she said, lifting her hands. "No pregnancies here!" she laughed. "But enough talk about the future. Let's have some fun tonight."

She suggested we skip the theatre and make our own "production" back at her place. She quietly admitted she hadn't had sex since her boyfriend's accident. It didn't take much prying and cajoling before Stacy and I were headed back to her place.

I slowly eased my hands up the sides of Stacy's body, stopping just shy of her breasts. She grabbed my hands and encouraged me to cup her breasts. She moaned in my ear. From that point on, my hesitance vanished.

After our lovemaking session ended, I headed to the bathroom to clean up before gathering my clothes from the floor beside the bed.

"Where are you going, hon?" Stacy asked, lying naked on the bed, not a shy bone in her body. "Won't you stay with me tonight?"

I shook my head. "I have to get back to the girls. I told them I'd be in late, but I'd be in nonetheless."

Stacy tried to convince me to stay by offering another round of sex, but I declined. She didn't make it easy. She rose from the bed, leaving the sheet behind, walked over to me and rubbed my crotch as she nibbled my ear.

"Very tempting proposition, but I really have to go. This we will do again—a whole lot more, if the girls aren't opposed to you moving in with us."

"So does that mean you're okay with my moving in?"

"Well, let's just say I'm warming to the idea." I shrugged. "But I'm on duty early tomorrow, and my gear is at home."

How weak am I? How did I go from three or four dates to possibly letting this woman move in with me and my girls? Oh, the pleasures of the flesh.

"Oh yeah, De Luca," Stacy muttered. "How could I forget?"

I noticed the sudden hard edge to her voice, though she tried to disguise it behind a smile. I frowned.

"I'm on duty whether Detective De Luca rides with me or not. She's a coworker and nothing more; besides, this gentleman prefers blondes."

34

The engine noise woke Miranda. Again, she pulled at her restraints. She heard the front door open and close. Her heart thudded in her chest when she heard David's voice above her, talking to Stacy. She looked around the semi-dark interior of the basement until she found the source. The bitch had positioned a baby monitor on the small table behind her. The volume was low, accompanied by occasional static, but she heard every word. Just like Stacy wanted.

"David, I won't break. Don't be scared," Stacy was saying.

Miranda's stomach clenched as she was forced to listen to the moans and groans of Stacy, her captor, as she had sex with David. The tape over her mouth prevented Miranda from screaming in outrage. Defeated, she let the tears flow. David had always been a good lover, and now he was showering another woman with his passion.

Miranda lost her breath; she couldn't afford to hyperventilate. She struggled to gain control over her emotions, knowing she would die of a broken heart right here, right now, if she didn't get a hold of herself. She couldn't allow the bitch to see her pain. Then again, what was the point? Her daughters and her husband had been wiped out of her life by the psycho bitch, and now the woman talked of moving into her house! With her children! With her husband! Miranda moaned in despair. She remained trapped, unable to prevent it.

Her thoughts were distracted when she heard the front door close a while later. She did her best to quiet herself as Stacy opened the door to the basement stairs and walked down, one slow, satisfied step after another.

"Could you hear any of that?" Stacy ripped the tape from Miranda's mouth with a self-assured smile. "I told you, didn't I? I told you I would have your family. Was the intercom speaker loud enough? David is quite a man, isn't he? He has such a big . . ." She laughed. "Who's the smart one now? I stole your life and family. I'm about to steal your house, too."

"You're a cruel bitch!" Miranda sneered. "And you deserve what I'm going to do to you. I promise you that."

"And I'm the cruel one, right?" Stacy laughed again. "Do unto others as you would have them do unto you."

Miranda wondered what Stacy was talking about. She was nice to people, never crossed anyone or had run-ins with them. This had to be related to the story she'd been working on. Had someone found out the details? Had the people she would have implicated somehow become aware and arranged for her kidnapping to keep her quiet? How long did they think they could keep her hidden? Why didn't they just have her killed? Surely they knew it would be the only way to silence her for good.

"Bye-bye now," Stacy taunted, wiggling her fingers at Miranda. "How long do you think it'll take me to get pregnant?"

With that she was off. Feeling sick to her stomach, Miranda sank further into despair.

35

I walked upstairs and found Hilary asleep, headphones on, music blaring in her ears as usual. Karen was sound asleep as well, clutching her diary. I thought about taking a peek for a moment, but then I passed on the idea. *Some secrets are better left untold*, I thought. I walked to my room, undressed, took a shower, and then crawled into bed. I fell asleep the moment my head hit the pillow.

I rose the following morning, Miranda weighing heavy on my mind. I pillaged through one of her drawers and ran my fingers across her silky undergarments. A bra, a sexy thong, a camisole . . . I hadn't had the heart to get rid of Miranda's things. I still missed the love of my life deeply and mourned her often.

I finished dressing and headed downstairs to make breakfast for myself and the girls. The rustling must have wakened them both, as several minutes later I heard them upstairs. I made scrambled eggs, bacon, and toast and set the plates on the table as Karen edged into her seat.

"So, Dad, how did it go?" Karen said as she nibbled a slice of bacon.

"Well, actually I was going to talk to you and Hilary about that," I said. "Not really sure where to begin. Stacy really wants to be a part of our family. She asked me last night how I felt—how we felt—about her moving in here with us."

"She didn't waste any time with that, did she?" Hilary said as she walked into the kitchen, an angry scowl on her face. "I don't think I'm hungry anymore."

I hurried over and gently grabbed her by the arm before she could head back upstairs. "Nothing's been decided, Hil," I assured her. "I told her I would talk to you girls, and we would make a family decision."

Hilary reluctantly came to the table. The girls picked at their food, and soon it was cold and inedible. I looked at both girls and asked what they thought of the idea. *The timing could have been better*, I thought, *but oh well*.

"I think Mommy would be okay with it," Karen finally offered with a shrug.

"I think you should date longer," Hilary said. "After all, you guys barely know each other. Why the rush?" She paused. "It's obvious you liked each other from the start, but it just seems fast, Dad. Don't you think? I mean, is this love or lust, really?"

I nodded. "I agree, and it definitely was my idea to date longer. But I slept on it last night, and I'm open to considering it, I guess. I ain't getting any younger. And it could be love . . . I think, or at least I might be headed there."

I knew it would be weird for everyone if Stacy moved in and maybe even unfair to the girls on some level. But I had convinced myself I was owed a woman—a partner. To be honest, Stacy was one hell of a catch, and she wouldn't stick around forever if I dragged my feet too much. I sighed.

"How about this," I suggested. "We can have Stacy come over and spend a weekend. Maybe next weekend? We'll see how it goes. Then we'll talk about it again after. Fair enough?"

I didn't wait for them to respond. I put my dishes in the sink and bent down to kiss each of them on the forehead.

"Bye, Daddy," Karen said.

"Bye, girls. I'll have my cell, as usual, if you need anything." I turned to Hilary. "You pick up your sister after school and then come right home."

She nodded without looking at me.

As I headed for my truck, my cell phone rang. Stacy, I assumed.

"Hello?"

"David, Captain Wilcrest here. Before you head out, come to my office. Some new evidence has turned up in Miranda's case."

I stopped, my heart thudding. "What kind of evidence?"

"Someone turned in some hairs and a note. The note said the hairs belong to Miranda and she's alive and they're holding her captive. It may be something; it may just be some asshole playing games with us. I don't know, too soon to tell. I just wanted to let you know and give you a chance to look it over before word about it spread."

"What?" I felt confused. "When did this stuff show up?"

"A farmer said he found the note in front of the station last night. He was coming in to pick up his son from the jail and said it was on the ground. It was just after midnight, so I elected not to wake you."

I stood stunned. Miranda, alive?

"David, it's been over six months. You know the numbers. I don't have to tell you. Chances are greater that this is just some kind of game someone is playing. A sick game, mind you, but a game nonetheless. Carter is serving the rest of his life behind bars for his involvement in her disappearance. I'm sure he didn't leave this in the hands of someone else for it to possibly turn up and bite him."

"You're right, and I know that," I said. "It's also possible Carter did just that—paid someone else to get their hands dirty so he and his goons wouldn't have to and it couldn't be traced back to them. As many enemies as I've made over the years, I'm sure it wouldn't have been hard for him to find a willing participant."

36

I drove quickly to the station. After I arrived, I rushed inside and blew by everyone, not slowing to say my customary good mornings and engage in gossip station talk.

"Something new came up in his wife's disappearance case."

I heard the comment from one of the other detectives as I brushed by.

"When is Porter going to realize she's gone?"

"I don't know why the guy tortures himself."

I ignored them all and walked into the captain's office, closing the door behind me.

"Good morning, Captain."

"David," Wilcrest said, looking up. "I didn't expect you so soon." He sighed. "The lab has been able to confirm that the hairs are . . . were indeed Miranda's. They're cross-checking the handwriting with local databases to see if any hits come up." He lifted a hand. "Still checking for prints and

DNA. You know DNA results could take weeks or even months to get a hit—if we get one at all. Beyond that, there isn't much more to tell."

"The note," I said. "What did it say?"

"It said Miranda is alive and watching her life play out—whatever that means." He glanced down, then back at Porter. "It closed with 'way to go, David.'"

I frowned. A deliberate taunt? "And that was it? Way to go, David? What the hell is that supposed to mean?"

Wilcrest shook his head. "It also said she was 'far enough away to not be seen but close enough to smell your aroma if the wind blew in the right direction.'"

"What the hell?" I muttered.

"Honestly, David, I don't know what any of it means. Sounds like some mumbo jumbo nonsense. Somebody's playing a cruel joke."

I wasn't so sure. "How did someone get hold of Miranda's hair?" I paused, my mind racing. "Cap, if Miranda . . . never mind. Stupid thought. I'll keep it to myself."

Before I realized it, I was ranting about something I knew wasn't possible. I knew Carter or one of his goons had killed Miranda, or at least paid to have it done. Either way, Carter was behind bars. I needed to accept that Miranda was gone. I needed to move on, if not for my sake, then for the sake of the kids. There hadn't been one shred of evidence to the contrary and I knew that.

"That it, Captain?" I finally said, feeling emotionally worn out.

He shook his head. "One more thing."

I braced myself.

"At the bottom, the note also said, 'Porter, I saved the best for last. I'm going to enjoy you.'"

Again, I felt nothing but stunned amazement. For an instant, I thought of Prodinov. Then, I thought of the child-killer, the one who had been eluding capture for months.

"You have any idea what that means, son? Any of it?"

"Prodinov? The child-killer, perhaps?" I shrugged. "Just sounds like some stupid talk, Cap. It's probably somebody I brought down, getting back at me or trying to. I don't know what to make of it."

I left Captain Wilcrest's office and headed for my desk. We were definitely dealing with one sick bastard. I had leads to follow up on regarding a murder-suicide that had taken place several days prior. I'd be working on that most of the day.

Detective De Luca had watched me walk into the station moments earlier, but had not approached.

"Good morning," she said as she approached my desk.

I just needed to grab some addresses, and then I planned to head out. Still, my head swam with possibilities.

"Morning to you," I said. I gestured toward the squad room with my chin. "I take it you heard about the—"

"Yeah, I heard about it. Asshole. Whoever he is, we'll catch him. If he keeps it up, we'll get the bastard, David—Detective Porter."

We both stared at one another. I'd sensed a hint of attraction between us before, but now I felt sure of it. The way she said my name, the way she looked at me sometimes. It wasn't something I would act on, of course, but it was there all the same.

After a few seconds of idle staring, I spoke.

"Yes, we'll catch him sooner or later. He'll make a mistake if he keeps this up; they always do. But I have to wonder if this asshole is messing with my brain, or if Miranda is actually alive out there. That's probably his intention. I guess it's working." I frowned as another thought struck me. "Maybe the asshole Carter paid to get rid of Miranda kept her. Like a personal trophy of some sort. I know it sounds stupid, but on some level . . ."

"I don't want to agree with you and say it sounds stupid, but you know the likelihood of her being alive after all this time is slim to none. Heavy on the none."

37

"Hilary, hurry up. Let's go!"

Karen tried to get off the phone so they could go to the park. Karen enjoyed taking bike rides to the park, and their dad didn't mind letting them go together. It gave them something to do. Before their mom died, Karen went to the park with her nearly every day.

Hilary was trying to talk her boyfriend into meeting them there. He knew this park trip wouldn't lead to as much as a kiss, so he was reluctant. Plus, he had been busy trying to hack into a new FBI program all morning.

"I'm coming, Karen!" she snapped at her little sister. "The park isn't going anywhere, you little twerp." She disconnected her call to Rodney. "He might meet us there."

"Great. He's a super guy," Karen said, rolling her eyes—a gesture she'd learned quite well from her big sister.

"You don't have to like him," Hilary said. "He's my boyfriend. Just come on."

"He's a geek! A nerd! A loser!"

"Yeah, I get it. Now out."

As much as Hilary hated to admit it, she too enjoyed the bike rides with her sister. It was a way for them to remember their mother, something they all used to do together.

On the way to the park, they passed a firearms store. For a second, Hilary thought she saw Stacy's car parked there. At least, it looked like Stacy's car. Their dad had told them Stacy would be on shift at the hospital for twenty-four hours. Why would she be at a store like that anyway?

Rodney lived near the park and was waiting when she and Karen rode up, perched atop of a park bench.

"Hey, Karen. How are you?" Rodney said, climbing off the bench and walking toward them.

"Hi, Rodney," Karen said. "I'm going to the swings, Hil. Some of my friends are over there!"

She darted off across the playground.

"Wow, look at you," Rodney said, a hungry leer on his face. "Come on over here and give Daddy some sugar. Nice shorts. A little too long, though."

"Daddy?" Hilary snorted. Maybe Karen was right. She walked over to Rodney, who wasted no time wrapping his arms around her neck. He had barely put his lips to hers when they were interrupted.

"What is this, young lady?"

Hilary heard the familiar voice at the same moment she felt a finger tap her shoulder. She turned around in dismay to find Stacy standing behind her, an ugly look on her face.

"Oh hey, Stacy," she said, forcing herself to remain calm.

"Don't 'hey Stacy' me," Stacy snapped. "What are

you doing with this boy?"

She shot a glare toward Rodney. Hilary stood speechless. She'd never seen Stacy act this way.

"Who is this?" Stacy demanded.

Hilary had held her anger in for as long as she could. Just as she was about to let Stacy have it, Karen came running to give her a hug.

"Look, Hil," Karen said, out of breath. "It's Coach Stacy."

"Yeah, I see her, Karen," Hilary said, grabbing Rodney's arm. "Let's go, Rodney."

"Excuse me, young lady, what was that?" Stacy asked.

Hilary turned to Stacy and rolled her eyes. She was ready to argue with her, but Rodney tugged her arm.

"C'mon, Hilary," he said. "Let's get outta here."

Suddenly, Stacy rushed forward and grabbed Hilary's arm, jerking her around to face her.

Hilary yanked her arm out of Stacy's grasp, eyes wide with surprise.

"Look, kid," Stacy snapped. "You need to listen and listen well. I'm going to be a part of your life. It appears you need a mother figure. I can't believe David puts up with you and your disrespectful attitude. You're out here slutting around in front of your little sister. If I was your mother—"

"Fuck you," Hilary said. "You'll never be anything like my mother! How dare you try to tell me who I can or can't kiss or whatever?"

"C'mon, Hil." Rodney urged her away from Stacy. "Let's just go."

Karen stood watching, wide-eyed. The two had garnered the attention of a few other park visitors as well. Stacy took a step back and laughed.

"You know what, Hilary my dear? You're right. I'm

not your mother. You can make out with anyone you'd like. If that's your thing, so be it. Hey, let's go make out in the park so everyone can watch us."

Hilary was dumbfounded. What was wrong with the woman?

"It was just a hello kiss," she said. "Don't you think you're overreacting just a bit? Either way, you don't have a right to question me or put your fucking hands on me. Come on, Karen."

She held out her hand for her little sister. For a second, Karen stood still. Stacy stared at Hilary with a strange look in her eyes.

"Karen can come with me if she'd like," Stacy said, holding out her hand. "Would you like that, Karen?"

"Hell no, she won't," Hilary said. "She came with me, and she'll leave with me. Let's go, Karen, now!"

Karen reluctantly walked past Coach Stacy and grasped Hilary's hand. Stacy smiled at them as they turned to walk away. It was a weird grin Hilary would have to work hard to forget.

"Bye, girls! Be careful," Stacy said, as if nothing had happened. "Nice to meet you, Rodney."

"You see? I knew it," Hilary said to Rodney as they reached the opposite side of the park. She looked over her shoulder to find Stacy still staring after them. She hadn't moved.

"Knew what?"

"Knew she was a bi—" She bit her tongue, aware her little sister was listening. "I mean, I can't believe she was all in my business like that. Can you imagine how it would be if she moved in with us?"

38

De Luca and I ultimately decided to work the new evidence regarding Miranda's case instead of following up my earlier leads on the other case—that could wait. This couldn't. We read and reread the note left behind at the station. We checked the baggie it had been left inside and both came to the same conclusion: someone was messing with me. Miranda was dead. Still, I wanted to catch the asshole who thought it would be funny to toy with me. It had now become more about catching him than finding Miranda's body. Yes, I wanted to find Miranda, give her a proper burial, but for now, I'd take what I could get.

We decided to call an impromptu press conference, officially closing the case. This had not been done before, even though the case had, for all intents and purposes, been shelved. We hoped the perp would watch the press conference and strike again so we could catch him. I always suspected someone other than Carter was involved. He wasn't smart enough to pull off a kidnapping and murder by himself. I wanted the accomplice.

"Detective Porter, are you sure you want to do

this?" the reporter asked as I approached the podium.

No one knew our real intentions in regard to the announcement. At the station, only De Luca, Wilcrest, and I were in on the plan.

My hands were a sweaty mess. A small group had gathered at the courthouse to witness the announcement. As I stepped up to the podium, I was surprised to see Stacy in the gathering. How did she find out about it? I had not mentioned my plan to her or the girls. The two of us made eye contact, and I offered a wan smile. I glanced to my right and got the go-ahead nod from the reporter.

"Good morning," I said, my hands tightly clenching the sides of the podium. Fake or not, making the announcement caused an upheaval of emotion in me. "My name is Detective David Porter. On behalf of the Harris County Police Department, we would like to first offer thanks for the support this community has lent us in the disappearance of my . . . of my wife, Miranda Porter. Initially, we decided the closure of this case would remain in-house for several reasons, but recently, new evidence turned up in the case. After careful analysis, we have determined that this evidence is a hoax and an attempt to dredge up horrible memories for myself and my family. So, we're making it publically official that the case into the disappearance of Miranda Porter is now closed. I will not be taking any questions today. Thanks for your time."

A handful of reporters crowded around me, spouting out question upon question, all of which I ignored.

I walked over to Stacy. I gave her a quick hug, and we walked off hand in hand. Stacy told me she needed to talk to me about something, but the timing was bad. I had work to do. Anything else could wait.

CHAINED GUILT

<u>39</u>

Miranda had wanted to quit so many times, just give up and die. She was down to nothing but skin and bones, and her body ached all over, all the time. She was literally sick and tired—tired of the hell she was forced to live in and tired of life, such as it was. This was not the way her life was supposed to go. She wasn't supposed to die tied up in some woman's basement for doing her job. She wasn't supposed to lose her family and die alone.

She heard rustling at the door and turned listlessly toward it.

"Miranda, dear, you're not going to like me today," Stacy said as she slowly walked down the stairs. "Well, I'm sure by now there are no days when you fancy me, but you're really not going to like me today. I have to take something from you. You see, I have a problem."

Miranda didn't give a rat's ass about Stacy's problems. She could stick—

"Today, the police officially closed your case. Do you know what that means? Do you? It means they honestly believe you're dead. The hair and the note I left for them last week were considered a hoax—a terribly distasteful hoax. What super cops they are, right? I want them to know you're alive. I want them to acknowledge that I'm too good for them to catch me. I want them to beg me for your life." She chuckled. "And your Detective David will believe you're alive, but David the man will still lust for me, and he'll make love to me every chance he gets. He's such a fool!"

Miranda watched Stacy walk around the edge of the basement near the old worktable, looking for something. She heard her captor place something down on the workbench, it sounded wet.

"I'll deliver the package this afternoon while it's still fresh. Maybe the police will take me seriously this time."

She took a step toward Miranda, metal snips in one hand as she reached for Miranda's hand, bound to the chair.

"They'd better."

By this point, Miranda was almost oblivious to pain . . . or so she thought. She screamed as her captor snipped repeatedly at her finger, hacking away at it till it finally fell to the floor. She focused her hate-filled gaze at Stacy as she dropped her bleeding finger into a sandwich baggie filled with ice, and then moved to tie a strip of cloth around the stump of her finger to stop the bleeding. If the bitch made even one small mistake, Miranda would take no mercy when killing this woman. Unfortunately, everything the woman did was well thought out and meticulous.

"All done." she said, laughing. "Good girl. All that screaming, but not a single tear?" She moved back to the workbench, returning moments later with needle and thread and skillfully sutured the skin together.

"Cry? Why should I?" Miranda muttered. "I won't give you the pleasure. You can't hurt me anymore, you bitch."

"Oh, I don't know about that," Stacy said with a smirk. "I may be able to kill two birds with one stone this afternoon. I'll bring you some pictures, don't worry. I wouldn't want you to miss out on the fun. To be completely honest I don't have a problem with you Miranda. I mean I do think you're a spoiled prissy little bitch don't get me wrong. Ultimately though you are just a tool I am using, a very special tool. By the way I'm willing to bet I can and will still hurt you."

40

My cell phone rang. I barely had a chance to say hello when my daughter broke in.

"Dad how much longer before you get home?" Hilary's tone was clipped and angry.

"I'm actually getting into my truck now," I replied. "Everything okay?"

"No, everything is not okay, Dad. But we can talk about it when you get home."

She hung up. I was confused, but whatever boy problems Hilary had with Rodney couldn't be that bad. Before I could slide my key into the ignition, my cell phone rang again. This time it was Stacy.

"Hey, David, how did the rest of your day go?"

"Pretty well." I sighed, sitting back in the seat. "I'm glad to have all that stuff with Miranda and the case behind me. What did you want to talk to me about earlier? Is everything okay? You seemed concerned about something."

"Well, I'm not sure where to start."

I waited.

"I ran into the girls at the park, and . . . well, I saw Hilary kissing some boy. It was pretty intense stuff. I mean, his hands were up her shirt and she was rubbing on his privates." She paused. "I can barely even talk about this, David."

I sat quietly, my blood pressure rising.

"There was some pretty loud moaning going on, and there were lots of people around. I mean, it looked like they were about to have sex right there in the park. So I kindly walked over and got Hilary's attention and—"

"What? She was doing what? Making out in the park?" I couldn't believe it. Not Hilary. Sure, she was a normal teenager, but she'd never gotten this far out of bounds. "Damn that d-bag kid, Rodney," I said. "I told her he was no good. Where was Karen while the X-rated video was being filmed?"

"I'm so sorry, David. I don't want you to be mad at me." She paused again. "Still, you should know."

"Know what?" I asked, growing alarmed now.

"I found Karen talking to some strange old guy about a hundred yards from where I found Hilary. After I grabbed Karen, I walked back to where Hilary and her boyfriend were. David, I just picked up Hilary's bra and handed it to her. That's it. She turned around and pushed me and then . . . No, I've said enough."

"And then what, Stacy?"

"She . . . she cursed at me. Told me to stay the fuck out of her business. Karen asked to leave with me, but Hilary insisted they go home together. I tried to calm Karen, but she was pretty upset, and Hilary wouldn't let me get close. Then she yelled at Karen to shut the fuck up."

I sat stunned. I knew Hilary had been struggling

since her mother's death, but I had honestly thought she was handling things pretty well, all things considered.

"Stacy, I'm so sorry you had to witness that. I'm also sorry she talked to you in that manner. I didn't raise my girls to be that way. I'll be home soon, so I'll talk to you later. Thanks for letting me know."

I drove home, my anger reaching the boiling point. I burst through the front door like an armed gunman on a home invasion. I took the stairs two at a time, heading straight for Hilary's room. In the back of my mind, I wondered if her behavior had something to do with the possibility of Stacy moving in with us, but that was a discussion for another time.

As I barged into the room, Hilary stared up at me in surprise, cell phone in hand. I snatched the phone, opened the back, removed the battery, and tossed it back to her.

"Let me guess . . . Rodney?"

"Dad? What's wrong?"

I was having no part of it. "Hilary, I'll ask the questions here. I believe yes or no answers will suffice. Got it?"

She nodded.

"Were you kissing Rodney in the park today?"

"Just a—"

"Yes or no?"

"Yes, sir."

"Did you curse at Stacy? Something along the lines of 'stay the fuck away from me?'"

Hilary swallowed hard. "Yes, after—"

"Quiet! The park is not an appropriate make out spot, not that there is such a place. Stacy said your bra was off, and you were damn near having sex right there. Even worse, you left your sister alone, and she was off talking to some old guy!"

Her eyes grew wide, and then she scowled. "That's a lie! That's not what happened!"

"You are not to leave this house or talk to Rodney by phone, email, IM, text . . . hell, not even a fax. Do I make myself clear?"

Tears formed in Hilary's eyes as she turned away from me and stared out the window.

"So you don't want to hear my side of it?" she muttered. "You don't want to hear the truth?"

"I asked you a question, Hilary."

"You told me to be quiet," she snapped. "Now you want me to talk? Make up your mind. Or do you need to call Stacy so she can make it up for you?"

"Okay, your one month restriction just went up to two."

"Make it until I move out; I really don't care," she said. "Close my door when you leave."

I stood staring at Hilary. I had come full circle; my emotions ranged from anger to confusion and sadness. I knew all too well how tough the last year had been for everyone. I somehow felt responsible for this whole thing. If I hadn't asked about Stacy moving in, this probably wouldn't be happening. Hilary was rebelling. I knew that. Maybe I had been too damn selfish about the whole thing.

I closed Hilary's door and walked into my bedroom. I found Karen lying in my bed watching cartoons.

"Daddy, I heard you yelling at Hilary. I don't want to talk about what happened at the park today. Is that okay?"

"That's fine, Karen. We can talk about it later. You didn't do anything wrong."

I climbed in bed with my little angel, cuddled up, and held her tight.

After Karen fell asleep, I got up to check my email. I wanted to see if De Luca had come across anything new. I grabbed my laptop and logged in. The first thing I saw was an email from Hilary. I could only imagine what it would say. To my surprise it was short and sweet—well . . . not sweet, exactly, but short.

"Dad, is this what I can expect if Stacy moves in? If so, I may have to take my chances elsewhere. Good night."

I had some soul-searching to do. I didn't want to lose my daughters. I needed to decide if this whole thing with Stacy was real or just a live-in booty call, as the kids called it.

41

I rolled over toward the window. The blinds had a crack in them, and the sun was beaming in full-force. Stacy was supposed to come over to begin her weekend stay today. I hadn't talked to her since she and Hilary had gotten into it at the park. I figured I should talk to Hilary to see if it was worth even trying our little experiment or not.

I took care of my morning business, dressed, and walked down the hall to Hilary's room. Her door was ajar. I knocked on it.

"Hilary?"

"What, Dad?"

"Wake up. I want to talk to you."

I stepped into her room and sat down at the foot of her bed.

Hilary slowly rolled over, but she didn't sit up or even make eye contact with me. She kept a pillow over her head and gave me a thumbs-up.

"Look, I'm sorry I came down so hard on you the other night," I said. "You know we made a statement regarding your mom's case the other day. Remember when I told you someone had sent us a note saying your mom was still alive?"

She nodded. The kids had taken it hard at first, but I'd decided they'd be better off hearing about it from me than some kid in school, especially since we'd held a press conference.

"And?" she said, her voice muffled beneath the pillow.

"I admit I was pretty scatterbrained that day." I paused to gather my thoughts. "That doesn't excuse your behavior, but I could have handled it better, and I admit that. Furthermore, I should have at least given you the chance to tell your side of the story. I'm sorry. I was wrong about that. You want to tell me your version of what went down the other day?"

"No. When I wanted to talk, you didn't want to hear it. Now I don't want to talk."

"Okay, Hilary, fair enough. Stacy is supposed to be coming over today to stay the weekend with us. She's supposed to call me before she comes to make sure everything is still a go."

"Do whatever you want, Dad."

"Hil, I don't want it to be this way. All I'm asking is that you give it a chance. A real chance."

Hilary finally moved the pillow from her face.

"She hates me, Dad. And I don't know . . . there's just something about the way she looks at me sometimes. I can't put a finger on it, but it gives me the creeps."

"She doesn't hate you. She actually admires you. She's told me as much." I smiled. "She thinks you're a smart and talented girl. Please give this a chance. For me."

I got up, waiting to see if my daughter would respond. Nothing.

"I'm going down to cook some breakfast. I love you, kiddo."

I went downstairs, prepared breakfast, and held my breath to see if Hilary would come down to join Karen and me at the table. I was pleased when I heard her footsteps on the stairs.

Just as the three of us settled at the table, the doorbell rang.

"I'll get it," Karen shouted, scrambling from her chair to race to the front door.

She opened the door and there stood Stacy, bags in both hands, obviously prepared for her weekend stay.

"Good morning, everyone!" Stacy called out.

I almost spit out my orange juice. *She was supposed to call*, I thought. Pushy little thing, she was.

"Stacy?" I sputtered. "I thought you were going to call."

"Oh, I just thought I'd surprise everyone."

"Well, you accomplished that goal," Hilary muttered under her breath.

Hilary turned to me.

"You should tell your girlfriend not everyone likes surprises. I'm going to my room. I'm not hungry anymore."

I sighed and got up to greet Stacy, whose eyes were fixed on Hilary's retreating back.

"She thinks we're moving too fast," I explained. "She's just going to need a little more time, Stacy. She'll be okay."

I leaned down to give Stacy a peck on the cheek. Then I took her bags to my bedroom. I hadn't even reached the door when Karen started in on Coach Stacy. I strained to overhear their conversation.

"I like you, and I like you and daddy hanging out, but I'd rather you and Hil not fight," Karen said.

"I know, sweetie and I'm sorry," Stacy said. "I should have butted out the other day. It really wasn't any of my business. Do you forgive me?"

I returned to the kitchen in time to see my teary-eyed daughter give Stacy a big hug.

"Aww. You okay, Karen?" Stacy smiled.

"Yes, I'm okay," she said, wiping her eyes with the back of her hand. "I just want a mommy so bad sometimes. I miss my mommy. And yes, I forgive you, but you need to apologize to Hilary, too."

I raised my eyebrows. Out of the mouths of babes . . . A sense of failure washed over me, followed by sadness for my girls. I cleared my throat to let the ladies know I'd reentered the room.

"Karen, you okay, baby?" I said.

"Yeah, I'll be fine, Dad," she grinned.

"Great! Now how about you help me get this kitchen cleaned up?"

We'd barely cleared the table when the doorbell rang. I frowned. We weren't expecting any more company this morning.

When I opened the front door, no one was there. I glanced down to find a certified package wrapped in brown butcher paper. The words *Open Immediately—Perishable* were printed across the top in bold, red letters.

I frowned, examining the box as I nudged the door closed with my foot. The package was addressed to me, but it had no return address except for a street, Sycamore, and a local zip code. I was surprised the package had made it through with such sparse return address information.

No sooner had I closed the door when I heard voices outside. I peeked out again to find my in-laws, Tom and Grace, standing there.

"Tom, Grace, what a surprise," I said, startled. Then I grew nervous.

It had been a few months since their last visit. Why had they decided to show up unannounced the weekend Stacy was supposed to stay with us? What next?

I offered to take their bags and placed the package on the entryway table, temporarily forgotten as I invited them in.

"I hope we're not intruding, David," Grace said as she handed me her bag.

"Hello, David," Tom said, casting a wary glance in Stacy's direction. "I told her we should have called first."

"Granny!" Karen yelled in excitement, running into the entryway for a hug.

"No problem. Tom, Grace . . . uh, this is my . . . friend, Stacy."

It was not how I had planned to introduce Stacy to the family. I didn't need anyone's approval, but I still felt a strong sense of uneasiness. I was sure they would, too. I thought I'd waited more than long enough to start dating. But now I was questioning myself, and I felt sure Tom and Grace were doing the same.

Miranda's parents continued to stare at Stacy unapologetically. I cleared my throat. Deep down, I'm sure they both knew the girls and I would eventually move on, but I could tell the shock was affecting them. I got the feeling neither of them really fancied Stacy. Still, that would have been true no matter what woman was trying to fill their Miranda's shoes, I'm sure.

Hilary heard all the chatter downstairs and peeked out to see what was going on. When she saw her grandparents, she ran down to greet them.

"Boy, am I sure glad to see you," Hilary muttered as

she hugged her grandmother.

Hilary didn't wasn't any time and quickly dragged her grandmother upstairs to her room.

"Grace," Tom called after her. "I think we should get a hotel room for the next few days."

"Don't be silly." I jumped in, though I didn't want to. They had been so good to me and the girls. I had no problems with them at all, but the timing was bad this trip—really bad.

42

Tom and I left the ladies at the house and went to the store to pick up what we needed for a barbeque later. I wondered what kind of trouble Hilary might create while I was gone. She had apparently lost all fondness for Stacy, and I was sure Grace didn't care for her too much either.

"So where'd you meet this Stacy, David?" Tom wasted no time asking once we were in the garage.

We climbed into the truck. I didn't answer until we were on the road, headed toward the store. I didn't think it prudent to mention I'd first met her at Miranda's memorial service.

"She was Karen's softball coach. She's a really nice girl." I needed to make the point right away. "I'm not trying to replace Miranda, Tom. She's the mother of my children and always will be. I'll never be able to replace her." I sighed. "But at some point . . ."

"At some point what, David? At some point you'll have to move on? Forget about Miranda? Start a new life?"

I glanced at my former father-in-law. His face was red with anger, and I saw pain in his eyes. I knew I was the cause of his discomfort. I waited a few seconds before I spoke up and considered my words carefully.

"Tom, we all lost someone dear to us. I won't sit here and pretend I know what it feels like to lose a child because I don't. But I do know what it feels like to lose your best friend and wife. It hurts like hell. It hurts every day. Stacy allows me to be myself again. I feel more alive when I can share time with an adult companion. I'm sure you can appreciate that."

"Let's just drop it, David," he said, staring out the window. "How have the girls been?"

"They're doing okay. Karen is as sweet as ever, and Hilary is . . . well . . . still Hilary. If she changed at this point, I'd have to seriously consider admitting her somewhere."

We rode the rest of the way in silence. The brief conversation had left me questioning myself again. When we arrived at the meat market, we picked up ribs, charcoal, and a tub of potato salad. It wasn't until we got back in the truck that Tom spoke again.

"Just take it slow, David. You're still a young man. No need to rush."

I nodded, but Tom continued before I could reply.

"And make sure she loves my granddaughters as much as she loves you. Do you know much about her? Her past and so forth?"

Tom spoke softly, and his words sounded sincere, not angry as before.

"Not sure what you mean about her past," I said. "I mean, we all have a past. I know she's a small town girl, a college grad, a nurse, and she was a foster child." I glanced at him. "How's that for starters? Oh, and she's an ex-softball player, hence the coaching."

"Any run-ins with the law?"

"Really, Tom? The law?" I shrugged and shook my

head. "Hell, I dunno. I didn't run a criminal background check on her, if that's what you're asking. For what it's worth, I didn't run one on Miranda either."

As quickly as the words spewed out of my mouth, I wanted to yank them back in. Tom shot me a go-to-hell look I felt all the way to my bones.

"It'd just be nice to know more about someone who could potentially be spending lots of time with my grandkids," he snapped.

"I'm a pretty good judge of character, Tom," I said, trying to keep the peace. "She's just a normal girl, as far as I can tell. I am a detective, you know, and a pretty good one."

Back at the house, Hilary had taken her grandmother up to her room and told her all about her mix-up with Stacy.

"So all you did was give him a little peck, and she acted all crazy? And that's it, Hilary?"

"Yeah, I swear to it, Grandma. And Dad wouldn't even let me tell my side of the story."

"Well, dear, your dad is a good man and a good father. I don't want to get in the middle of how he decided to handle this." She frowned. "And it's not that I don't believe you, because I do. It just wouldn't be fair to your dad."

"I understand. I just don't want that cow moving in with us and marrying Dad."

"Moving in? Marriage? What are you talking about, Hilary? How long have they been dating?"

"Well, she said she knows Dad's *the one*," Hilary said, rolling her eyes. "And she claims she loves me and Karen and wants to be a part of our family. I think Dad is lonely, and I really liked her at first. I mean, I even pushed Dad to go out with her in the beginning, because he wasn't sure. Boy, do I regret that now."

"You're young, Hilary, but this can be an important life lesson for you. Sometimes you get something you really wanted, only to find out it's not what you needed after all. I love you."

Hilary knew her grandmother was right. She had really wanted her dad and Stacy to start dating, but now that it had become a reality, she second-guessed the idea. Too bad the wheels had already been put into motion.

I walked into the house with Tom not far behind and saw my mother-in-law standing at the bottom of the staircase.

"Good conversation I just had with Hilary there, David," Grace said, cutting her eyes in Stacy's direction.

"Well, that's good, I think," I replied, though I had an inkling the conversation hadn't been good at all.

I took the meat I'd just bought into the kitchen. To my surprise, Hilary walked in behind me and made a beeline for the spice cabinet.

"What's up, Hilary?"

"I'm going to season the meat and get it ready for the grill. That okay with you, Dad?" Her unexpected smile blinded me.

"Uh . . . yeah, I guess."

Her mood change took me by surprise, but I quickly recovered. "I mean, that's a good idea. Thanks. I'll go out and get the pit ready then."

What exactly had my mother-in-law said to her upstairs? Maybe she should drop in more often, I thought. As I passed through the living room, I wondered if I should invite Tom out to help me with the preparations. After glancing at the awkward stares between Tom, Grace, and Stacy, I opted for it.

"Tom, wanna grab a couple cold ones and help me tackle the pit?"

Tom looked a bit dumbfounded but appeared to welcome the idea. I headed outside, Tom not far behind.

"Nice day," Tom said as he stepped outside with two frosty longnecks.

I nodded as I scraped the grill. "Yeah, it's a gorgeous day."

"Nice grill you got there, David."

"Yeah, well, it hit my pocketbook pretty darn good, too. The salesman did his job, I guess. Maybe if I was in a cooking contest somewhere I would use all these bells and whistles, but I hardly cook on this ol' girl at all."

I finished cleaning the grill, and then the two of us sat around making small talk for a while. We stuck to work and politics and steered clear of personal stuff. I enjoyed our talk; in fact, it was probably the longest, most normal conversation the two of us had ever had.

Just as I was thinking I should go inside to see how the ladies were doing, Hilary walked out carrying a tray loaded with seasoned meat.

"Wow! Good job, Hil," I said. "It looks great, and I bet it'll taste even better."

Tom and I grilled the ribs while the ladies prepared side dishes to go with the meal. I thought maybe things might turn out okay after all.

We all sat down at the dining room table, which Hilary had set, and I blessed the meal. As we ate, everyone was on their best behavior. The conversation was civil, and, surprisingly, no one threw any barbs.

"Hilary, have you decided on a college major yet or where you want to go to college?" Tom asked.

"Not sure on either," she said. "I mean, I want to go, I think. Just haven't been putting much thought into it lately."

"Ever thought about nursing?" Stacy asked. "It's a

great career with a high demand and pretty good pay."

"Not really," Hilary replied. "Like I said, I really haven't thought about any of it in too much detail."

"Well, there are classes you can take now, while you're in high school, to get a head start on college. If you'd like, I'll help you look at some of them," Stacy said.

Hilary stared at her a moment, then frowned and glanced around at the table. She caught my eye. I looked at her as if to say *answer the woman*.

"Yeah, maybe," she finally muttered.

"David, I think Grace and I are going to go into town and catch a show," Tom said as they finished eating. "The food was great. You ladies did an excellent job on the sides."

Tom and Grace excused themselves from the table and soon left the house. David, Stacy, Hilary and Karen stared at each other in silence, a blanket of uncertainty threatening to smother them.

43

David, can I talk to you for a minute?" Stacy said as she moved her chair back from the table.

I nodded and we stepped into the kitchen. With the door closed, Stacy spoke quietly. "David, I want to take the girls out shopping and maybe get our nails done or something. I want to show them I'm just as dedicated to them as I am to you."

She reached down to touch me seductively. I instantly backed up.

"Whoa," I said. "As much as I'd love to, that's out of the question. I'm not sure about taking the girls out either. I mean . . ."

"David, trust me. The girls and I need some bonding time. We have to build a relationship. They have to be able to trust me."

"I'm just not sure about Hilary right now."

"David, relax," she said, smiling. "Trust me on this.

It'll be fine."

Stacy leaned in to give me a kiss.

"You'll have the house all to yourself. We'll be fine."

She left me standing there wanting more. I followed her back into the dining room.

"Girls, I had to beg, but your dad finally gave in to the three of us going into town to do some shopping."

I stood back and waited to see their response.

"Really?" Hilary said with a confused frown. "You want to take us shopping? Why?"

"Of course I do." Stacy grinned. "Why not? Go get ready so we can get out of here before he changes his mind."

Moving slowly, as if in disbelief, Hilary trudged up the stairs to her room, Karen dancing along ahead of her. Stacy looked over her shoulder at me. I was still concerned, but perhaps it would work out.

"See? I told you it would be fine," she said.

"Well, you haven't returned in one piece yet, so let's reserve the verdict until later." I grinned back at her.

What a turn of events. I had gone from a house full of people—in-laws, two kids, and a soon-to-be-live-in-girlfriend—to just me in under two hours. I sighed, shaking my head. I glanced at the dining room table, which still needed to be cleared, and knew the kitchen was a mess as well. I'd keep busy.

As I stacked the plates and headed to the kitchen, I spotted the package I'd left on the table in the entryway. I'd forgotten all about it in the hustle and bustle following Tom and Grace's arrival. I tried to recall if I'd ordered anything recently. Perhaps Hilary had. I set the dishes in the sink, grabbed the package from the table, and sat down on the couch to open it. It was lightweight, about the size of a cell phone box. I frowned. If Hilary had ordered a new phone without asking me first, she'd be in trouble. As I ripped open the box, a Ziploc baggie tumbled out. I opened it and removed the Bubble Wrap inside. As I unrolled it, something pale and familiar-looking tumbled onto the couch beside me. It called to me, taunted me to touch it. My heart pounded, and my stomach rolled as a cold sweat enveloped me. I sat in frozen horror, transfixed by what rested on the cushion beside me.

44

The girls were quiet on the ride to the mall, so Stacy decided to attempt some small talk.

"So, what fun things did you guys enjoy doing with your mom?"

Both girls seemed hesitant to answer. Stacy glanced in the rearview mirror and saw them exchange a puzzled look with each other.

"I don't know . . . I mean, regular mother-daughter stuff, I guess," Hilary said. "Softball practices, soccer practices, movies." She paused. "That's kind of a weird question to ask."

"I didn't mean anything by it," Stacy said, glancing between the road and the rearview mirror. "I'm just trying to see if I can come close to doing as good a job as she did. I know I can't replace her. I mean, not that I'd even want to. But I want to do the best job I can."

"You don't have to worry, Coach Stacy," Karen said.

"Just be yourself. That's what Mom always used to tell us."

"About that . . . Coach Stacy, that is," Stacy said. "I don't want you to call me that anymore. I mean, you don't have to call me that. Call me Stacy. Stacy is fine. Maybe one day you'll even call me Mom." She smiled at them in the mirror. "I plan on being around for a long time, if that's okay with you guys."

For some reason, the girls did not respond. Stacy wasn't sure if she'd done more harm than good with her little chat. She considered pushing the issue, but they arrived at the mall before she got the nerve.

"Listen, girls," she said. She pulled into a space, put the car in park, and turned off the ignition. As she slipped her keys into her purse, she twisted in her seat so she could look at them. "Let's just go in here and have some fun. Some girl time. We'll buy some clothes, get some make-up, maybe get a pedicure. Sound like a plan?"

Hilary and Karen nodded, climbed out of the car, and followed her into the mall without a word.

As they walked through the mall, Hilary passed several people she knew. She gave them a friendly wave but didn't stop to talk or to introduce Stacy to them. She saw them watching, though, and it made her uncomfortable. She knew they probably wondered who the lady was, and it didn't take a far stretch of the imagination to figure it out. Most of her friends had known her mom and liked her, which made being with Stacy all the more awkward. Hilary felt like she was betraying her mother by socializing with Stacy. And why did Stacy have to look so pleased about the three of them being out together? Hilary frowned and held back, allowing Stacy and Karen to take the lead. Stacy noticed.

"Hil, you okay?" Stacy said.

"Yeah, I'm fine." She gestured toward a nearby

store. "I think I ate too much. I'm going to go in there and see if I can find some new jeans."

Hilary ditched Stacy, more than aware the woman continued to eye her. She imagined her staring holes into her back. Her heart sank. Deep down, she knew something wasn't quite right about the woman. She heard Karen urging Stacy to move.

"Stacy, come on! Coach Stacy? Can we go to the toy store now?"

Hilary glanced once over her shoulder in time to see Karen take Stacy by the hand and tug her toward the store on the other side of the large, crowded aisle. She also noted the undisguised glare Stacy sent her way before she turned to follow Karen into the toy store.

45

I grabbed a Kleenex from the side table. Using it to prevent leaving my prints behind, I slowly reached down and picked up the severed finger. It was thin and feminine-looking. I studied it for several moments, frowning, before I glanced again at the box it had been sent in. I noticed a piece of paper folded into the bottom. I placed the finger back in the baggie, grabbed another tissue from the box, and carried both box and baggie upstairs to my bathroom. The light was better there, and the last thing I needed was for the girls to come home and find me sitting there with my little "gift."

I set the box and the baggie on the counter and rummaged through Miranda's vanity for the tweezers. I reached the tweezers into the box to retrieve the note. Using the tissue and tweezers, I unfolded the note and spread it flat on the counter.

I scanned the note with growing disbelief. The note said the finger was Miranda's. The finger showed no signs of decay, meaning Miranda had to be alive when the finger was severed. I stood, allowing a rush of emotions to surge through me: hope, despair, joy, and a deep, deep agony. I forced my attention back to the note, which ended with a strange phrase: *"Come on and play, come on and play. No one will believe a word she'll say."*

I sat down on the bed, my legs no longer able to support me. What if this was true? Was this really Miranda's finger, or was someone still playing a cruel game with me? Did I dare hope Miranda was actually alive? And what did the nonsense at the end of the note mean? I was beyond confused. If Miranda was alive, why was someone keeping her? Why would he wait so long to begin taunting me? The more logical explanation was the finger came from another body and had been frozen or preserved somehow. This guy was good. He knew which buttons to push and, even better, knew exactly when to push them. Every killer leaves a trail; I just needed to figure out where to look.

I ran my fingers through my hair as I paced across the bedroom. I had more questions than answers. I wanted to tell the girls there was hope their mother was alive, but before I could even think of doing so, I had to determine if the finger was Miranda's. I did my best to bury my emotions and willed the cop in me to take over. I pulled my cell from my pocket and dialed the captain. After two rings, he answered.

"Hey, Cap, it's Porter."

"Porter, what can I do for you?"

I skipped the pleasantries. "The asshole who sent us the last package has sent another one, this time to my house. A finger in a Ziploc bag."

"What?"

"There was a note inside saying the tissue is still alive. There's no way the tissue would be alive if . . . The finger looks fresh, Cap."

"David . . ." Then Captain Wilcrest swore. "If I had to guess, I would say the kidnapper didn't like us officially closing the case the other day. I think we rattled him.

"If the DNA from the finger matches Miranda's, it only tells us she was still alive when the finger was severed. And if, as you said, the tissue hasn't decayed, it could mean she's still alive. But where is she, and, more importantly, why is someone still holding her?"

"I'm thinking it might be our child-killer," I said. "This is personal. The notes left at the scenes of those crimes were directed at me as well."

"The cuts made on the kids were surgical, too," the captain added. "We knew that much already. He's smart. He's also a sick bastard."

I sighed, my thoughts in turmoil. "We need to figure it out and determine for certainty whether the cases are connected."

"I'll send a unit to pick up the evidence and get it over to the lab," Captain Wilcrest said. "I'll get them to priority test it, David, and then we'll know for sure."

When I didn't respond, he continued. "You'll be okay? If the finger does turn out to be Miranda's, you shouldn't be involved. Conflict of interest and all."

To hell with conflict of interest, I thought. "I'm fine. Let's just determine if the finger came from Miranda. We'll go from there."

I lied to Wilcrest and told him what he wanted to hear. I wasn't okay. Not by a long shot. I carried the box and its grisly contents downstairs and stored it in the back of the refrigerator until the officers came to pick it up. I had to know whether Miranda was dead or alive. Even the slightest possibility that she was alive caused my heart to pound with excitement, with hope, with utter relief at the very idea that we could get through this nightmare. I reined in my thoughts and focused on the task at hand. Wait for the DNA results, and then catch the asshole. I sat on the couch as my emotions brewed. It wasn't long before the doorbell jarred me from my wishful thoughts.

I slowly rose to my feet and headed for the door. To my surprise, I opened it to find Detective De Luca on the other side. I stared. She carried a small Igloo. A wisp of dry ice vapor oozed out of the lid.

"Don't look so excited to see me, David. Geez." She tilted her head and stared back at me. "Well, are you just going to stand there, or are you going to ask me in?"

"Oh yeah. Come on in. I'm sorry."

"So what do you want to do about this?" she asked as she stepped inside the foyer. "Are we reopening the case?"

"Well, that will be up to Cap," I said. "At any rate, we won't publicize this package. No need to give this maniac the glory by doing that."

I sighed as I led her through the dining room to the kitchen. "While my rational self doesn't think she's alive, and I think this asshole's getting off on making me wonder, there is the possibility—"

"But David . . . never mind. I'm not going to push you on this."

"I appreciate your concern. I guess I'm really still trying to process it all. It's hard to make heads or tails of all this. I swear, if I'm quiet enough and lie still long enough, I can hear her heartbeat in my mind."

I glanced at De Luca, but she didn't meet my gaze. "I know that sounds stupid, but—"

"David, I know losing her so suddenly, and in such an awful manner, must have been terrible beyond belief. But I honestly think she's gone. You gotta quit doing this to yourself."

I pulled the box out of the fridge and gently placed it in the cooler for the trip to the lab. Whoever's finger it was, it deserved respect.

"Here's what I think happened," De Luca continued. "I think he cut the finger off before he threw her into the lake. This was obviously with the intention of doing what he's doing right now—torturing you."

I remained silent.

"There was a serial I helped track a few years ago, and he did the same thing," she said. "You know how sick some of these guys are, David. You've been a detective long enough to know irrational people do irrational things. You're trying to rationalize this and you can't."

I didn't know what to think. The finger was fresh. Would it look so vigorous after months on ice? I doubted it. But with all the new technology out there, anything was possible. One thing was certain—whoever was behind this was sinister and very, very clever.

46

"Well, girls, we've almost spent our first full day together, so what do you think?" Stacy asked as she started her car. "Am I really all that bad?"

She'd hoped to win them over and kill them with kindness, and she was pretty sure she had after all she'd bought them. She could pretend to be a good girl . . . if that's what it took.

"I don't suppose so," Hilary said with a laugh.

"You don't suppose?"

"I'm kidding. You're pretty cool, I guess. Thanks for all the clothes you bought me and the pedicure," Hilary said.

Of course, Stacy knew Hilary could play nice too, and it was doubtful she'd gotten over the park episode of a few days ago. Still, the jaunt to the mall had served its purpose.

Stacy pasted on a smile and drove the girls back to the house. Ever so slowly, her plan was coming full circle. She had almost completely infiltrated the Porters' lives. She had David right where she wanted him. Best of all, she was forcing Miranda to watch it all; she couldn't have scripted it any better.

As Stacy pulled into the driveway, she noticed a car parked at the curb. Then she saw David on the front porch with Detective De Luca, who reached out to hug him. David returned the gesture, a smile on his face. *What the hell was the bitch doing here?*

She had barely turned off the car before the girls climbed out with their bags. David approached to help, but Stacy kept her eyes on De Luca as she paused by the car and said hello to the kids.

David reached for one of the bags Karen struggled with and turned to the detective. "De Luca, thanks for everything. I'll catch you back at the station."

De Luca nodded and continued down the driveway. Stacy glowered at her, certain she'd seen a smirk on the detective's face.

"So, did you girls have a good time?" David said.

"Yes, we did. Looks like you had a good time too," Stacy snapped as she nudged her way past him toward the house.

"David, don't hesitate to call if you need anything else. You have my number. Don't be afraid to use it," De Luca said, waving as she slid into her car.

Stacy watched David acknowledge the comment with a nod.

"Daddy! Daddy, look what I got!" Karen jumped up and down as she pulled her father into the house behind her.

"Good job, cupcake." David smiled down at his daughter.

After they made several trips back and forth to the car, David eyed the pile of bags on the couch.

"Stacy, all this stuff must have cost you a fortune,"

he said.

"They're good girls, David. Nothing wrong with doing something nice every now and again is there? I don't have daughters of my own to spoil, so is it okay if I spoil yours?" She cocked her head and eyed him. "I might have gotten something for you too!"

The girls promptly gathered their booty and headed to their rooms to sort out their new clothes. Stacy knew David was probably waiting for her to ask about De Luca and why she'd been at the house. She certainly wasn't going to be the first to bring it up. The anticipation and suspense was killing her.

"Can we talk for a second?" he suddenly said, glancing upstairs to make sure the girls were still in their rooms.

Here it comes, Stacy thought, holding back a grin.

"I don't really know how to talk to you about this, but I'll try," he began. "You know we had pretty much closed Miranda's case, but things keep popping up. We've received a few new pieces of evidence and potential clues."

He paused with a sigh, shaking his head. "Think me crazy, but there's a part of me that thinks she's still alive out there." He glanced at her. "I really don't know what to think. I mean, I know how crazy that sounds. I don't want to mention any of this to the girls right now, but I'm kind of torn."

Stacy was beside herself and struggled to contain her glee. This was even better than she'd expected, listening to him grovel about his poor Miranda. Now she would begin to play with David's mind even more. She'd wanted to make David emotionally dependent on her, and so far her plan had been successful. Time to kick it into high gear.

She feigned sadness. "So what are you saying,

David? You want to break up with me? I mean, if you want to, I understand." Stacy glanced down at the floor to hide her smile. Then she gathered herself, forcing tears to her eyes.

"It almost sounds like you want me to make this easy on you and just walk out of your life."

"Stacy—"

"I'm right here in front of you, David. Whatever is going on with the case is just to throw you off—throw everyone off. No one can magically be alive after so long, David. She had an accident. She's gone, baby. If you need more time, I understand, but I don't know how much longer I can wait."

David stood in silence for several moments, staring down at her. She put on her most sincere expression and waited.

"What the hell am I thinking?" he finally muttered. "You're right. Miranda is gone. You're standing right here, waiting."

He leaned down and kissed her.

"There. How's that for wanting to break up?" he said. "Good enough? I'm just really confused. The asshole keeps sending stuff, taunting me about Miranda. If it makes you feel uncomfortable, I won't talk about it with you."

"I can understand your confusion and where you're coming from, but I don't think it would help our relationship for us to be talking about the case." Stacy mustered a fake grin. "David, will you let me love you?"

He didn't have to say a word; his expression said it all. Oh, how badly she wanted to laugh out loud, right there in David's face. Mr. Super Cop had been even easier to fool than she'd hoped.

47

"Girls, come on down. We're running late!" I yelled up the stairs. I had to get to work, and I still needed to drop the girls off at school.

"You know, Dad, we were never late when Mom was here," Hilary said.

"Well, I'm doing my best, and as you can see, I'm definitely *not* Mom."

While a part of me was pleased the girls had become more comfortable talking about their mother in the past tense, I felt a great sadness that they were able to do so. It was necessary, yes, and I was glad they were beginning to heal, but it also symbolized their moving on, starting over. More than ever, I was determined to say nothing about the new development in Miranda's case until I had definitive proof. The three of us sat at the table scarfing down bowls of Frosted Flakes and Captain Crunch. I figured this was as good a time as any to see what the girls thought of Stacy after a full weekend with her. She had left earlier that morning.

"Now that Stacy is gone, you guys tell me how you really feel about her moving in and being a part of our lives on a full-time basis. She spent the whole weekend here, even in the midst of your grandparents. I thought it went pretty well, considering."

"Maybe with her here we would get to school on time," Karen said.

"Very funny." I feigned a frown. "I'm serious. I don't want to commit to this, for me or for us, unless you guys are one hundred percent on board with it. Come on now, help me out here."

"Well, it seems like it'd be okay," Hilary said. "But we'd all have to be on the same page with house rules and all that. I mean, that whole park thing . . ." She sighed and put down her spoon. "I don't want her coming in and changing things. I don't want us to change who we are. Either she's gotta be okay with that, or I'm not sure it would work."

"Okay," I said. "Well, thanks for telling me how you really feel."

"Dad, you asked," Hilary said. "And I'd rather tell you exactly how I feel than hold it in. Trust me, it'd be much worse that way."

"And little one?" I said, looking down at Karen. "Your thoughts?"

"I think Coach Stacy will fit into our family just fine," she said without looking up from her cereal. "I've wanted a new mommy for a long time." She paused, plucking a piece of cereal from the side of her bowl and popping it into her mouth. "Coach Stacy said she's always wanted a family."

"Thanks, princess." I pushed away from the table. "Stacy and I have a date tonight. We'll talk about it and take it from there."

We downed the last of our cereal and stacked the dishes in the sink. As I waited for the girls to grab their backpacks, I stared at my reflection in the hallway mirror.

I still wasn't sure I'd waited long enough. Stacy seemed like a great girl, but I knew you don't really know someone until you'd lived with them. And I wasn't certain if lust and lust alone was making decisions for me.

<u>48</u>

"Hello?" Miranda called out. She heard someone coming. She had never asked for anything the entire time she'd been in captivity, but she hadn't eaten in at least three days, and the hunger had grown unbearable. She didn't have much room to move, seeing as her captor had placed a manacle around her left wrist and chained her to the wall. She sat on a soiled mattress—another improvement over being restrained in a chair. She had also been given a covered diaper pail to use when she needed to take care of her business. She liked it much better than the old way they'd been doing things. Before, the bitch had given her a bell to ring when she needed to go. But if her captor didn't come, she had no choice but to do what she had to do. It gave her some satisfaction to watch the bitch clean it up. Sometimes, though, the woman would just let her sit in it for days. Miranda was relieved when the bitch finally tired of the cleanup and put an adult diaper on her. She figured nowadays the bitch was too busy to tend to her, thus the diaper pail.

Stacy appeared at the bottom of the stairs. Miranda swallowed her pride, prepared to voice her request.

"Hello, dear," Stacy cooed. "Are you hungry? Oh, I bet you are. It's been a few days now, hasn't it? I bought you some new dog food. I think you'll like this more than the last brand I bought. This is supposed to have more flavor and vitamins, too. Gotta keep you alive."

Dog food, cat food . . . at this point it really didn't matter. Miranda swallowed, her throat parched from lack of water.

"I don't understand what I did for you to be so cruel to me."

"Aww, you sound so sweet and innocent," Stacy said. "Well, shit happens, Miranda! I didn't deserve what happened to me either, but hey, that's life. Right? Moving on. It's all about moving on. I'll be moving in real soon now. Maybe I'll come down one day and we can talk about baby names. Think you could help me pick one out? I hope we have a little boy, and then David will really forget all about you."

Miranda reminded herself to remain in pure survival mode. Eventually, the bitch would make a mistake, and she had to be ready to jump on it. Whatever it took. She just had to think of a way to set herself free.

"Sure," Miranda said. "I'll help you pick out a baby name. I know which ones David prefers. I hope you have a boy, too, and a healthy one."

Stacy frowned. "You yanking my chain?" she asked. "You feeling okay? Need more sunlight down here or something?" She laughed. "That was not the answer I was expecting, but I may just take you up on it."

She turned around to pour dog kibble into a bowl

and then placed it on the mattress within Miranda's reach. "Can I get you anything else while I'm here, seeing as how we're being so nice to each other?"

Miranda looked away. As quickly as Stacy had come, she headed back up the stairs, leaving Miranda alone in the cold, dimly lit basement with only her thoughts to keep her company.

49

De Luca sat in the ladies' locker room, contemplating what she would say to Porter when they rode together today. At this point, she knew she had to say something to him. She didn't trust Stacy. Something just didn't seem right about her. She didn't want to come across as jealous, but with her obvious dislike for Stacy, she wasn't really sure that was possible.

She had even taken one more look at the last bits of evidence to make sure she hadn't missed anything.

He's late, De Luca thought as she waited at the front of the station for him. Five minutes later, he pulled in and slowly eased his truck to a stop in front of her. She opened the door and climbed in.

"You're late, sir," she said as she fastened her seat belt. "Girlfriend trouble, Porter?"

"No, and good morning to you too." He glanced at her. "I had to drop the girls off at school. We got a late start, that's all."

She sighed. "Porter—"

"David."

She nodded. "David, I'm not sure what's going on between me and Stacy. I have no clue what I did to make her dislike me, aside from having breasts, but she clearly doesn't. Which is okay by me, because I really don't care. But beyond that, something just doesn't seem right with her."

She glanced at him. He looked out the windshield, features bland. "Don't get me wrong; I'm not trying to hook up with you or anything." That brought a smile. "But the cop in me says she's got issues. To be honest, I think she's trying too hard to seem perfect."

"Well, thank you, Detective De Luca, for that rousing, in-depth, fact-based report on my girlfriend," he said, finally glancing her way. "It seems everyone except Karen has a problem with her."

She shrugged. "Maybe you should listen to them. Everyone can't be wrong, can they?"

"Yeah, well, I think I'm going to take my chances. Thanks anyway."

De Luca hadn't wanted to piss him off, but it appeared she had. She thought about apologizing, but that just wasn't her style. She'd said what she felt about the matter, and the truth was always best. Right? It was going to be a fun day.

<u>50</u>

Stacy looked out the window and saw David pulling into the driveway. She had forgotten to turn the basement speakers on and hurried down to do so. She heard the distant thud as David got out of his truck and closed the door. He'd be at her front door any second.

"Don't mind me, Miranda," she announced. "Just taking care of some administrative details. You just lay there and listen."

Stacy quickly returned upstairs, closing the basement door just as the front doorbell rang.

"Hey there," she said as she opened the door.

"Hey," David said, looking at her. "You okay? You sound winded."

She waved a hand. "No, no, I'm okay. I just left a pan on the stove and had to turn it off."

"You cooking? I thought we were going out to eat."

Again she waved him off. "Yeah, we are. I'd made

some tea earlier and realized I'd forgotten to turn the burner off. You're early."

"It's 7:00. I'm right on time. If you want to sit down and have that tea, we can."

"No . . . we have reservations, so we should get going."

"You look amazing, as usual," David said as he leaned forward to give her a kiss.

"Thank you, sir. You're pretty dapper yourself."

"I clean up well, or so I've been told." He gestured toward the door. "You ready to go?"

"You bet."

Stacy grabbed a sweater from the hall closet and shrugged into it as she followed David out to the truck. She thought he seemed oddly subdued, but didn't question him about it. She turned to the window and smirked. After all, the man had a lot on his mind lately.

They pulled up to the restaurant and left the car with the valet. They walked inside, arm in arm.

"What name for the reservation, sir?" the host asked.

"Porter," Stacy said before David could reply. "Table for two."

"Already using my name, huh?" David teased.

"Just practicing, babe. Hopefully one day . . ."

They were seated promptly. Stacy pretended to study the menu, though only one thing was on her mind.

"So what did the girls have to say about my weekend stay?"

David shrugged, his gaze still riveted on the menu. "Well, we talked about it, and we'd like you to move in with us."

He glanced up at her, and she struggled to contain her amusement. She nodded instead, as she could tell he had more to say.

"I think it would be good for all of us. Hilary was a little afraid you'd want to change all the household rules, but I don't see that happening, personally. If anything, she may need someone to be a little harder on her than I have been at times."

Stacy pretended to be overcome with emotion and dabbed at her eyes with her cloth napkin. She even managed a tear. He fell for it.

"What's wrong?" he asked, placing his menu on the table, his eyebrows furrowed in concern. "What did I do?"

"Nothing." She sniffled. "This is just all . . . too perfect. I've wanted a family of my own forever. That's why, from the beginning, I was so upfront with you about what I wanted. And now it looks like it's finally happening." She flashed him a dazzling smile. "I couldn't be happier, David."

He reached out for her hand. "I hope you won't change your mind once you move in and become immersed in Porter family life twenty-four hours a day."

"No, never," she said. "And I'll be careful with Hilary. I was a teenage girl once. I know things can be kinda crazy at that age. I want this to work in the worst way. You have no idea."

Later, after a pleasant dinner, she and David headed back to her house. She could hardly wait. The speaker was on, and she fully intended to make the most of it. "I do have a question for you," David said as Stacy hung her sweater in the entryway closet. "What exactly are your plans regarding kids? You said you wanted more at some point?"

He sounded reluctant and she caught on.

"Not right away, David," she said, smiling sweetly. "I think every girl wants a kid or two of her own, but I'm years away from that. Let me get it right with the two we have first."

He smiled at her response. She could see the relief oozing out of him. Stacy had no intention of telling him she'd been off her pills for weeks in anticipation of getting pregnant as quickly as possible.

"Don't just stand there," she said with a coy smile. "You're coming in, right? You don't have to ask to come in, David. Besides, I have something for you."

She reached out her hand and led him through the kitchen toward the back bedroom, located right over Miranda's head. *Better acoustics in this room*, she thought. She felt a twinge of alarm when she realized she had forgotten to place a kettle on the stove, as per her earlier excuse. He apparently didn't notice, which was just fine with her.

She made sure she was extra loud and exuberant during their lovemaking, imagining Miranda just below them, weeping her stupid little eyes out.

51

I relaxed in my tub, filled nearly to the brim with hot-as-I-could-stand-it water. My knees and back ached. I wasn't the twenty-something-year-old man I once was, and after moving Stacy's belongings over to the house all day, I felt my age. We had already said good night to the girls. I opened my eyes and smiled as Stacy came into the bathroom and closed the door.

"There's my superman," she said, eyeing me. "You tired, honey?"

"Yeah." I chuckled. "Guess I ain't as young as I used to be."

My thoughts caught on the word *superman*. That's what Miranda used to call me.

"Okay, well since you're tired . . ."

She untied the belt of her bathrobe and allowed it

to slip off her shoulders. She wore nothing underneath it.

"Well I'm not *that* old or tired, ma'am," I said. I pulled my knees to my chest as she stepped into the tub.

Later, as we lay in bed, I flipped through the channels on the TV. Stacy had fallen asleep in my arms. My channel-flipping stopped at channel 31, the one Miranda worked for before she disappeared. My heart skipped a beat when I realized the station was airing a telethon created in Miranda's name to fund resources for families of kidnapping victims. How ironic to see it on the air tonight— the first night I brought another woman to live in my home and made love to her in the bed I once shared with Miranda. I clicked off the TV, closed my eyes, and grieved silently.

**

The bedroom door burst open and I awakened instantly. The sunlight shone through the curtains, casting the room in a warm glow as Karen rushed in, jumped into the bed, and hurled herself into my arms.

"Daddy! Daddy, wake up!"

"Good morning, sugarplum!" I laughed as I kissed her forehead.

"What the hell is going on?" Stacy moaned, burying her head under her pillow.

"Oh, Stacy, don't mind Karen," I said, nudging her. "You'll have to get used to this. She does it every morning."

"Whatever happened to knocking before you came into someone's room?" Stacy muttered.

Karen looked at me and shrugged. I smiled at her.

"Come on, honey. It's going to take Stacy a while to get used to your very special morning greeting." I winked at her. "You know she's been alone forever."

I set Karen on the floor and shooed her out of the

room so I could dress. Stacy remained motionless and silent, head still buried under her pillow. I chuckled as I left the room and went downstairs to fix the girls' breakfast.

"Hilary!" I called upstairs. "Come on down."

Karen giggled as Stacy staggered into the kitchen, bathrobe tightly belted around her waist.

"Well, look what the cat drug in," I said, smiling at her.

"Where's the coffee?"

I gestured toward the counter while Stacy eyed Karen.

"You have way too much energy in the morning, little girl." She poured herself a cup of coffee. "I'll pour you a bowl of cereal. What kind do you like?" she asked, opening the cupboards in search of cereal.

"Captain Crunch," Karen said. "I'm the only one who'll eat it. Dad and Hilary both hate it."

"Yeah, she can have that crap," Hilary added as she entered the kitchen, collapsed into a chair, and eyed her little sister with a disgusted scowl.

"No crap, young lady. Say stuff, if anything," Stacy said. "Women don't use the word *crap*."

Before Hilary could reply, I turned to her with a grin, though I hoped I wouldn't be playing referee all the time. "Yeah, I don't like that crap—I mean, stuff—either." I winked at Hilary.

"So Karen is the only Captain Crunch eater in the house? I'll eat it too, Karen, but I prefer Cinnamon Toast Crunch," Stacy said.

She turned to me. "David, I know I said I would take the girls to school, but I have the worst headache known to man. Would it be too much trouble if you took them?"

"Not a problem at all. Why don't you go up and rest before your shift at the hospital starts?"

I gave her a kiss, rounded up Karen's gear, and we were off.

Stacy smiled. With the house finally to herself, she ran through her to-do list. There was a pregnancy test to take and some hidden cameras to install—the ones she'd purchased from the firearms store a few days before. She would also take the opportunity to contaminate Karen's Captain Crunch, now that she knew she was the only one who ate it. This would be easier than she'd thought—much easier.

She had stolen a bottle of Baclofen from the hospital. It wouldn't take long for the drug to affect Karen's little body. The Baclofen would make her disoriented and dizzy at first. Then she'd begin forgetting things. It might even kill her over time since she was so young. Even better, no one would know what was making her sick. Let's see if Miss No Feelings Miranda would react to her precious little brat getting sick . . . deathly sick.

But first things first. Stacy installed the hidden cameras and tested them using the laptop she kept in David's bedroom. Then she pillaged Hilary's room looking for anything that would prove valuable. She found what she was looking for in a small notebook stuffed in the back of her desk. She copied down a few passwords for her computer.

Finally, she headed into the bedroom with the pregnancy kit. She stuffed the box and wrappings into her purse to dispose of later. Then she sat on the toilet and peed on the stick.

"Oh my God!" she gasped. She had done it! She was pregnant.

She couldn't believe her luck. She took care of business, dressed, and then pulled out her cell phone, unable to erase the grin that curved her lips. She'd previously rigged her answering machine to the speaker down in the basement so Miranda could hear incoming messages. All she had to do was press a code on her phone and the message would record on the machine, preventing the need to drive over every time she wanted to inform her prisoner of important news. This was the first time she'd actually used it. She punched in the number and waited for the beep.

"Hello, Miranda. I hope you weren't sleeping, dear. Just wanted to give you the good news. I'm officially moved in. Yay for me! And even better news . . . I'm pregnant! I just found out this morning. Such news is too good not to share, don't you think? I hope your day turns out as good as mine will be! Toodles!"

52

"Rodney, stop it," Hilary said, laughing.

"Why do you always tell me to stop? You know you don't really mean it."

"I do mean it. What if my dad comes home early or something? Or she comes home early?"

After many weeks of nagging, Rodney had finally convinced Hilary weed wasn't a drug. The two had begun smoking together, and Rodney was trying to take their sexual relationship to the next level at the same time.

"We really shouldn't be doing this at my house," she said. "What about the smell? We're gonna get caught, and then I won't be able to see you."

"Don't worry about that. I got some stuff that'll get rid of the smell."

He climbed off the bed and gestured toward her

dad's bedroom.

"Your new mommy keep a laptop in there, by any chance?" he asked.

Hilary nodded. "Why?"

"I want to show you something."

Rodney was always trying to prove he was the ultimate computer hacker and could get into anything. As usual, he was out to prove it again.

Hilary sighed. "Rodney, that's my dad's room," she protested as he crossed the hallway and entered the master bedroom. "What are you doing?" she hissed. "Get outta there!"

"Don't worry," he said as he surveyed the room. He found Stacy's laptop on the desk in the far corner, flipped open the lid, and pressed the power button. "Just watch the window for me. I'm going to log into her laptop and see what I can find. I'm sure there's something juicy on there. Maybe she has naked pics on it or something."

"Hey, asshole, that's my dad's girlfriend. We are so gonna get busted. Hurry up!"

"Sorry, but she's still hot."

"Whatever." Hilary shrugged, stepping toward the window. "You want to look at naked pictures of an older woman, go for it. Just hurry."

Within a matter of seconds, he had bypassed the password lock and busily tapped the keys, working his way through her files.

"What the heck are you looking for anyway?" Hilary asked, still watching out the window.

"I told you—naked pics. Everybody does it nowadays."

A few moments went by as Rodney opened file after file looking for a hidden gem.

"Hey, what school did your dad go to? Texas Tech,

right?"

"Yeah why?"

"I don't know. Maybe it's nothing, but I'm finding a lot of files named Texas Tech on here. I thought Stacy went to some nursing school on the East Coast." He frowned. "Why should information about Texas Tech be in here?"

"Maybe my dad put some files on there. I don't know, Rodney, maybe— Oh crap! I see her car turning the corner. Stacy's coming!"

"Are you sure? I thought she—"

"Yes, I'm sure!" Hilary said, hurrying away from the window. "Get the hell outta there. C'mon! Shut it down. She's pulling in the driveway."

Rodney frantically closed the files he'd been scanning and shut the computer down. They made it to the safety of Hilary's room just as the front door slammed. Rodney rushed to the window and opened it, hoping to rid the room of the stale, sweet smell lingering in the air.

"I hope I closed everything down properly," Rodney muttered.

"What the hell, Rodney? What do you mean?" Hilary asked, eyes wide.

"I mean, you scared the shit out of me, and I don't know if I closed everything out."

"Hilary, you here, hon?" Stacy called up the staircase.

"Oh shit! She's coming up! Go stall her or something," Rodney said, fanning the air toward the window.

"That your master plan for getting rid of the smell? Open a window?"

"Just go stall her!"

"Hey there, Stacy," Hilary hollered as she stepped into the hallway. She closed the door to her room just as

Stacy reached the top step.

"You here alone?"

"Uh . . . no, Rodney's here. That okay?" Hilary tried hard not to sound defensive.

"Yeah, sure." Stacy shrugged. "What are you guys up to?"

"Nothing much, just hanging out."

"I bet," Stacy snickered. She glanced at Hilary's closed door, sniffed the air once, and headed for the master bedroom. She closed the bedroom door firmly behind her.

As soon as Stacy was out of sight, Hilary flipped her off.

"Hi, Stacy!" Rodney yelled.

"What are you doing?" Hilary spun around to find Rodney standing behind her.

"Idiot! Get back in there!"

In the master bedroom, Stacy paused on the other side of the closed door. She sniffed the air, detected the faint hint of weed. They had been in the bedroom. She looked around, but it didn't look like anything had been touched. She was on a short break from her shift at the hospital, but had wanted to pop in to see what that sneaky bitch Hilary might be up to. Snooping in her stuff, most likely. She reached down to open her laptop to check on the camera feeds and noticed it was warm. She hadn't used her computer for hours.

"Those little bastards!"

She hadn't set up hidden cameras in the master bedroom yet, but she was pretty sure Hilary and her boyfriend had been on her laptop. Or maybe it was just warm from sitting in the sunshine that filtered in from the nearby window. Either way, she was sure they had been up to something.

"Hilary, there was a file with a Texas Tech transcript

in it on her computer. The name on the transcript was Lisa somebody. Why would Stacy have somebody else's transcript in her computer?" Rodney said.

"How the hell would I know?" Hilary said, rolling her eyes at him. "I'll tell you what I do know. I think the weed is playing with your mind. And you'd better hope this freakin' smell is gone by the time my dad gets home!"

Rodney and Hilary stood by her window and watched Stacy head back to her car. They both ducked away from the window when she glanced up at Hilary's room. They stayed out of sight until they heard the squeal of her tires as she peeled out down the road.

Rodney wasted no time working on Hilary again. He was captain of the swim team and had the abs to prove it. He took off his shirt and tossed it across the room. This time, Hilary wouldn't tell him to stop.

53

"Karen Porter," a nurse called out.

"Come on, honey let's go," I said to Karen.

Over the past few weeks, Karen had been experiencing horrible headaches, chest pain, and muscle weakness. She'd missed several days of school. During the last week, she'd been throwing up and coming close to blacking out. Even Stacy couldn't put her finger on what was making Karen so sick. I thought I'd waited long enough, and a trip to the pediatrician was in order.

"So, Dad tells me you haven't been feeling so well?" the doctor said, smiling at Karen.

"No," she told him, eyes filling with tears. "And I hurt, too."

"Well, we're going to run some tests, nothing painful, and see what we can do to get you feeling better. That sound good to you?"

The pediatrician ordered a battery of tests and told

me it could be a few days before the results were ready. In the meantime, he suggested children's Tylenol and a diet of soft food and fluids.

"Karen, you did a great job at the doctor's office," I said as we got back in the car. "You feel like getting some ice cream or something?"

"No, Daddy. I just want to go home."

Once back at the house, Karen headed for her room. When I went in to check on her fifteen minutes later, I found her fast asleep, her notebook open on the bed beside her. I couldn't help but read what she'd written.

Hi mommy,

It's me! I dont feel so well. Everee thing has been hurteing. Stacy has muved in with us. I like her shes nice. I hope you are not mad at me for that. I hope the dr can fix me. I did not tell daddy but I hurt so bad I think I want to die some times and come see u in heven not all the time but jest some time. I know u r watshing me from heven!Luv you mommy – im going to take a nap now.

Karen.

**

I had been reading a criminology book, analyzing the behavior of copycat criminals. I couldn't put in much time on Miranda's case while I was at the station, and I didn't want to work on it around Stacy. I didn't want to make her feel uncomfortable, so this was as good a time as any.

I hadn't told the girls or Stacy about the severed finger the perp had sent me. Eventually, this perp would make a mistake. It happens every time. I was way too good not to catch him. Obviously he didn't know that, or he wouldn't be playing games with me.

As I let my mind wander, I heard Stacy call my name from downstairs.

"Stacy?" She wasn't supposed to be home for a few hours. I gathered the papers strewn over the bed and stuffed them into a folder, "Yeah, I'm up here!"

A moment later, she came into the room. Her smile faded when she saw the folder.

"You bringing work home again?"

"You're early," I said with a shrug.

"You want me to go back to work?" She laughed. "Don't answer that, mister."

She sat down beside me on the bed, still smiling.

"I have a surprise for you," she said.

She placed her hand over mine gently interlocking our fingers.

"I know you said you wanted to wait on another kid, and I agreed . . ."

"Whoa," I murmured, staring at her. "Hold on. You aren't going to tell me that after a few weeks you're ready to start trying, are you?"

"No . . . better than that."

She leaned over to kiss me. I wasn't prepared for the words that came out of her mouth next.

"I'm going to tell you I'm already pregnant!"

I stared, my mouth agape. After several seconds, I gave a slight shake of my head. In no way did this please me. We had all been trying to adjust to her moving in and now another hurdle. It was way too soon.

"You're not happy," she said, her grin fading.

"Well . . . it certainly happened sooner than we wanted, but I guess we can't change it now. How did this happen anyway? I thought you were on the pill?"

Stacy scowled. "Don't worry about it, David," she said, climbing off the bed. "I can clearly see you're not happy about this. Maybe I'll just move out and raise the baby alone. I knew you weren't going to be ecstatic; I mean, you already have your own kids, but I didn't expect this."

"Gimme a break, Stacy," I said gently. "You sprang this on me pretty fast. I don't do well with surprises. I just never expected this in a million years. Cut me some slack here, would you?"

She continued to frown at me. I plunged ahead.

"And let's face it. We've been moving at warp speed for quite some time now. I want you here, you and the baby."

Just as the words left my mouth, the door flew open. Karen stepped into the room, her face pasty and slack.

"Baby?" Karen whispered as she crumpled to the floor.

I leapt off the bed, scooped her up, and laid her gently on the bed.

"Hey don't you worry about any of that," I whispered. "We've got to take care of you right now."

"Worry about any of what?" Hilary said, standing in the doorway.

"Stacy's pregnant," Karen mumbled.

Hilary cast a wary glance at Stacy. "Surprise, surprise," she mumbled. "But I suppose that's what happens when you don't even open your birth control pills. You sure as hell can't be taking them if they aren't even open."

Hilary glared at Stacy again and headed down the hall. I ran after her, determined to hear what she had to say.

"Hilary, what are you talking about?" I asked.

She glanced over her shoulder at me. I was startled by the mix of emotions I saw on her face.

"Dad . . . nothing. Whatever. Congratulations, I guess. I mean, if that's what you wanted. If you—"

Before she could get another word in, Stacy lunged past me and slapped Hilary. I stared in disbelief. This was worse than a horror movie. What in the hell was going on? My life was spiraling out of control.

"You ungrateful, spoiled, little bitch!" Stacy barked. "That's no way to talk to me and your father!"

I stepped between Hilary and Stacy, prepared to wrap my arms around my daughter. Hilary stared past me; the look of fear on her face froze me in my tracks, and I turned around to find Karen in a full-blown seizure. Hilary ran over to her at the same time I did. I picked her up and ran downstairs, leaving Stacy and her news behind. Hilary was right behind me, grasping her little sister's hand. Stacy caught up to us at the bottom of the stairs.

We scrambled to the truck, and I eased Karen's now-limp body into the back seat. Hilary climbed in next to her. I slid behind the wheel, backing down the drive before Stacy could get her door closed. My mind was racing a hundred miles a minute. I couldn't even begin to process what had happened back at the house. At the moment, all I could think about was my sweet Karen.

We got to the hospital in less than five minutes. I slammed the truck into park at the emergency room entrance, lunged out, and took Karen from Hilary's arms as she scrambled out. I burst through the doors of the ER, Karen lifeless in my arms.

"Do something! Help her now!"

"Sir, calm down, please," one of the hospital staff urged as she approached and took Karen from me. She whisked her behind the curtain of one of the trauma bays.

Several minutes later, Stacy entered the ER to find me huddled with Hilary in a corner of the waiting room. She approached slowly.

"Hilary," she said, her voice soft and apologetic.

"I'm sorry I snapped. I wasn't brought up to talk to adults that way, so it set me off. I'm sorry. It wasn't my place. We can talk about it later."

Hilary refused to look at her.

I was, however, unprepared for what she said next.

"Nothing to talk about," Hilary replied calmly. "You're not my mother, and if he won't say anything to you, I will."

She'd jerked her head in my direction.

"And one more thing. Don't you ever put your hands on me again."

And with that, Hilary walked away, moving to the opposite side of the waiting area.

"Let her go," I said when Stacy moved to follow her.

Both of us sat quiet and motionless. How had my life gotten so screwed up? Karen was terribly ill. Stacy and Hilary seemed to hate each other. And to top it off, Stacy was pregnant. Why had I foolishly believed Stacy moving in would make things better?

About forty-five minutes later, a doctor came out. I still hadn't said one word to Stacy. I had never been angry at her before, but I was now. She had slapped my daughter. As frustrating as Hilary could be, neither Miranda nor I had ever raised a hand to her. If what Hilary said was true, Stacy had gotten pregnant on purpose. There were worse things than your girlfriend wanting a baby; it was the deceit that made me angry.

"She's going to be just fine," the doctor said. "The tests came back negative. There are many reasons why people have seizures. We don't know what caused Karen's seizure, but she's doing fine now. We have the technology and medicine to help with the severity and frequency of them. As a precaution, we're going to keep her overnight."

"Can I see her?" I asked.

He nodded. "Just for a few minutes. We'll be moving her to a room soon. She's sleepy. That's common post-seizure."

I followed the doctor through the double doors, leaving Stacy and Hilary behind. When I got to the treatment room door, I almost lost it. Once again, I'd been unable to protect my family. I didn't understand why the doctors couldn't find the cause of Karen's seizure. I peered down at her, so small and fragile in the big hospital bed. I felt deep sorrow for my little girl. Then her eyes opened and she attempted a smile. My brave little girl.

"Hey, Daddy."

"Hey there, champ. Don't talk; just rest."

"Dad, can I see Grandma and Grandpa?"

Her request surprised me. "Sure," I said. "If you'd like, you can stay with them for a little bit, when you're feeling up to it." I brushed a stray hair from her cheek. "Maybe Grandma has some old magic remedy that will get you feeling better."

"I'd like that, Daddy. When can I go?"

"Just rest for now. I'll call Grandma first thing in the morning and see if she'd like some company for a few days."

"Thanks, Dad. I'm gonna sleep now."

I sat there and watched my daughter sleep. I had never really believed people could die from a broken heart. I'd read about old couples who died within hours of each other, one just giving up, no desire to remain behind after the other had passed. Being a detective, I relied on physical evidence to do my job. I lived a life based on things I could taste, touch, and feel. But now I understood. My heart ached. My mind was numb. There was a strange buzzing in my head, like static, as if my brain was about to shut off at any minute. I could feel my heart skipping beats and my hands sweating, my fingers tingling. If my daughter died right this moment, I couldn't be sure I wouldn't follow. I wheezed, trying to catch my breath, as if breathing had become a chore, something I had to think about doing. I needed to regain control of myself and my life. And I needed to do it fast.

54

De Luca watched to make sure Stacy was completely out of sight before she got out of her car. She hurried over to David's truck and snatched the note Stacy had left under the windshield wiper. She didn't feel the least bit guilty for invading David's privacy. Stacy was up to something; she was sure of it. To that end, she wanted their expert to do a handwriting analysis on it. She took it to the lab and watched as the technician, Barb, scanned it into the national database.

When Barb asked her if she wanted it crossed with anything in particular, she shook her head. She didn't want to alarm anyone or have David find out she was investigating Stacy. She just didn't trust the woman.

"I don't have a name," De Luca said. She hated to lie, but it was the best she could do at the moment. "Just notify me if you come up with a match, okay?"

Barb nodded and De Luca left the lab.

**

I nodded at De Luca as she passed me in the hallway. I was

walking toward the door, ready to head out. She had come from downstairs, where the labs were located.

"Hey, Porter. Whatcha got going today?"

"Hey there," I said. "Actually, I'm headed home to drop Karen off at her grandmother's for a few days. She's not been feeling well and wants to visit."

"Oh? What's wrong with her?"

I shrugged. "The doctor's aren't sure, but if visiting her grandparents will make her feel better, I'm all for it. By the way, what are you doing in? Didn't you take today off?"

She nodded. "Oh, I was just catching up on some paperwork. I'm done now."

De Luca kept looking away from me like she was distracted. Maybe it was my imagination; God knows it'd been working overtime lately.

"Well, I'm out of here," she said. "Tell Karen I hope she feels better soon."

I nodded. "Will do."

I left the station. I had just climbed into my truck when my cell phone rang. I reached into my pocket, saw the call was from Stacy, and sighed.

"Hey," I said.

"Hey, honey. Did you get the note I left for you on your truck? What do you think?"

I frowned. "Uh . . . no, I didn't see a note."

"I left it under the windshield wiper."

I checked. "Nope. Maybe the wind caught it and blew it off. What did it say?"

"Oh, it wasn't important, just a love note to say I'm sorry again for the other night. I really do have to work on my patience with the girls. I'm—"

"Yeah, I agree you do" I said, not happy to be reminded of the other night. "Their young minds are fragile, and it won't take much for them to shut you out. I'm not going to lie to you. I was angry at you, and still am, a little. I don't treat my girls that way, and I certainly don't expect you to."

I paused, as she hadn't said anything.

"Look, I know we haven't had a chance to talk much about the baby. How far along do you think you are?"

"A few weeks, at most."

Her tone changed instantly.

"I'm so excited, aren't you? I hope it's a boy!"

Stacy didn't say another word about her encounter with Hilary. It was as if she didn't remember it. I frowned. Had I made a mistake? Was this the first indication that perhaps I had moved into this relationship too fast? We chatted about the baby for a few minutes, and then I told her I was in traffic and needed to concentrate on the drive. She needed to get back to work as well, her break over. I hung up, mildly disturbed. The memory of her striking Hilary didn't set well with me at all. I knew I needed to talk to Hilary and Karen about the baby and what had happened between Hilary and Stacy.

I drove home, deep in thought. Once inside, I yelled for both girls to come downstairs, still fighting with myself over exactly what to say.

"Karen, you packed for your visit with Grandma and Grandpa?"

She nodded, still looking terribly pale. "Hilary helped me."

"Dad, that's not why you called me down here. What's up?" Hilary said.

"Sit down here, both of you," I said, gesturing to the couch. "First off, I want to say that having another baby came as a surprise to me, as it did to you guys." I paused to gather my thoughts. "I'm not sure what happened," I said, casting a meaningful glance at Hilary, who remained silent.

"But she's pregnant, and now, as a family, we have to deal with that and make the best of it. Stacy and I talked, and she feels horrible for reacting the way she did to you, Hilary. I told her that can't happen again." I shook my head. "We all know no one is perfect, and that includes Stacy."

"She hit me, Dad," Hilary said, her voice barely above a whisper. "And right in front of you!"

"I know. I've talked to her about that. She promised it would never happen again."

"There are only so many of her apologies I'm going to be able to take, Dad."

"I know," I said with a heavy sigh. "Trust me, I know. Come here."

We all leaned in for a group hug, and I promised them no one—not even Stacy—would break up our family. I told them I loved them.

"Hilary, I'll take Karen to Grandma's house, and then let's go out for pizza or Mexican food or something. Just the two of us," I suggested. "Would you like that?"

She nodded.

"Try to find it in your heart to forgive Stacy and give her another chance. This is our family now, and we have to make it work."

I gathered Karen's bags, and the two of us headed out the door. The drive to my in-laws' house would take a couple hours, and I took the opportunity to spend some one-on-one time with Karen. I was eager to get her take on how things were going with Stacy.

"Dad, do you think you can handle another baby at your age?" Karen abruptly asked.

"Is that a joke? I'm not that old!"

"Well, you were sore for days after helping Stacy move in. Remember?"

"Hey, it was hard work moving all the heavy stuff by

myself."

I chuckled. Karen could always make me laugh.

"The baby will be here in less than a year, whether I'm ready or not. Can you make me a promise though?"

"Maybe," Karen said, smiling. "Is this a big promise or little promise?"

"Well, I need you to keep a secret."

"A big secret or a little one?"

"Medium, I suppose. Can we hold off on telling your grandparents about this whole baby thing for now?"

She looked up at me. "That's a big secret. I think I'm going to need some kind of payment. Maybe stopping to get some ice cream?"

"Done."

I smiled. My little girl sure knew how to wrap her Daddy around her little finger. And ice cream was a small price to pay to keep her quiet.

**

Once Karen was settled with her grandparents, I got back on the road. The drive back would give me some alone time to make heads or tails of the last twenty-four hours. I took out my phone to call Stacy.

"Hey there. Just dropped Karen off. I'm heading back. I know you're at work, so I won't keep you long. Hilary and I are going to dinner. Gonna try to get things back on even keel."

I waited, Stacy's silence heavy in my ear.

"Hello?"

"I'm sorry, David. Someone walked in, and I had to take the phone down from my ear. What were you saying?"

"Nothing. I'm heading back. I'll see you later."

I wasn't big on repeating myself. Besides, I found myself quickly irritated by Stacy. It didn't take much these days. I guess deep down I still hadn't fully forgiven her for raising a hand to Hilary.

I texted Hilary and let her know I was twenty minutes away so she would be ready. I was already starving.

When I pulled into the driveway, Hilary was waiting on the porch, phone in hand as always. She walked down the drive and climbed into the passenger seat.

"Hey, Dad."

"Hey, yourself. Texting Rodney?"

"Maybe. So what are we eating? Gringos, right?"

"Gringos it is, sweetie. What have you been up to today?"

"Nothing much. Been working on a paper for my English class."

"Oh yeah? What's your topic?"

"The effects of stepparents and blended households on children."

I looked at her—not angrily but direct enough.

"Okay, I deserved that. This how tonight's going to be?" I laughed, sort of.

"No. It should be, but after some reflection . . . this whole Stacy thing was mostly my idea."

"Wow! Are you okay, Hil? And this was more like ninety-nine percent your idea, not *mostly*. I remember actually pushing back and not being sure."

"Okay, I sorta brought this on myself. Now that that's outta the way, how do we coexist? Can we?"

"Stacy will have to assert her demands, wishes, and expectations a lot more slowly than she has, for one. And I'll tell her so. She'll have to listen more and talk less, which is apparently difficult for all women," I said, ribbing back at her.

"Ha freakin' ha, Dad!"

We both shared a laugh. Maybe this night would turn

out okay after all.

55

"David, it's the middle of the day," Stacy pleaded, a seductive grin on her face. "Karen is gone and Hilary is at school and won't be home for hours. Come on, let's have some fun."

I sat on the couch, looking up at her. I didn't really want to and found myself making every excuse I could to get out of it. Still, it seemed Stacy wasn't going to back down. I had noticed that when she wanted something, especially from me, she usually got it.

I got up and took her hand, attempting to head for the stairs. Instead, she pulled away from my grip, took off her clothes right there in the middle of the living room, and laid down on the couch.

Why am I so weak? I wondered. *Why in the world couldn't I tell this woman no?*

Ten minutes later, I heard a key in the door. I froze, lying naked on top of Stacy. Before I could recover from my surprise, Hilary stepped into the foyer and saw us *in flagrante* on the living room couch.

"What the hell are you doing?" Hilary gasped, wide-eyed.

I did my best to cover our private parts while I responded, my voice cracking with surprise.

"Hilary! What are you doing home so early?"

If it wasn't so embarrassing, I might have thought the situation funny.

"We got out early today," she explained, staring unabashedly at the two of us. She glared in Stacy's direction. "I gave her the early release letter two days ago!"

I looked down at Stacy, who offered a sheepish grin as she squirmed beneath me.

"I thought the early release date was for next week," she said.

"Well, surprise, it's today," Hilary said as she headed for the staircase. "You guys do have a bedroom, you know."

She offered a parting shot over her shoulder.

"I'll never sit on that couch again!"

"This is our house, Hilary," Stacy said, her voice snappish rather than embarrassed. "We're both consenting adults. I believe we're free to have sex wherever we please. You, on the other hand . . . now that's a different story."

Hilary paused halfway up the stairs. I remained frozen atop Stacy, not daring to move lest I expose a part of myself I never wanted my daughter to see.

"What are you talking about?" Hilary demanded.

"The other day when I came home on break and Rodney was here, you guys were having sex and smoking weed up in your room."

Hilary didn't have to respond. The guilt was written all over her face. My heart crashed to the pit of my stomach in utter disappointment. Before I could say a word, Stacy continued.

"Did you think I couldn't smell it? And don't tell me you two weren't having sex. Maybe you'll be pregnant next," she said. "We can be pregnant together."

She looked up at me with a catty grin.

"That would be great, right, David?"

"That won't happen," Hilary said as she made a mad dash toward her room. "I actually take my birth control pills!"

Hilary slammed her door behind her. I peeled myself off Stacy and got dressed. She did the same. Again, I was stunned. What the hell was going on around here? I really didn't have an answer for any of this. Every day brought new drama. Nothing was easy anymore. Maybe it wasn't supposed to be. Maybe God was punishing me for something. Whatever it was, I might need to smoke some weed of my own if things didn't improve—and fast!

I turned to Stacy. "If you knew about Rodney and Hilary, why didn't you tell me? I'm her father. You can't keep things like that from me. I can't deal with it if I don't know about it."

Stacy plopped on the couch and pulled on her shoes. She offered not a word of explanation.

"I don't like secrets in any relationship," I said. "I don't have skeletons in my closet, and I don't like surprises, especially of this nature."

"I'm sorry, David," she said, looking up at me. "I was trying to ignore it. I mean, it was just weed, and I'm sure you had sex before you got married. After all, you were a jock in college. I'm sure you fooled around with lots of girls, probably just for fun. I bet you got any girl you wanted. Am I right?"

I shook my head. "We aren't talking about me.

Maybe I didn't make myself clear. If one of my girls does something, I need to know about it immediately. Do you understand?"

I couldn't believe I was talking to Stacy in such a harsh tone, but I was extremely frustrated and confused. For the first time, I really felt her moving in was a huge mistake. It was never going to work.

"Got it, captain," she replied, miffed. "Well, now that you know, you can go upstairs and talk to your teenage daughter about premarital sex and drug use."

She rose from the couch and marched into the kitchen, somehow managing to get the final word. Again.

I stood there in her wake, wondering once again what the hell I'd been thinking when I asked Stacy to move in with us. I had no answer. I headed upstairs, knocked on Hilary's door, and entered without waiting for an invitation.

"Hilary, I'm not mad about the sex. Concerned, yes, but not mad."

She sat on the edge of the bed, staring at me. She looked miserable.

"We need to talk about it," I said. "We should have talked long before now."

"Mom and I already talked about it," she mumbled. "That's when she decided I needed to start taking the pills. I told her I could see myself doing something soon."

I schooled my expression. No sense in going off half-cocked. "Okay, well, you and I can still talk about it. But I am very angry and concerned about the drugs."

"Dad, it was just weed. I only tried a few puffs. I didn't like it, anyhow."

"Hilary, I'm a cop. I've seen weed turn into much more over time. I'm more concerned that Rodney might be able to talk you into more."

"Yeah, yeah, the whole gateway thing," she

mumbled. "How do you know he talked me into it in the first place?"

"However it came about, Hilary, I'm still upset about it. I'm not sure what your punishment is going to be, but it will be severe. You really haven't left me much choice here. I would also like to set up a time to meet with Rodney. Maybe the three of us can sit down and have dinner one night. It's my fault we hadn't met before, I know that, but I'd like to meet him now."

She stared at me, a doubtful expression on her face.

"The three of us, right? Meaning you, me, and Rodney? I don't want your psycho girlfriend to join us—"

"Hilary!"

She shook her head. "I'm telling you, she hates me! And I don't believe she thought I was coming home early next week. I just gave her the note two days ago. Speaking of being talked into something, I'm willing to bet she talked you into that . . . that little display downstairs on the couch. Am I right? So, no Stacy?"

I didn't answer right away, but Hilary was right. Stacy had talked me into it, but there was no way I could believe the episode had been intentional. I couldn't put Stacy down on that level of manipulation no matter how mad I was at her. Still, her behavior left me wondering if parenthood would work for her, regardless of whose child it was. But she had been so good coaching those girls in softball.

"Okay," I said. "No Stacy this time. But if she's going to be part of this family, she'll have to be involved at some point. The three of us need to sit down one day, too. Soon . . . very soon. You two are going to have to figure out how to make this work."

I sat down beside her and gave her a hug. To my relief, she offered one in return. I sat with her for a few moments longer. Finally, I kissed her on the forehead and left her room with a parting sentiment.

"I love you, Hil."

"Love you too, Dad," she replied, already reaching for her headphones.

I knew my next move was to talk to Stacy. I went into our room and found her lying facedown on the bed. My anger dissipated, and I sat down next to her.

"I don't know if this is going to work, David," she mumbled. "It seems like I'm getting this wrong. Hilary hates me. You probably even hate me now."

"No one hates you," I assured her. She turned over to look at me. Her face was flushed, her eyes wet, but she had not shed tears. "I'll tell you a little secret my mother told me before we had Hilary. 'Parenting doesn't come with an instruction book,' she said. 'You're going to make mistakes, but own them quickly, ask for forgiveness, learn from it, and start over. Lastly, realize you're going to learn far more from them than they will from you.'"

When Stacy didn't respond, I kept going.

"Maybe I should have passed on that little pearl of wisdom before you got here, right?"

She reached out for me, and, once again, I found myself unable to resist her.

CHAINED GUILT

56

"Miranda?"

Stacy slapped her face.

"Miranda, wake up, you stupid bitch. Your little slut daughter is ruining my plans. You did a fine job raising her, by the way."

Miranda finally opened her eyes and stared at her captor, her gaze listless.

"What are you talking about?"

"Shut up and eat your dog food. I have something for you to watch."

Stacy had already set up the playback recording of Hilary in her room smoking weed and having sex with her boyfriend. She opened the laptop in front of Miranda and shoved it closer to her face. She pressed the Play button.

"You see that?" she sneered at her hostage. "That's your offspring. I guess the apple doesn't fall far from the tree, does it? You and David into drugs, too? Y'all do 'em together?"

Miranda shrugged as if she didn't care. "Hilary has always been her own person. She's a tough little girl. I'm sure she's giving a stupid inbred bitch like yourself hell. She too smart for you?"

"Whatever." Stacy chuckled. "We get along just fine, thank you very much. And I was smart enough to get you here. Oh, and here are some pictures of your little princess. She looks like shit, doesn't she? That's because I'm giving her a teensy-weensy dose of something to make her . . . Hmmm. Let's just say she's dying. Slowly. Don't worry, it will take a long time before she's gone."

"You're a sadistic whore!" Miranda yelled, struggling against her restraints.

Stacy let Miranda yell her little heart out as she crossed the room with the laptop under her arm, laughing in glee as she headed upstairs.

**

"Porter, are you coming in today or what?" De Luca snapped. She'd gotten his voicemail again.

De Luca had news. Her hunch had paid off. The handwriting analyst had matched the taunting letters left for David to the note left on his windshield by none other than Stacy. A ninety-eight percent match! What was the bitch up to? She had to let David know, but where was he? She stared down at her phone for several seconds and then decided to head over to Stacy's house. She'd already gotten the address of the estate. Perhaps David was over there. She was so intent on her task, she failed to notice the car that passed her and then pulled a U-turn behind her, gradually allowing several cars to separate them.

De Luca parked her red SVT Mustang in the driveway. She knocked on the door several times but got no answer. She looked around and peeked into the garage window. Stacy wasn't home.

She rang the doorbell twice for good measure. Nothing. She had just stepped off the front porch when she thought she heard someone yelling. She paused and listened some more. Definite yelling, but it sounded muffled and far away. She knew the sound was coming from inside.

She took the porch steps two at a time and, without waiting, kicked open the front door.

"Police!" she called out.

The muffled yelling continued. De Luca pulled her gun and moved slowly into the house.

"Police!" she yelled again. "Show yourself!"

"Help!"

The sound came from somewhere below her. She hurried into the kitchen, and the cries got louder. She spied a padlocked door near the pantry and put her ear to it. Bingo! De Luca used the butt of her gun to smash the padlock. Her heart pounded.

"I should call for backup," she muttered, but the cries for help from below grew more frantic.

"Who's down there!" she shouted.

"Miranda!"

De Luca swore, reaching for her phone.

"I'm Miranda Porter! Please help me!"

"I'm coming!" De Luca rushed down the stairs, dismayed when she saw the skeletal frame of a woman lying on a dingy, stained mattress, one bony wrist manacled to a metal ring cemented into the wall. Miranda Porter. The woman stared at her in wide-eyed dismay, tears streaming down her face.

"It's okay." De Luca attempted to reassure her as she stepped closer, holstering her gun. "It's okay. I'm going to get you out of here."

The woman whimpered.

"I'm Detective De Luca. I work with your husband, David. Don't you worry; I'm going to get you out of here."

Miranda's eyes filled with tears as she sobbed softly. "You found me. You found me."

She repeated the words over and over.

"Where's—"

"She's gone," Miranda said, her voice trembling. "She left a little while ago. She comes down here to feed me, and usually doesn't come back for a day or two." She jerked on the chain with what little strength she had left. "Please take this off me!"

De Luca hurried over to Miranda, her heart aching. The woman had apparently been held here for months. She looked at the handcuff attaching her wrist to the chain. Perhaps her cuff key would open it.

"Behind you!" Miranda yelled.

Too late. The words had just registered in De Luca's brain when she felt the blow hit the back of her head. She fell facedown beside Miranda, her head throbbing and her vision blurred.

"Almost busted me, didn't you?" a voice above her said mockingly. "You little nagging bitch; I knew I didn't like you. Now you get a new home here with Miranda. I should just put a bullet in you and be done with it."

De Luca felt her gun being removed from the holster at her waist but was in no condition to stop it. With ears buzzing and her vision dancing crazily, De Luca rolled over to find Stacy standing above her, a shovel in her hand. She swore and attempted to rise, but Stacy lunged forward and kicked her in the head. Darkness threatened as Miranda's cries echoed around her.

By the time De Luca regained her senses a bit, she'd been restrained next to Miranda, both wrists manacled to the metal ring in the wall. Then Stacy began tearing the detective's clothing from her body piece by piece. When De Luca thrashed about and tried to kick off her attacker, Stacy smacked her hard in the head. The darkness returned. As De Luca hung limply from her restraints, Stacy used a knife to hack away at the detective's hair. Miranda watched, deathly still and silent.

"Well now," Stacy finally said, sitting back on her heels. "This wasn't how I intended on spending my morning. Kidnapping a detective?" She laughed and shot Miranda an evil look. "Well, at least now you'll have some company."

57

Stacy had taken care of De Luca, but now she had to ditch the detective's car. All at once, a brilliant idea came to her. She would ditch De Luca's car in the same manner and in the exact same spot she'd ditched Miranda's. She had to hurry. She knew David and Hilary had gone for a bike ride. He'd told her of their plans earlier and said he wanted no distractions, which meant no cell phones. She'd have to hurry back to the house to make sure De Luca hadn't left him a message about where she was going or what she'd found.

At David's house, she found two cell phones on the dining room table, just as expected.

"He's so damn predictable," she mumbled, a satisfied grin on her face.

Picking up David's phone, she accessed his text and voicemail messages and deleted those De Luca had left. Once that little detail was taken care of, she carefully placed the phone back on the table exactly where she'd found it.

**

"Thanks for the bike ride, Dad," Hilary said as the two coasted into the driveway an hour later. "I have to admit, I didn't want to go at first, but I'm glad we did. Can we do it again soon?"

"Of course we can do it again," I said, beaming. "It's good 'us' time, and it sure doesn't hurt to get out in the fresh air and get some exercise."

We climbed off our bikes and stored them on the side of the house.

"I'm gonna go take a shower," Hillary said as we headed inside. "I love you, Dad."

"Love you too, honey." I smiled till my cheeks hurt. I was glad to see her in such a good mood.

"Oh, and Rodney said dinner one night, just the three of us, sounds good."

I gave her a thumbs-up, and she disappeared up the stairs. I headed to the dining room to get my phone. As expected, Stacy had left me a note. She wrote that Captain Wilcrest had called twice. She had to go to work and would be done with her shift later that evening. I decided to call the captain to see what was up.

"Hey, Cap."

"David, where've you been? I've been trying to get ahold of you for over an hour."

"Hilary and I went for a bike ride. I told her we were leaving modern technology behind, so we left our cell phones at home." I frowned. "Why? What's up?"

"Our guy is back. That's what's up."

My heart plummeted to my stomach. Another taunt regarding Miranda? Another bit of flesh or hair? "More evidence left?"

"No, worse."

"Worse? What do you—"

"I need you to come down to the same spot where Miranda had her wreck, David. Over the bridge. There's been another accident."

I rushed upstairs to tell Hilary I was leaving and sped over to the scene of the accident. I couldn't believe my eyes. There was De Luca's car, in the exact spot where we'd found Miranda's nearly a year ago. The similarities were mindboggling. The scene was almost identical. The same skid marks on the street. Every detail copied. My heart skipped a beat.. What the hell was going on?

"Any sign of her?" I asked as I climbed out of my car and approached the captain, who stood nearby in deep discussion with several patrol officers. He turned to me and shook his head.

"No, David." He gazed over the lake. "Of course, we're going to comb this area. We're looking for witnesses now—the usual."

"So this is a copycat?"

"Way too early to make any assumptions," he said, scratching his head. "But it looks like that's exactly what it is. You okay? I know you guys are new partners and all, but . ."

I gazed at her car and then at the lake. This had to be linked to Miranda's case, and I said as much to the captain.

"But why?" Wilcrest said, perplexed.

"I have no ideas at the moment," I admitted.

Another officer approached and gestured for the captain. I waited, examining De Luca's car while he spoke with the officer. No sign of foul play, no sign of blood, no sign of my partner.

"David, De Luca's phone was found in the car. While

her latest messages and voicemail had been deleted, we were able to pull De Luca's phone records for the last ten hours." He paused, looking at me. "She called you five times today. You know what that's about?"

I swore. "Like I said, Cap, Hilary and I went on a bike ride, and I left my phone at home. That won't happen again."

I glanced at the captain. I didn't like the look on his face.

"Can they trace her movements from the GPS on her phone?"

"We may be able to. Working on that now." The captain sighed wearily. "I don't know what the hell is going on, and I have no idea why De Luca's disappearance is linked to Miranda's, but it appears someone is playing games with us, David . . . with you."

58

"Hello, sweetie!" I smiled as Karen got on the phone.

"Hey, Daddy!"

"You sound great today," I said, relieved. She was getting better.

"Yeah, I'm all better! Grandma fixed me all up. A few cans of Campbell's soup was all I needed!"

I laughed. "So the doctors couldn't figure anything out, but Grandma fixed everything with soup, eh?"

"Not just soup, Dad. *Campbell's* soup!"

"Okay, I get it," I said. "Well, I'm glad you're feeling better. I need to take care of a few errands, and then I'll be over to get you."

"Okay, Daddy. I missed you, but I had fun with Grandma and Grandpa.

I disconnected the call and decided now was as

good a time as any to settle the mess between Hilary and Stacy. I found Stacy sitting on the living room couch, a magazine in her lap.

"Hilary, could you come down here, please?" I hollered up the stairs.

"What are you doing, David?" Stacy asked.

Hilary came downstairs, hovering at the bottom step. "What is it, Dad?"

"Listen, I'm going to head over to Grandma and Grandpa's to pick up Karen. I also have to make one stop to check out a new lead I'm working on. While I'm gone, I want you two to talk. We're a family now. Not to mention, Stacy and I have a baby coming. Talk like adults and work this out." I eyed each of them. "I'm not asking you. This is not a request. I insist on peace in this house. I love you both."

With that, I grabbed my car keys and moved to the front door.

"I'll be back with Karen in a few hours."

I wasn't sure if this was the right call, but I was desperate. I hoped they could both be adult enough and cared for me enough to see I was at my wit's end with their relationship. Maybe both would cave a little, do some compromising. Either it would work as planned, or I would return to find one of them standing over the other's body. Probably not much gray area with this one.

I needed to go back down to the bridge where Miranda and DeLuca had wrecked their cars. Miranda's accident happened at night, so there wasn't much hope of eyewitnesses on passing boats or barges. DeLuca's crash, however, had occurred in broad daylight. I was hoping someone might have seen something. I know the cops assigned to the case had asked around, but something in my gut told me to give it another shot.

I walked down and asked a few questions to the crew

members milling about the boats docked along the waterway. Nothing. They all said the same thing—the bridge was too high, too far away to hear anything.

"Excuse me, Detective?"

A middle aged-man approached me. His clothes and the stench that followed told me this guy was definitely a full-time deckhand.

"Yes? What can I do for you?" I said.

"Well it might be nothing. I didn't hear the wreck or nothing, but . . ."

"Did you see something?"

"Well, I did but I didn't. I didn't actually see the crash or hear it, but I looked up not long after. Couldn't have been long after because no one else from down here had even noticed, and there wasn't no cops or ambulances yet. Eventually a few cars stopped to help, but when I first looked up I saw a woman. Looked like she was dragging whoever had wrecked. I figured she was trying to help, so I didn't think much of it at first. Long ways up to that bridge. I don't have no description, I just know it wasn't no man. I could tell that much. Only reason I'm saying something now is I'm hearing they didn't find no body and maybe it was a kidnapping."

I thanked him for telling me what he'd seen, and he went on his way. I stood where he told me he was standing that night, and it was definitely too far away for any meaningful descriptions to be given. It wasn't much to go on, but it was something. I conducted several more interviews but no one else had seen a thing, or they weren't talking if they had. I believed I'd gotten everything I could from my visit and decided to head for my Karen.

Several hours later, I returned with a vibrant Karen in tow. She offered an enthusiastic greeting to Stacy as well.

"Karen!" Stacy said after she burst through the

door. "We missed you, kiddo!"

"Where's Hilary?" I asked when she didn't appear.

"She's okay," Stacy said. "We had a good talk. I think we're going to be able to make this work. I let her go over to Rodney's to hang out. I took her over and dropped her off myself."

I was shocked that Stacy had allowed her to go to Rodney's, but maybe earning the teen's trust was a step in the right direction.

When Stacy left to pick Hilary up, I tucked Karen away to sleep. With the travel, it had been a long day for all of us.

"Good night, princess."

"Good night, Daddy. I love you."

I closed her door and went back downstairs to wait for Stacy and Hilary's return. As I waited I turned my attention back to DeLuca's disappearance. I had to start making heads or tails of this. I needed to find out what DeLuca had been working on. Could she have been working on Miranda's case? What had she been doing in the lab when we crossed paths at the station? I didn't want to jump to conclusions, but maybe this perp knew of our relationship and was looking for another way to punish me, toy with me.

And then I snapped. This was never about Miranda or her story. Her story was a coincidence. That meant Carter had been telling the truth about his involvement or lack thereof. This perp, whoever he was, was hurting people I cared about. DeLuca had figured it out, or was getting close, but had somehow tipped off the maniac, who then had to get rid of her too. What had DeLuca found out? Where had she been digging? I heard keys fumbling in the door.

"Hey, Dad," Hilary said as she kissed me on the forehead. "I'm off to bed. Probably gonna listen to some music before I go to sleep. I do have a science project I need to finish too."

"Okay. Good night," I said, kissing her on the cheek. "I want to take you and your sister canoeing tomorrow, so don't make any plans, okay?"

"Sounds good. See you in the morning."

I grabbed Stacy's hand, and we walked upstairs to our room. I didn't want to talk or rehash whatever she and Hilary had spoken about. We got into our pj's and climbed in bed. I put my arm out, and Stacy snuggled into my chest.

I believed the best things in life were acquired through hard work. I'd learned that early, back when I played football in high school. You lift hard, you gain muscle. Doesn't come overnight but it comes. I could finally see a glimmer of light at the end of this Stacy-Hilary tunnel, and it warmed my heart. The good times would be like gaining that muscle back in high school—slow and steady, but worth the effort. And I'd probably have to be the glue for a while longer until they trusted each other. I could handle that. As my eyes closed, my mind drifted to Miranda. I still longed for her. Even as Stacy lay in my arms, pregnant with my child, I wondered if the longing, the ache, would ever go away. I loved Stacy, but it was different. I guess nearly two decades of affection for someone didn't simply disappear overnight.

The next morning, the four of us sat down for breakfast. We each ate our cereal in peace.

"This ain't so bad now, is it?" I asked.

"No." Stacy smiled. "It's good. I like it. Glad I'm a part of it."

"I'm taking the girls canoeing today while you work your shift," I said. "Tonight maybe we can all catch a movie or something."

"Don't you have to work?" Stacy said.

I didn't answer. I needed to think, and being away from the station made that easier. Cap knew about my preference for working alone, and as long as I kept him updated, he didn't mind. I didn't want to think about Miranda. I didn't want to think about De Luca. I didn't want to think about the link between the two, or that a serial killer had somehow worked his way into my life. For just a little while, I wanted to forget.

"Sure, we can do that, honey," Stacy said.

I glanced down at Karen with amusement as she worked on her second bowl of cereal. After breakfast, the girls and I headed for the car. The lake would be beautiful today, and hopefully a few canoes would be available for rent before it got too late in the day.

After the girls and David left, Stacy waited for Rodney to show up. She had snatched Hilary's phone the evening before while she was in the shower and texted Rodney an invite to come over today. She'd erased the outgoing message and affirmative reply and replaced Hilary's phone before leaving her room, a satisfied smile on her face. He should be here any minute now.

When the doorbell rang twenty minutes later, she answered it, feigning a disapproving look.

"Hi, Stacy, is Hilary here?" a nervous Rodney asked.

She was ready for him. She'd removed her bra and replaced her collared blouse with a tight T-shirt. She saw his eyes widen when he glanced at her breasts, and then he quickly backed up, his face reddening.

"Come on in," she said. "I wasn't expecting company. You'll have to excuse my clothes. Hilary should be back any minute now. She ran to the store."

Rodney took a seat on the far edge of the couch.

Stacy smiled and made him sit there for a minute before she plopped down on the sofa next to him.

"I want to show you something, if you promise you can keep a secret."

He glanced at her, confused. She leaned closer to him, making sure her breast brushed up against his arm. He blushed again but didn't back away.

"Okay, I guess." He shrugged.

She stood and reached out her hand to him. With a confused frown, he took it. She hid her smile. Like a puppy, he followed her to the master bedroom, where she knew he would see the bag of weed and the ecstasy pills.

"Want to have some fun while we wait?"

"N-No . . ." he mumbled. "I couldn't. I don't mess with that stuff."

"Oh, come on," she said with a sexy wink. "Hilary told me you two have fun with it."

She licked her lips and leaned her head toward his.

"Besides, why can't we? I won't tell if you don't."

She watched his defenses slowly crumble. He chewed his bottom lip, glancing from her breasts to the drugs and back again. Stacy reached down and plucked a pill from the plastic baggie and slowly pushed it into his mouth with her fingers. She trailed her finger seductively across his lips, reaching for his crotch with her other hand.

"What are you—?"

"Shhh," she whispered, her fingers caressing him through his jeans. "You have to learn when to talk and when not to, young man. Hilary also told me you have an incredible . . . gift, shall we call it?"

It was obvious to her that Rodney couldn't believe what was happening. He was scared they would get caught, but his hormones raged. She could barely contain her glee. She pushed him gently down on the bed. He didn't resist.

She disrobed and then helped him out of his clothes. She caught every second of it on tape.

**

The girls and I were enjoying our afternoon on the lake. It had been several months since I'd taken them out. I glanced at Karen, frowning when I realized how pale and clammy she looked.

"Karen, are you feeling okay? You look kind of tired."

Before she could respond, Karen collapsed into the bottom of the canoe, stiff as a board and jerking.

"Quick, Hilary, grab the other paddle!" I ordered. "She's having a seizure. We have to get to shore!"

Hilary and I paddled as quickly as we could. Once back on shore, Hilary and I scrambled out of the canoe. I reached for Karen, cradling her in my arms as I ran toward the truck. As before, Hilary rode in the backseat next to her sister, keeping a protective hand on her limp body as I sped to the hospital.

I pulled up to the emergency entrance, slammed on the brakes, and grabbed Karen from Hilary's arms. It was déjà vu all over again. I rushed through the emergency room doors hollering for help, Hilary only steps behind, tears of worry streaking her sunburned cheeks.

"What's wrong with her?" an ER nurse asked as we burst through the door.

"I don't know! She had a seizure about twenty minutes ago. She's been unconscious ever since."

The nurse called for a gurney, and I gently placed my daughter on it. She was no longer stiff, but still looked so pale and still.

"Oh my God," I said, nearly choked on my fear. "Please save her!"

The nurse quickly pulled Karen behind the trauma doors, leaving Hilary and I staring after her in stunned dismay.

"Dad, what's wrong with her?" Hilary asked. "Why

does she keep having all these seizures?"

"She was fine, I thought . . ."

I decided to find Stacy and walked to the wing where she usually worked. I didn't see her anywhere and headed for the nurse's station.

"Is Stacy here today?" I asked a nurse sitting behind the desk. I recognized her, but in my current condition I couldn't recall her name.

"Hi, David. I haven't seen her," the nurse said. "She's been missing a lot of work lately. That morning sickness can be nasty stuff."

"Thanks," I said, not giving her words another thought. I hurried back to the ER waiting room.

Just as I returned, a doctor emerged and headed for us.

"How's Karen?" I asked, my emotions in an uproar.

"She's going to be fine," the doctor said. "She's just going to need some rest. I want to keep her here till she's at least forty-eight hours seizure-free. Is there anyone who could stay with her? We'll run some more tests and get to the bottom of why this little girl is so sick all of a sudden."

"I can stay," Hilary said.

"You're awfully young," the doctor said.

"Dad, I want to stay with her."

The doctor finally agreed, as long as I stayed as well. Karen was stable and asleep, soon to be taken to a room in the pediatric ward. I was proud of my oldest daughter, but a bit wary.

"This is a big deal, Hil. If anything happens . . . I mean, you just need to be alert in there. I'm going home to get you some clothes. Anything else you want? Your laptop or anything?"

"Yes, clothes and my laptop should be good. And my phone," she said. "Thanks, Dad. Oh, and grab Karen's journal for her. I'm sure she'd like that."

"I'll get it all. No problem."

I gave Hilary a quick hug and was on my way.

I pulled into our driveway and noticed Stacy's car still there. It hadn't moved. *I thought she was going to work.*

"Stacy?" I called as I walked through the door.

She appeared at the top of the stairs, dressed in her scrubs.

"Hey there," she said, smiling. "Where are the girls?"

"Karen had another seizure," I explained, heading upstairs. "They're both at the hospital, where I thought you'd be."

She shrugged nonchalantly. "I was supposed to go, but after you guys left I didn't feel well, so I called in. I was going to call you, but I didn't want to bother you. I didn't want you to stop canoeing with the girls and come home for little ol' me."

I nodded, brushing past her toward Hilary's room. "Hilary is going to stay at the hospital with Karen. They're keeping her for at least forty-eight hours to try to get to the bottom of what's causing the seizures. I have to get some stuff to take back to her."

I wasn't so sure I bought Stacy's explanation, but what did I know about pregnancy and morning sickness? She seemed fine when we left earlier that day, and she looked fine now. Actually, I thought I smelled a hint of liquor on her breath as I passed her at the top of the stairs. I shook my head. *What was I thinking?* I focused on my tasks and gave her the benefit of the doubt.

I grabbed the things Hilary had requested—all but her phone, which was nowhere to be found. I grabbed my toothbrush and a change of clothes for myself and stuffed it all in a backpack. I planned to drop it off at the hospital and then head over to the station to fill Cap in and check on a few things before returning to the hospital for the night. I said as much to Stacy. She held the door open for me.

"I love you, but I need to be with the girls tonight. You understand, right?"

She nodded but didn't say anything. I could wait and try to assuage her obviously hurt feelings, but decided against it. I threw Hilary's backpack into the truck and backed out of the driveway. I looked up to see Stacy watching me through our bedroom window. Only then did I realize she hadn't asked if Karen was all right. Come to think of it, I know I smelled liquor on her breath. I frowned. Why would she be drinking if she was pregnant?

.

59

De Luca woke with a pounding head. She blinked hard to clear her vision, and focused on Miranda.

"David was right about one thing," De Luca said.

"Right about what?" Miranda's voice was weak and raspy.

The two lay side by side on the mattress.

"He told me how pretty you were." De Luca gently shook her head, every move eliciting new pounding. "What the hell happened?"

"She came up behind you and hit you over the head with a shovel. She gave you a pretty good shot. I thought you were dead for a while."

"I'm Italian." De Luca grinned at her. "It's going to take a hell of alot more than that to take me out."

"How long have I been down here?" Miranda asked. "Do you know?"

"Almost a year," she replied, eyeing the handcuffs that bound her.

Miranda sighed. "I lost count a long time ago."

De Luca struggled to sit up. "So let me get this straight. She wrecks your car and then locks you up down here? Takes over your life? You have any idea why?"

"I was working on a story. It would have sent some people to jail. But no one knew the details—not even David. Maybe it was compromised; I don't know."

"Yeah, about the mayor," De Luca said, scanning her surroundings for a way out. "Somehow, David figured it out and chased Carter clear out of the country. He's in jail now. The judge gave him thirty years without the possibility of parole."

"Well, I'm glad he's locked up, but I have no idea why this bitch has taken over my life. I don't even think what she's done to me is a result of my story. She has my husband, my house, my girls . . . and to top it off, she's pregnant. She taunts me every time she comes down here. That story uncovered a lot, but I'm not sure it has anything to do with why I'm down here."

De Luca wondered if she should fill Miranda in. After all, there was no telling when they'd get out of here. If they ever did. Still, hope was a wonderful thing.

"Miranda, David believes you might still be alive. Stacy sent hair samples and . . ." she glanced down at Miranda's now-healed hand. "And your finger. They tested and confirmed the DNA. He knows they came from you. Problem is, he can't even begin to figure out who has you or why."

"He'll figure it out," Miranda said, her confidence renewed by the news that David thought she might be alive.

"He'll figure it out."

<u>60</u>

Rodney's high ebbed. His head throbbed. He couldn't believe what he'd done. He was lucky his parents were out of town so he could recuperate without answering their questions. Still, he was lucid enough to be concerned about Hilary. She'd never showed up at her house. It wasn't like her to text him to come over and then not be there. He frowned. That Stacy was a freak.

The transcript he had seen on Stacy's laptop the other day still bothered him. After his recent experience with her, he didn't trust her one bit. Thank God he didn't remember much of it. The thought turned his stomach. He knew he should call the police, but he couldn't handle the embarrassment.

He decided to try his luck hacking into Texas Tech's

records. It took him twenty minutes—longer than he'd hoped—but he was in. First, he looked up David's transcript. He had dropped out midsemester. He queried the school's website for hits on David's name and was linked to numerous articles he'd appeared in over the years.

He downloaded the files to his laptop and kept digging. Then he focused on the woman whose name had been on the transcript on Stacy's computer: Lisa Crease. He typed in her name, followed by the year David had attended the university.

"Lisa Crease, huh? Who are you, Lisa?" Rodney muttered as he waited impatiently for his computer to do its thing.

Finally, a file opened. He read with interest and increasing alarm. Lisa Crease had dropped out of school after filing charges against several members of the football team—charges of rape. He sat back, stunned. Then he came across a newspaper clipping and clicked on the file. It read:

> Student Lisa Crease has accused four members of the Texas Tech football team of rape. She described what allegedly occurred to the police in great detail. Her physician stated that his examination did indeed confirm that an act of violence had occurred.
>
> Crease insists the main perpetrator in her attack was none other than David Porter, an eighteen-year-old co-captain of the team.

Porter and the other players allegedly involved told police Crease was a willing participant. Porter alleges he did not have sex with Crease but was there and aware of what was happening in the other room.

Crease alleges Porter handpicked her as part of the football team's hazing ceremony. It should be noted that Porter has been cited twice for public drunkenness and drug use while a student at Texas Tech and is currently on team probation.

According to reports, Crease said Porter had sex with her and then forced three other players to have sex with her against her will, all part of a hazing ritual carried out by the team. She's quoted as saying, "I cried and cried and begged them to stop, but they kept taking turns, and finally I stopped fighting. I had nothing left. I didn't report it at first, because I believed what David Porter said—that because of my past, no one would believe me. Yes, I worked at a few strip clubs, but that has nothing to do with what they did to me. It will be with me for the rest of my life. As for his claims that he wasn't involved, he's lying. I'll never forget the chain he wears around his neck. It has a locket on it. That locket hit me in the face over and over as he raped me. I'll never forget it."

As of today, no official charges have been filed. Our calls to campus authorities and school administrators have, to date, gone unanswered.

Rodney read the story again, trying to make sense of everything. Then he clicked on another file and looked at the newspaper photograph of an eighteen-year-old Lisa Crease. Stunned, he found himself staring at a younger version of Stacy, with blond hair instead of red and blue eyes instead of green.

"Oh my God!" he mumbled.

She'd undergone minor cosmetic surgery on her nose and had an obvious boob job in the intervening years, but it was her, no doubt about it.

He grabbed his cell phone from the nightstand and punched in Hilary's number.

"Come on, come on! Pick up the damn phone!"

When the call went to voicemail, Rodney texted her.

Stacy ain't who you think she is. You gotta get outta there now and find your dad.

Rodney didn't know what to do next. He had no idea where Hilary was, and she wasn't responding to his messages. Maybe she was in trouble. He saved the files to his computer and sent them to Hilary's email as attachments.

About a half hour later, he heard a noise downstairs. Rodney knew his parents weren't due home for hours. He grabbed a bat from behind his door and crept out of his room, pausing at the top of the stairs. He saw nothing. He moved downstairs, checked the front door, and found it unlocked. He locked it and headed for the kitchen.

"Hello, Rodney."

Stacy's voice echoed from the alcove beneath the stairs. She stepped out, a gun pointed at his chest. Rodney felt his heart skip a beat.

"Stacy? What are you doing?"

"Too bad you figured it out," she said, shaking her head.

"What? How—"

"Hilary left her cell phone on her bed. You can imagine my surprise when I read your message."

"Stacy, I—"

He heard the gun go off, felt the bullet slam into his chest. Then all went black.

Stacy shot Rodney twice in the chest, killing him instantly. He fell to the floor in a heap. She thought about leaving a clever note behind for David, but since this little episode hadn't been planned, she didn't want to make a mistake. She quickly left Rodney's house by the back door, the same way she'd entered. She'd been careful not to touch anything.

She walked around the side of his house and headed down the sidewalk to her car, parked six houses down. She slid inside, stuffed the gun under the seat, and drove back to David's house.

61

David returned to the hospital as quickly as he could. When he entered Karen's room, he found Hilary sitting at the foot of her bed.

"Dad, she just went back to sleep," Hilary said.

"How's she doing?"

"I think she's going to be fine. The doctor came in and said they were going to try a new seizure medicine for her."

I handed her the backpack I'd brought.

"Here's the stuff you wanted, but I couldn't find your phone. I'm sorry; I was just rushing around grabbing—"

"That's okay, Dad. I was just going to tell Rodney what was going on. I can email him. You did bring my laptop, right?"

"Yes, I did get that, but I don't know how much battery life you have left, and I forgot to grab the power cord. Sorry."

"It's okay, Dad. We're both upset. Can I use your phone to call him?"

I handed her my phone and sat down on the bed next to Karen. I took her little hand in mine. She looked so tiny.

"He's not answering," Hilary said, a look of concern in her eyes. She left him a voicemail.

"Rodney, Karen had another seizure, and we're at the hospital. I'm going to stay here with her tonight. I'll talk to you tomorrow."

"I'm going to stay up here tonight too," I said. "I'll watch her for a while. Why don't you try to get some rest?"

She nodded and moved to the recliner in the corner of the room. I found a spare blanket in the closet and covered her with it.

"Your mom would be so proud of you, Hilary. I'm proud of you, too. I wouldn't have made it through this without you."

Hilary thanked me, pulling the blanket up to her chin. Before long, she was sound asleep.

I spent the next few hours pacing the room and then did something I rarely did—I prayed. I prayed God would allow my daughter to come out of this healthy and stronger than ever.

62

The next morning, as the sun's early light sliced through the blinds and warmed my face, I woke up and peered over at my little girl. Then I looked at Hilary, sleeping in the recliner. I stared at both of them, my heart bursting with love for my girls.

Finally, I unfolded myself, stretched, and made my way to the bathroom. Spending the night in a hard bedside chair had its drawbacks. I changed clothes and brushed the fuzz from my teeth.

"Hilary, I have to go in to work for a little while," I whispered as I nudged her awake.

She nodded, sitting up and rubbing her eyes. She immediately glanced toward her sister.

"When Karen wakes up, make sure she eats some breakfast, whether they send her oatmeal or eggs. Tell her I love her."

"Okay, Dad. I'll take good care of her."

I drove to the station, taking it slow. I thought about all the things I would do with my daughters when Karen was healthy again, the extra time I would spend with them. One thing Miranda's death and Karen's sickness had taught me was that life should not be taken for granted; it could be over in an instant.

When I got to the station, I headed straight to my desk.

"Hey, Porter. Sorry to hear about your daughter, man," one of my fellow detectives said.

I nodded my thanks. "She's on the mend."

I saw Captain Wilcrest gesturing for me to step into his office. I did so, closing the door behind me.

"I heard," Cap said. "She gonna be okay?"

I nodded. "Thank God."

"David, you've been through hell and more this year—first Miranda, and now this thing with Karen. Why don't you just take the rest of the week off? Take care of your kids, and then we'll reassess our priorities. Sound good to   you?"

"Cap, I need to work."

"You're not able to focus right now, David. Just take care of your kids. I'll call you if anything important comes up."

I nodded and left the captain's office. I went back to my desk to straighten a few things and returned to my car. I moved slowly, zombie-like, the air a heavy, hazy blanket around me. As I buckled myself in, I realized I hadn't called Stacy to update her. Even more strange, she hadn't called me. Not once.

I pulled my cell phone from my pocket to call her and then suddenly lacked the urge. I only wanted one thing—to get back to the hospital to be with my kids. In the end, they were all that really mattered.

**

Karen began to shift in the bed, and Hilary anxiously waited for her sister to open her eyes. When she did, she felt an enormous sense of relief.

"Hey there, you little creep," she said. Karen returned the smile. "How do you feel?"

"I feel okay—a little sleepy but okay." She glanced around the room. "Where's Daddy?"

"He had to go to work for a little while, but he'll be back soon. He told me to tell you he loves you." She gestured toward her laptop. "Dad brought my laptop for me last night, but he forgot the power cord and the battery is dead. I have an assignment due today, but I can email it to my teacher."

"Call Stacy and have her bring it here for you," Karen suggested.

Hilary shook her head. "I'd rather not. Plus, Dad forgot my cell at home too."

"Wow. What *did* he remember to bring?"

Hilary laughed at her sister's snarky question. She was definitely feeling better.

"Look, Karen, they should be serving breakfast soon. You will eat something, you hear me?"

Karen nodded. "I am hungry, but no Captain Crunch!" she insisted. "It tastes funny to me now."

"I'm sure they won't be serving Captain Crunch. Will you be okay by yourself for a little while? I think I'll go ask around and see if there's someone who can drive me home real quick. I don't want to bother Dad at work, but I need to find my cell phone and pick up the power cord so I can email my assignment to my teacher. I can't afford another late paper."

"Okay," Karen said. "Just put the TV on Dora for me, and I'll be good."

Hilary grabbed her laptop and scampered out into the hallway to see if she could find one of the nurses who might be able to suggest something. With no one in sight, she walked to the nurse's station, where a kind-looking middle-aged woman greeted her with a smile.

"Hi, sweetie, what can I do for you?"

"I need a big favor. Is there any way you can help me arrange for a ride home to grab a few things? My dad's at work, and I'm not sure when he'll be getting back here. And I don't have money for a cab."

"You're with Karen Porter, aren't you?"

"Yes, ma'am."

She raised her eyebrows. "You know, I think one of the aides is ready for a break. It's not standard procedure, but I bet she wouldn't mind. I can ask her if you want me to."

"Thank you so much! I'd sure appreciate it," Hilary said.

"Sure thing," the nurse said. "You ready to go now?"

Hilary nodded.

The nurse made a few calls, and before long, a young woman strolled over to the nurse's station.

"Janice, you're taking your break now, aren't you?" the nurse said.

Janice nodded.

"Would you mind taking this young lady back to her house to pick up a few things? She's sitting with little Karen Porter."

Janice looked at Hilary and smiled. "Sure, no problem. Do you live close by?"

Hilary nodded again. "About ten minutes away. I'll

be quick, I promise."

Within minutes, Hilary and Janice were on their way.

"I really appreciate you giving me this ride," Hilary said for the third time. "I can have my boyfriend bring me back to the hospital, so you can just drop me off."

"No problem," Janice said. "I needed to run an errand anyway, and you're along the way. You sure you won't need a ride back?"

"I'm positive, thank you. You've done enough."

They pulled up to the house, and Hilary scrambled out of the car. She leaned down through the open window as she shut the door.

"Thanks again!"

Hilary hurried up the walk and to the front door. The door was unlocked, and she rushed inside, intent on getting to her bedroom. She plugged her laptop in and found her cell phone. While her computer booted up, she checked her phone for messages. No texts from anyone but a few calls from Rodney. She hated voicemail, so she didn't listen to it. She tried calling him back but got no answer.

She logged into her email account and found ten emails from Rodney.

63

Stacy walked into the hospital and quickly scanned the boards to find out which room Karen was in. Her plan was coming to fruition—sooner than she'd planned. *Time to tie up all the loose ends*, she thought. She walked into Karen's room and found her eyes glued to some silly cartoon.

"Hey there, Sweetie. How you feel this morning?"

"Hi, Stacy!" Karen replied. "I'm feeling much better."

"Where's your sister?" Stacy asked. "Why isn't she here? David . . . your Daddy said she was staying with you. She downstairs in the cafeteria or something?"

"No," Karen said, her attention back on the television. "One of the nurses took her home to get something for her computer."

Damn it! Stacy thought. She still didn't know if Rodney had sent Hilary any of the information he'd found about her true identity, but she couldn't take the chance. Not just yet. She forced a smile.

"Oh, okay, Sweetie. Well, I have to make my rounds now. I'll see you in a little bit. By the way, how long ago did Hilary leave?"

Karen shrugged. "Not long. Maybe ten minutes or so."

Stacy hurried out of the room. Without speaking to anyone, she took the stairs down and ran to her car. By the time she pulled out of the parking lot, she was flushed with anger. Time to take care of Hilary before all her plans were ruined.

**

Sitting on her bed with her laptop, Hilary opened the last email from Rodney. She was still trying to figure out why Rodney had sent her the article about Lisa Crease. She opened up the last attachment and felt her heart drop to the pit of her stomach. She read through it again, and then it clicked. She grabbed her phone and punched in Rodney's number again. No answer.

She ran downstairs, but just as she got to the bottom step, she saw Stacy's car pull into the driveway. She froze for an instant, hoping Stacy hadn't seen her through the window. Racing back upstairs, she frantically called her Dad's cell phone, her fingers trembling.

"Come on, Dad, pick up the phone. Pick up the phone!" she muttered.

No answer. She heard a car door slam outside. She ran to the master bedroom, hoping to find one of her dad's spare guns. She knew he kept one on a high shelf in his closet. She had never fired the weapon before, but her dad had shown her how it worked. She had told him a hundred times she'd never need to use one, but he'd insisted she at least know how it worked, just in case. Now she was glad he'd done so.

She snatched the gun and ran back to her bedroom, shutting the door just as she heard Stacy slam the front door. Hilary wedged herself into the far corner, facing the door, her knees pulled up tight to her chin. She held the gun with both hands, resting her forearms on her knees to steady herself. The gun felt heavy in her grip. She waited.

She heard Stacy's footsteps on the stairs.

"Hilary," she said in a sing-song voice. "I know you're here."

Suddenly, the door to Hilary's room flew open with such force it rattled the windows. Hilary jumped, nearly losing her grip on the gun. Stacy stood in the doorway, a sick smile on her face. Hilary had never seen her look so . . . so out of it.

"Get out of my room!"

"Hilary," Stacy said, a pouty look on her face. "Don't hate me. I had to do it." She frowned and shook her head, staring hard at Hilary. "I had to teach him a lesson. Do you understand that? You ever been raped before, Hilary? Well, have you?"

"You're a crazy psycho bitch! I was right not to like you. I knew you were crazy! You stay away from me. I have a gun!"

Stacy just stared at her. The look in her eyes frightened Hilary.

"My dad didn't do anything to you!"

Stacy laughed, a high, crackling sound that cut through the room like a knife.

"Do you think I screwed myself that day? Do you

think what he did to me was right?" She took a step into the room. "You know it was your dad's idea, right? What would you have done? Just let it go? I had to teach him a lesson. I had to give him a taste of the pain I've lived with for so many years, the pain I still have today. You know what else?"

She smiled, but the smile didn't reach her eyes. Hilary watched her warily, her hands trembling.

"Your pretty little mother is alive." She chuckled. "But you'll never see her again, Hilary, dear. You won't make it out of this house alive."

"My mom is dead!" Hilary wailed. "You're nothing but a crazy liar."

"You poor thing. That's what I wanted you to believe," Stacy said, leaning casually against the doorjamb as if she'd just stopped by to say hello. "This whole thing was perfect. You think I would kill her and make her miss all this excitement?"

She laughed again, her head tossed back, her eyes wild.

"I took her life. Yes, I took her life, her home, her kids, and I even had sex with her husband in her bed. After all, payback is so sweet. No, she's nice and cozy in my basement."

Hilary stared at her. Was she telling the truth? She shook her head.

"You're a liar!"

Hilary stood, her legs shaking, and braced herself against the wall. She lifted the gun and pointed it at Stacy, only ten feet away.

"Get out of here. Now! If you take one more step, I'll blow your head off and feel good about doing it." Her heart pounded with terror. Could she? Could she pull the trigger?

Stacy shook her head. "You've never killed anyone before, Hilary. You don't even know how to use that thing."

She took another step toward Hilary.

"Don't bet on it, bitch."

Stacy grinned and took another step.

"I'm warning you, Stacy . . . or Lisa, or whoever the hell you are."

Stacy paused, eyeing the gun. "You think I've hurt him enough yet? You do have to admit this whole thing was brilliant, wasn't it? I mean, wow! Oh, and I'm sorry, but you'll have to find another boyfriend. I didn't plan on killing him, but he was too damn smart."

What? Hilary blinked hard. *Rodney? She'd killed Rodney?* She felt lightheaded and her legs were numb and tingly. No! No, she had to be strong. No matter what. She had to save her dad, and if the bitch was telling the truth, her mother. Her mother was alive . . .

"We had a wonderful romp in bed though," Stacy said. "Been a long while since I've had such a young one in my bed."

"Liar!"

"You want to see the video?"

Hilary choked back a sob. At that moment, Stacy lunged forward. Startled, Hilary moved to the side, banging hard into the desk next to her and losing her grip on the gun.

Stacy's momentum propelled them both to the floor, and Hilary landed hard on her shoulder. Her heart raced as she desperately tried to get up, but Stacy lay on top of her, laughing. Hilary struck blindly, balling her hands into fists and trying to strike Stacy's nose. Stacy slapped her hard, and Hilary gasped as her head struck the floor. She had to get away!

Hilary groped the floor for the gun, reaching

beneath her desk where she thought the gun had landed. Stacy grabbed her hair with both hands and slammed her head into the floor.

Hilary cried out in pain. She tried to lift herself off the floor, but Stacy was too heavy.

"Bitch!" Stacy swore each time she slammed Hilary's head into the carpet. "Bitch! Bitch!"

Hilary's vision wavered. Blackness crept in, and she knew if she didn't do something, she'd be unconscious . . . and dead soon after. She reached a little further with her right hand, trying to scratch at Stacy's eyes with her left, but the woman managed to keep her head out of Hilary's reach.

Suddenly, Hilary felt the grip of the gun. She clenched her hand around it.

Without thinking, Hilary aimed blindly and pulled the trigger. She fired one round. Above her, Stacy's eyes widened in surprise. A trickle of blood oozed from her mouth, and then she tilted to the side and slowly toppled over.

Crying hard and gasping for breath, Hilary dropped the gun and crawled toward the bed. She grabbed the bedpost and pulled herself up, her legs unsteady. She looked at Stacy, a pool of blood soaking the carpet beneath her. She saw no rise and fall of her chest, heard no sound whatsoever.

Hilary snatched the gun from the floor and took a deep breath. She had to find her dad! She had to tell him what had happened and, more importantly, that their mother was still alive. She wiped the tears from her face as she reached for her phone and called him. Still no answer.

She hesitated and then searched Stacy's pockets for her car keys. Once in hand, she took one last look at the lifeless body on her bedroom floor and raced down the stairs and out of the house.

<u>64</u>

I was in the middle of a conversation with Captain Wilcrest when Hilary burst into his office, her eyes wild. Her nose was bleeding, and her face was pale and frightened. I jumped to my feet.

"Hilary! What's—"

"I just killed Stacy! She—"

"What?" I gasped. I glanced at the captain, who had risen to his feet.

"Hilary—"

She burst into tears. "Her name's not Stacy, it's Lisa. Dad, she said Mom is still alive!"

I had never felt so confused. "Hilary, slow down."

The captain moved around his desk and helped Hilary into the chair I had just vacated.

"Take your time, Hilary. Tell us what happened,"

Wilcrest said.

Her eyes wide with panic, she tried to explain. "Dad, we have to go! Stacy is really some other person. She tried to kill me. She said you and a bunch of guys raped her a long time ago, and she was punishing you. I killed her! I got your gun and—"

"You shot her?" I placed my hands on Hilary's shoulders, felt her wild trembling beneath them. I was too stunned to make sense of it.

"Dad!"

She looked up at me with an intensity I'd never seen in her eyes before.

"Listen to me!" she insisted. "She said Mom is locked in her basement!"

I could see she was distraught, but she was talking crazy and way too fast. None of it made much sense to me.

"Hilary," I said, trying to sound calm. "Hilary, slow down. What are you talking about?"

She paused for a moment and tried to catch her breath. I crouched down beside her chair while the captain hovered over her.

"Dad," she tried again, her voice filled with anguish. "Stacy is . . . she was someone else." She choked back a sob. "Rodney left messages for me last night, but I didn't get them because . . . Anyway, he hacked . . . he found the truth about her. He emailed the files to me, and I saw them this morning when I got home."

"Wait. How did you get home? You were supposed to be staying with Karen at the hospital!" I still couldn't make sense of anything.

"I wanted my computer cord and cell phone," she explained, her voice rising with increasing emotion. "I saw the files, Dad, and then Stacy got there and she was crazy, and . . . I shot her, Dad! She's dead!"

I didn't understand it, but I knew Hilary was telling the truth. She wouldn't—

"Wait," I said, glancing first at the captain and then down at Hilary. "You said Stacy told you mom—is alive?"

Hilary nodded and lunged out of the chair. She pulled at my arm.

"She said Mom is alive, down in her basement! We've got to go!"

Hilary literally dragged me into the hall. Wilcrest followed. When I finally understood what she was trying to tell me, we all ran for the door.

The three of us hurried to Wilcrest's car and took off. I rode shotgun and Hilary sat in the back. I grabbed the mic and had dispatch send backup and an ambulance to both my house and Stacy's.

My mind raced. It was simply too much to process.

Wilcrest drove as fast as he dared through town, sirens following us in the distance. I hung on for dear life. I wanted to ask Hilary a million questions, but I doubted I would have heard her over the pounding of my heart.

We pulled up to Stacy's isolated house outside of town, and I was out of the car and racing toward the door before he turned off the engine. Hilary and Captain Wilcrest followed close behind.

I didn't wait, but kicked open the door.

"Miranda!" I yelled as I ran through the house and into the kitchen. There, I saw the door leading down to the basement.

"Miranda!" I yelled as I kicked that door open, too.

I paused only for an instant at the top of the stairs.

"David! We're down here!"

The captain and I exchanged a glance. *De Luca!*

I ran down the stairs and into the basement. Finally! Finally I saw my Miranda again. She was slumped on a filthy mattress, handcuffed to a chain bolted to the wall. I saw Detective De Luca beside her, restrained in the same manner.

With a choked cry catching in my throat, I approached the mattress, and then sagged to my knees. I reached for my wife and wrapped her gently in my arms. She was nothing but skin and bones, surely near death, but she was alive. She returned my embrace with all the strength she could muster. Tears of joy spilled down my cheeks, and in the next instant, Hilary was there too, crying and wrapping her arms around both of us.

"I found you," I said, cradling Miranda's face in my hands. I couldn't stop saying it. "I found you. I found you!"

Wilcrest stepped over to De Luca as the house came alive with police officers and paramedics. Soon, the handcuffs were removed from both women, but I barely noticed the commotion as I held my Miranda in my arms again. She wept into my shoulder, whispering words of love for me and Hilary.

"Good to see you again, Detective," Wilcrest said to De Luca.

"Hey, David," De Luca said.

I glanced at her and noticed her grin.

"I told you she was no good for you, didn't I? You should have listened. Italians always know!"

I smiled at her through my tears, glad she was safe as well.

"How did you know . . .? Why didn't you tell me you'd found . . .?" I shook my head, unable to put the pieces together or form a coherent question. I knew I'd find out all the details later. Having Miranda in my arms was enough for now.

"Is Karen okay?" Miranda asked. "That bitch told me she was poisoning her!"

It all made sense now, why Karen had been getting sick. I felt my stomach turn. Stacy had fooled me through and through. I'd put my kids in so much danger . . . and for what? Love? Hardly. I felt so stupid.

As cops and medical crew crowded into the basement, I looked around the room. Stacy had done this. Stacy had abducted my wife and kept her down here for months while I . . . It made my stomach churn. I wanted to kill her, but my daughter had been forced to do it for me. I reluctantly relinquished my wife to the paramedics, then turned and retched. Hilary placed a comforting hand on my back, and I felt like screaming in anguish.

"Stacy did this . . ." I muttered, disbelieving.

Then I noticed the speakers and realized Miranda had been forced to listen to everything that had occurred between Stacy and me. I swore and turned to her. The paramedics had inserted an IV into her arm and attached leads in order to monitor her heartbeat on the portable EKG machine they'd brought down with them. I watched as an ambulance crew carried a gurney down the narrow staircase.

"Miranda." I choked out the words. "I'm so sorry."

"Stop," she said, resting her hand on my arm. "You didn't know. You thought I was dead."

I watched, my arm wrapped tightly around Hilary, as the paramedics lifted my wife onto the gurney. Detective De Luca stood nearby, slapping away the ministrations of another medic.

"You guys ready to get out of here?" Wilcrest said.

"More than anything in the world," Miranda said.

Hilary and I rode in the ambulance with Miranda. I held her hand and refused to let go. Hilary wept quietly, her hand never leaving her mother's arm.

"I thought I'd never see you again," Miranda

whispered.

The siren wailed as I stared down at her, my heart bursting with love and gratitude. What a fool I had been.

We pulled up to the hospital. Hilary and I climbed out and followed her gurney into the emergency bay.

"I want to see Karen," Miranda insisted.

The emergency room doctor quickly approached, prepared to whisk Miranda into one of the trauma bays.

"I want to see Karen!"

At that moment, I was willing to give my wife anything she wanted. I turned to Hilary.   "You stay here. I'll go get Karen," I said.

Hilary nodded. I hurried to the elevator, waited impatiently for it to open, and pushed the button for the pediatric ward.

"I need to take my daughter down to see her mother!" I yelled as I ran toward the nurse's station.

"Detective Porter?" the nurse said, moving around the edge of the counter. "What's wrong?"

"My wife is downstairs," I explained. "She wants to see Karen."

The nurse frowned. "But we released Karen to Stacy about twenty minutes ago."

I froze. "What did you say?"

"Stacy came up, not looking too well, mind you, but said you wanted her discharged."

I shook my head. No! This couldn't be happening. Stacy was dead.

"No," I mumbled. "That's not possible."

"What do you mean?" the nurse asked. "You didn't want your wife—"

"Stacy is not my wife!" My voice rose as panic washed over me. "My wife is downstairs! I want Karen! Now!"

"Calm down, Detective. Please."

The nurse hurried behind the desk and called for security.

"Stacy didn't look well, but she said you wanted Karen discharged. Something about trying a different hospital." She glanced down at a paper on her desk. "See? She brought your signed request for release. I wanted to wait for the doctor to see her this afternoon, but Stacy was quite insistent—"

I felt my blood pounding through my veins. This couldn't be. Stacy was dead! Hilary had killed her and—

"She left you a note, Detective."

She handed me the note. I took it and read the single line. I felt my knees weaken.

The _two_ of us will be good together. – Love Stacy

You just read Chained Guilt – Part 1 of the <u>Hidden Past Series</u> by Terry Keys.

Turn the page for a special sneak peek of Part 2 of the 3 Part Series - <u>Maximum Guilt</u> coming winter 2016!

1

I glanced around the room. There had to be hidden cameras recording me, my emotions. This had to be some sort of sick reality TV show featuring me as the star. *This can't be real,* I thought. But it was. After finally getting my Miranda back from the clutches of death, I somehow managed to lose another loved one to the same fate. I was happy and heartbroken all at the same time.

"Detective Porter, what's wrong? Is everything okay? You're as pale as a ghost," the nurse said as she watched my reaction to the note she'd just handed me.

I didn't feel like explaining to her that Stacy's little note wasn't some cute love letter; rather, it was a confirmation that she was every bit as sinister as Hilary had suspected all along.

"No, everything is not okay," I replied. "Take Miranda back. Get her checked from head to toe."

And then it was lights-out.

"David? David, c'mon! Wake up, kid!" Wilcrest shouted.

Florescent lights buzzed above me as I blinked my way back

to consciousness. My head pounded to the beat of my racing heart. I wasn't sure what had happened.

"David, look at me. Come on," Miranda said, leaning in close to me. "There you go. No, don't sit up. Just rest there a minute."

I had fainted. First time I'd ever done that. I guess the nurse had been right about my being pale as a ghost. I struggled to my feet despite the warnings from everyone around me.

"I'm okay," I said. "I . . . I just . . . I don't know. I fainted, I guess."

We all shared a chuckle at my expense. Miranda was even smiling. Boy was it good to see her smile. I stood there for a second longer, trying to shake off the cobwebs.

"David, you should go back with Miranda," Wilcrest said, shaking his head. "We'll get started at the house. Go with your wife.

When I didn't move fast enough to suit the captain, he continued. "That's an order, son. I have every cop and then some looking for Karen and Stacy. We're going to find them."

"Yes, David, please come back with me. I don't think I can be without you right now," Miranda said, her voice shaky.

The cop in me wanted to question my partner, Detective De Luca, to see what things she might be able to tell me about her brief captivity and the basement where she and Miranda had been held. The father in me wanted to set the streets ablaze and hunt Stacy down like a bloodhound. I knew the hot trail she'd surely left behind would become cold rather quickly. I was hoping to capitalize on any mistakes she might have made in her haste, as snatching my daughter was probably a spur of the moment act of desperation. I trusted Wilcrest, and I knew the boys would give this the highest priority.

Wilcrest, however, was right. Miranda needed me as a husband right now and not as a cop. It would be a balancing act from this point on, because I knew I needed to spend time tracking Stacy down before it was too late. I knew she wouldn't hesitate to kill Karen if it suited her plans.

I sat beside Miranda and held her hand as the doctor ran test after test. My mind, however, was traveling at warp speed. Hilary had felt uneasy about Stacy from the moment she'd showed up at Miranda's funeral. I'd considered her out-of-nowhere appearance a bit strange, but no one could have imagined this. How could I have been so blind? It all made sense now—her eagerness to become a part of our lives, to move in with us . . . And the pregnancy! *What about the baby? What did that mean for me now?*

And now I would have to explain it all to Miranda, including the college fiasco I thought I'd left behind. I wondered how Miranda would react to everything when I told her. Karen's kidnapping trumped all of it, and my wife had not even started the healing process following her own abduction. I had never taken advantage of the psychiatric counseling available to all police officers, but now seemed like as good a time as any—for all of us. I held Miranda's hand as tight as I could and just stared at her. It seemed unreal that she was here next to me again.

"David, we've given Miranda a once-over. Other than what's to be expected—dehydration and malnourishment—everything seems to be okay. I'll have you bring her back in a few weeks, and we'll take a look at the finger she lost. We can keep her here for a few nights, or you can take her home, but you'll need to make sure she gets plenty of rest. She's also going to need some type of counseling. Here's my cell phone number. I don't usually give it out, but I figured what the hell. Call anytime. I mean *anytime,* David."

I took the business card with Dr. Peter's information and stuffed it into my wallet. I reached out to shake his hand and thanked him for everything he'd done for my family.

"Please take me home, David," Miranda whispered to me.

I hated seeing her like this. She looked so weak, so fragile. I walked beside her wheelchair as the nurse wheeled her out to my truck, Hilary trailing close behind us.

After we got Miranda buckled in, I rounded the back of my truck, tears streaming down my face. Right now, when all should be right in my world, everything was broken. Shattered. Would our family ever be whole again?

ABOUT THE AUTHOR

Terry Keys is a novelist, songwriter and poet. He writes for Examiner.com and works as a project manager in the oil and gas industry. A native of Rosharon, Texas Keys spends his free time hunting, fishing and working out. He lives in Dickinson, Texas, with his wife and two children.

Please visit his website at www.terrykeysbooks.com

Twitter: @tkeys15

Facebook: terrykeysbooks

Email: terry@terrykeysbooks.com